Our Home In The Silver West
A Story Of Struggle And Adventure

by

Gordon Stables

Double9
BOOKS

Our home in the silver west
A story of struggle and adventure
by Gordon Stables

ISBN: 978-93-65782-32-5

Published by

DOUBLE 9 BOOKS

2/13-B, Ansari Road
Daryaganj, New Delhi – 110002
info@double9books.com
www.double9books.com
Tel. 011-40042856

This book is under public domain

ABOUT THE AUTHOR

Gordon Stables turn out to be a prolific nineteenth-century Scottish author, physician, and naval officer, whose works regularly revolved spherical maritime and journey troubles. One of his exceptional creations, "Wild Adventures spherical the Pole," continues to seize the imaginations of readers. Published inside the late 19th century, this e-book is a thrilling and innovative story of polar exploration. "Wild Adventures round the Pole" takes readers on a charming adventure to the Arctic, where Stables weaves a story filled with daring exploits, breathtaking landscapes, and encounters with the cruel realities of the frozen frontier. Gordon Stables' writing is understood for its shiny descriptions and his deep knowledge of the seafaring lifestyles. His reviews as a naval officer lent authenticity to his maritime narratives, permitting readers to feel the loosen up of the polar winds and the push of excitement as explorers braved the unknown. Stables' works often convey strong moral undertones, emphasizing courage, camaraderie, and the indomitable human spirit in the face of adversity. "Wild Adventures round the Pole" is not any exception, as it encourages readers to undertaking into the uncharted territories of their very personal lives with a feel of marvel and resolution.

CONTENTS

CHAPTER I
THE HIGHLAND FEUD

Why should I, Murdoch M'Crimman of Coila, be condemned for a period of indefinite length to the drudgery of the desk's dull wood? That is the question I have just been asking myself. Am I emulous of the honour and glory that, they say, float halo-like round the brow of the author? Have I the desire to awake and find myself famous? The fame, alas! that authors chase is but too often an *ignis fatuus*. No; honour like theirs I crave not, such toil is not incumbent on me. Genius in a garret! To some the words may sound romantic enough, but—ah me!—the position seems a sad one. Genius munching bread and cheese in a lonely attic, with nothing betwixt the said genius and the sky and the cats but rafters and tiles! I shudder to think of it. If my will were omnipotent, Genius should never shiver beneath the tiles, never languish in an attic. Genius should be clothed in purple and fine linen, Genius should—— 'Yes, aunt, come in; I'm not very busy yet.'

My aunt sails into my beautiful room in the eastern tower of Castle Coila.

'I was afraid,' she says, almost solemnly, 'I might be disturbing your meditations. Do I find you really at work?'

'I've hardly arrived at that point yet, dear aunt. Indeed, if the truth will not displease you, I greatly fear serious concentration is not very much in my line. But as you desire me to write our strange story, and as mother also thinks the duty devolves on me, behold me seated at my table in this charming turret chamber, which owes its all of comfort to your most excellent taste, auntie mine.'

As I speak I look around me. The evening sunshine is streaming into my room, which occupies the whole of one story of the tower. Glance where

I please, nothing is here that fails to delight the eye. The carpet beneath my feet is soft as moss, the tall mullioned windows are bedraped with the richest curtains. Pictures and mirrors hang here and there, and seem part and parcel of the place. So does that dark lofty oak bookcase, the great harp in the west corner, the violin that leans against it, the *jardinière*, the works of art, the arms from every land—the shields, the claymores, the spears and helmets, everything is in keeping. This is my garret. If I want to meditate, I have but to draw aside a curtain in yonder nook, and lo! a little baize-covered door slides aside and admits me to one of the tower-turrets, a tiny room in which fairies might live, with a window on each side giving glimpses of landscape—and landscape unsurpassed for beauty in all broad Scotland.

But it was by the main doorway of my chamber that auntie entered, drawing aside the curtains and pausing a moment till she should receive my cheering invitation. And this door leads on to the roof, and this roof itself is a sight to see. Loftily domed over with glass, it is at once a conservatory, a vinery, and tropical aviary. Room here for trees even, for miniature palms, while birds of the rarest plumage flit silently from bough to bough among the oranges, or lisp out the sweet lilts that have descended to them from sires that sang in foreign lands. Yonder a fountain plays and casts its spray over the most lovely feathery ferns. The roof is very spacious, and the conservatory occupies the greater part of it, leaving room outside, however, for a delightful promenade. After sunset coloured lamps are often lit here, and the place then looks even more lovely than before. All this, I need hardly say, was my aunt's doing.

I wave my hand, and the lady sinks half languidly into a fauteuil.

'And so,' I say, laughingly, 'you have come to visit Genius in his garret.'

My aunt smiles too, but I can see it is only out of politeness.

I throw down my pen; I leave my chair and seat myself on the bearskin beside the ample fireplace and begin toying with Orla, my deerhound.

'Aunt, play and sing a little; it will inspire me.'

She needs no second bidding. She bends over the great harp and lightly touches a few chords.

'What shall I play or sing?'

'Play and sing as you feel, aunt.'

'I feel thus,' my aunt says, and her fingers fly over the strings, bringing forth music so inspiriting and wild that as I listen, entranced, some words of Ossian come rushing into my memory:

'The moon rose in the East. Fingal returned in the gleam of his arms. The joy of his youth was great, their souls settled as a sea from a storm. Ullin raised the song of gladness. The hills of Inistore rejoiced. The flame of the oak arose, and the tales of heroes were told.'

Aunt is not young, but she looks very noble now—looks the very incarnation of the music that fills the room. In it I can hear the battle-cry of heroes, the wild slogan of clan after clan rushing to the fight, the clang of claymore on shield, the shout of victory, the wail for the dead. There are tears in my eyes as the music ceases, and my aunt turns once more towards me.

'Aunt, your music has made me ashamed of myself. Before you came I recoiled from the task you had set before me; I longed to be out and away, marching over the moors gun in hand and dogs ahead. Now I—I—yes, aunt, this music inspires me.'

Aunt rises as I speak, and together we leave the turret chamber, and, passing through the great conservatory, we reach the promenade. We lean on the battlement, long since dismantled, and gaze beneath us. Close to the castle walls below is a well-kept lawn trending downwards with slight incline to meet the loch which laps over its borders. This loch, or lake, stretches for miles and miles on every side, bounded here and there by bare, black, beetling cliffs, and in other places

'O'erhung by wild woods thickening green,

a very cloudland of foliage. The easternmost horizon of this lake is a chain of rugged mountains, one glance at which would tell you the season was autumn, for they are crimsoned over with blooming heather. The season is autumn, and the time is sunset; the shadow of the great tower falls darkling far over the loch, and already crimson streaks of cloud are ranged along the hill-tops. So silent and still is it that we can hear the bleating of sheep a good mile off, and the throb of the oars of a boat far away on the water, although the boat itself is but a little dark speck. There is another dark speck, high, high above the crimson clouds. It comes nearer and nearer; it gets bigger and bigger; and presently a huge eagle floats over the castle, making homeward to his eyrie in the cliffs of Ben Coila.

The air gets cooler as the shadows fall; I draw the shawl closer round my aunt's shoulders. She lifts a hand as if to deprecate the attention.

'Listen, Murdoch,' she says. 'Listen, Murdoch M'Crimman.'

She seldom calls me by my name complete.

'I may leave you now, may I not?'

'I know what you mean, aunt,' I reply. 'Yes; to the best of my ability I will write our strange story.'

'Who else would but you, Murdoch M'Crimman, chief of the house of Crimman, chief of the clan?'

I bow my head in silent sorrow.

'Yes, aunt; I know. Poor father is gone, and I *am* chief.'

She touches my hand lightly—it is her way of taking farewell. Next moment I am alone. Orla thrusts his great muzzle into my hand; I pat his head, then go back with him to my turret chamber, and once more take up my pen.

A blood feud! Has the reader ever heard of such a thing? Happily it is unknown in our day. A blood feud—a quarrel 'twixt kith and kin, a feud oftentimes bequeathed from bleeding sire to son, handed down from generation to generation, getting more bitter in each; a feud that not even death itself seems enough to obliterate; an enmity never to be forgotten while hills raise high their heads to meet the clouds.

Such a feud is surely cruel. It is more, it is sinful—it is madness. Yet just such a feud had existed for far more than a hundred years between our family of M'Crimman and the Raes of Strathtoul.

There is but little pleasure in referring back to such a family quarrel, but to do so is necessary. Vast indeed is the fire that a small spark may sometimes kindle. Two small dead branches rubbing together as the wind blows may fire a forest, and cause a conflagration that shall sweep from end to end of a continent.

It was a hundred years ago, and forty years to that; the head of the house of Stuart—Prince Charles Edward, whom his enemies called the

Pretender—had not yet set foot on Scottish shore, though there were rumours almost daily that he had indeed come at last. The Raes were cousins of the M'Crimmans; the Raes were head of the clan M'Rae, and their country lay to the south of our estates. It was an ill-fated day for both clans when one morning a stalwart Highlander, flying from glen to glen with the fiery cross waving aloft, brought a missive to the chief of Coila. The Raes had been summoned to meet their prince; the M'Crimman had been *solicited*. In two hours' time the straths were all astir with preparations for the march. No boy or man who could carry arms, 'twixt the ages of sixteen and sixty, but buckled his claymore to his side and made ready to leave. Listen to the wild shout of the men, the shrill notes of bagpipes, the wailing of weeping women and children! Oh, it was a stirring time; my Scotch blood leaps in all my veins as I think of it even now. Right on our side; might on our side! We meant to do or die!

'Rise! rise! lowland and highland men!
Bald sire to beardless son, each come and early.
Rise! rise! mainland and island men,
Belt on your claymores and fight for Prince Charlie.
Down from the mountain steep—
Up from the valley deep—
Out from the clachan, the bothy and shieling;
Bugle and battle-drum,
Bid chief and vassal come,
Loudly our bagpipes the pibroch are pealing.'

M'Crimman of Coila that evening met the Raes hastening towards the lake.

'Ah, kinsman,' cried M'Crimman, 'this is indeed a glorious day! I have been summoned by letter from the royal hands of our bold young prince himself.'

'And I, chief of the Raes, have been summoned by cross. A letter was none too good for Coila. Strathtoul must be content to follow the pibroch and drum.'

'It was an oversight. My brother must neither fret nor fume. If our prince but asked me, I'd fight in the ranks for him, and carry musket or pike or pistol.'

'It's good being you, with your letter and all that. Kinsman though you be, I'd have you know, and I'd have our prince understand, that the Raes and Crimmans are one and the same family, and equal where they stand or fall.'

'Of that,' said the proud Coila, drawing himself up and lowering his brows, 'our prince is the best judge.'

'These are pretty airs to give yourself, M'Crimman! One would think your claymore drank blood every morning!'

'Brother,' said M'Crimman, 'do not let us quarrel. I have orders to see your people on the march. They are to come with us. I must do my duty.'

'Never!' shouted Rae. 'Never shall my clan obey your commands!'

'You refuse to fight for Charlie?'

'Under your banner—yes!'

'Then draw, dog! Were you ten times more closely related to me, you should eat your words or drown them in your blood!'

Half an hour afterwards the M'Crimmans were on the march southwards, their bold young chief at their head, banners streaming and pibroch ringing! but, alas! their kinsman Rae lay stark and stiff on the bare hillside.

There and then was established the feud that lasted so long and so bitterly. Surrounded by her vassals and retainers, loud in their wailing for their departed chief, the widowed wife had thrown herself on the body of her husband in a paroxysm of wild, uncontrollable grief.

But nought could restore life and animation to that lowly form. The dead chief lay on his back, with face up-turned to the sky's blue, which his eyes seemed to pierce. His bonnet had fallen off, his long yellow hair floated on the grass, his hand yet grasped the great claymore, but his tartans were dyed with blood.

Then a brother of the Rae approached and led the weeping woman gently away. Almost immediately the warriors gathered and knelt around the corpse and swore the terrible feud—swore eternal enmity to the house of Coila—'to fight the clan wherever found, to wrestle, to rackle and rive with them, and never to make peace

'While there's leaf on the forest
Or foam on the river.'

We all know the story of Prince Charlie's expedition, and how, after victories innumerable, all was lost to his cause through disunions in his own camps; how his sun went down on the red field of Culloden Moor; how true and steadfast, even after defeat, the peasant Highlanders were to their chief; and how the glens and straths were devastated by fire and sword; and how the streams ran red with the innocent blood of old men and children, spilled by the brutal soldiery of the ruthless duke.

The M'Crimmans lost their estates. The Raes had never fought for Charlie. Their glen was spared, but the hopes of M'Rae—the young chief—were blighted, for after years of exile the M'Crimman was pardoned, and fires were once more lit in the halls of Castle Coila.

Long years went by, many of the Raes went abroad to fight in foreign lands wherever good swords were needed and lusty arms to wield them withal; but those who remained in or near Strathtoul still kept up the feud with as great fierceness as though it had been sworn but yesterday.

Towards the beginning of the present century, however, a strange thing happened. A young officer of French dragoons came to reside for a time in Glen Coila. His name was Le Roi. Though of Scotch extraction, he had never been before to our country. Now hospitality is part and parcel of the religion of Scotland; it is not surprising, therefore, that this young son of the sword should have been received with open arms at Coila, nor that, dashing, handsome, and brave himself, he should have fallen in love with the winsome daughter of the then chief of the M'Crimmans. When he sought to make her his bride explanations were necessary. It was no uncommon thing in those days for good Scotch families to permit themselves to be allied with France; but there must be rank on both sides. Had a thunderbolt burst in Castle Coila then it could have caused no greater commotion than did the fact when it came to light that Le Roi was a direct descendant of the chief of the Raes. Alas! for the young lovers now. Le Roi in silence and sorrow ate his last meal at Castle Coila. Hospitality had never been shown more liberally than it was that night, but ere the break of day Le Roi had gone—never to return to the glen *in propriâ personâ*. Whether or not an aged harper who visited the castle a month thereafter was Le Roi in disguise may never be known; but this, at least, is fact—that same night the chief's daughter was spirited away and seen no more in Coila.

There was talk, however, of a marriage having been solemnized by torchlight, in the little Catholic chapel at the foot of the glen, but of this we will hear more anon, for thereby hangs a tale.

In course of time Coila presented the sad spectacle of a house without a head. Who should now be heir? The Scottish will of former chiefs notified that in event of such an occurrence the estates should pass 'to the nearest heirs whatever.'

But was there no heir of direct descent? For a time it seemed there would be or really was. To wit, a son of Le Roi, the officer who had wedded into the house of M'Crimman.

Now our family was brother-family to the M'Crimmans. M'Crimmans we were ourselves, and Celtic to the last drop of blood in our veins.

Our claim to the estate was but feebly disputed by the French Rae's son. His father and mother had years ago crossed the bourne from which no traveller ever returns, and he himself was not young. The little church or chapel in which the marriage had been celebrated was a ruin—it had been burned to the ground, whether as part price of the terrible feud or not, no one could say; the priest was dead, or gone none knew whither; and old Mawsie, a beldame, lived in the cottage that had once been the Catholic manse.

Those were wild and strange times altogether in this part of the Scottish Highlands, and law was oftentimes the property of might rather than right.

At the time, then, our story really opens, my father had lived in the castle and ruled in the glens for many a long year. I was the first-born, next came Donald, then Dugald, and last of all our one sister Flora.

What a happy life was ours in Glen Coila, till the cloud arose on our horizon, which, gathering force amain, burst in storm at last over our devoted heads!

CHAPTER II
OUR BOYHOOD'S LIFE

On our boyhood's life—that, I mean, of my brothers and myself—I must dwell no longer than the interest of our strange story demands, for our chapters must soon be filled with the relation of events and adventures far more stirring than anything that happened at home in our day.

And yet no truer words were ever spoken than these—'the boy is father of the man.' The glorious battle of Waterloo—Wellington himself told us—was won in the cricket field at home. And in like manner our greatest pioneers of civilisation, our most successful emigrants, men who have often literally to lash the rifle to the plough stilts, as they cultivate and reclaim the land of the savage, have been made and manufactured, so to speak, in the green valleys of old England, and on the hills and moors of bonnie Scotland.

Probably the new M'Crimman of Coila, as my father was called on the lake side and in the glens, had mingled more, far more, in life than any chief who had ever reigned before him. He would not have been averse to drawing the sword in his country's cause, had it been necessary, but my brothers and I were born in peaceful times, shortly after the close of the war with Russia. No, my father could have drawn the claymore, but he could also use the ploughshare—and did.

There were at first grumblers in the clans, who lamented the advent of anything that they were pleased to call new-fangled. Men there were who wished to live as their forefathers had done in the 'good old times'—cultivate only the tops of the 'rigs,' pasture the sheep and cattle on the upland moors, and live on milk and meal, and the fish from the lake, with an occasional hare, rabbit, or bird when Heaven thought fit to send it.

They were not prepared for my father's sweeping innovations. They stared in astonishment to see the bare hillsides planted with sheltering spruce and pine trees; to see moss and morass turned inside out, drained and made to yield crops of waving grain, where all was moving bog before; to see comfortable cottages spring up here and there, with real stone walls and smiling gardens front and rear, in place of the turf and tree shielings of bygone days; and to see a new school-house, where English—real English—

was spoken and taught, pour forth a hundred happy children almost every weekday all the year round.

This was 'tempting Providence, and no good could come of it;' so spoke the grumblers, and they wondered indeed that the old warlike chiefs of M'Crimman did not turn in their graves. But even the grumblers got fewer and further between, and at last long peace and plenty reigned contentedly hand in hand from end to end of Glen Coila, and all around the loch that was at once the beauty and pride of our estate.

Improvements were not confined to the crofters' holdings; they extended to the castle farm and to the castle itself. Nothing that was old about the latter was swept away, but much that was new sprang up, and rooms long untenanted were now restored.

A very ancient and beautiful castle was that of Coila, with its one huge massive tower, and its dark frowning embattled walls. It could be seen from far and near, for even the loch itself was high above the level of the sea. I speak of it, be it observed, in the past tense, solely because I am writing of the past—of happy days for ever fled. The castle is still as beautiful—nay, even more so, for my aunt's good taste has completed the improvements my father began.

I do not think any one could have come in contact with father, as I remember him during our early days at Coila, without loving and respecting him. He was our hero—my brothers' and mine—so tall, so noble-looking, so handsome, whether ranging over the heather in autumn with his gun on his shoulder, or labouring with a hoe or rake in hand in garden or meadow.

Does it surprise any one to know that even a Highland chieftain, descended from a long line of warriors, could handle a hoe as deftly as a claymore? I grant he may have been the first who ever did so from choice, but was he demeaned thereby? Assuredly not; and work in the fields never went half so cheerfully on as when father and we boys were in the midst of the servants. Our tutor was a young clergyman, and he, too, used to throw off his black coat and join us.

At such times it would have done the heart of a cynic good to have been there; song and joke and hearty laugh followed in such quick succession that it seemed more like working for fun than anything else.

And our triumph of triumphs was invariably consummated at the end of harvest, for then a supper was given to the tenants and servants. This supper took place in the great hall of the castle—the hall that in ancient days had witnessed many a warlike meeting and Bacchanalian feast.

Before a single invitation was made out for this event of the season every sheaf and stook had to be stored and the stubble raked, every rick in the home barn-yards had to be thatched and tidied; 'whorls' of turnips had to be got up and put in pits for the cattle, and even a considerable portion of the ploughing done.

'Boys,' my father would say then, pointing with pride to his lordly stacks of grain and hay, 'Boys,

'"Peace hath her victories,
No less renowned than war."

And now,' he would add, 'go and help your tutor to write out the invitations.'

So kindly-hearted was father that he would even have extended the right hand of peace and fellowship to the Raes of Strathtoul. The head of this house, however, was too proud; yet his pride was of a different kind from father's. It was of the stand-aloof kind. It was even rumoured that Le Roi, or Rae, had said at a dinner-party that my good, dear father brought disgrace on the warlike name of M'Crimman because he mingled with his servants in the field, and took a very personal interest in the welfare of his crofter tenantry.

But my father had different views of life from this semi-French Rae of Strathtoul. He appreciated the benefits and upheld the dignity, and even sanctity, of honest labour. Had he lived in the days of Ancient Greece, he might have built a shrine to Labour, and elevated it to the rank of goddess. Only my father was no heathen, but a plain, God-fearing man, who loved, or tried to love, his neighbour as himself.

If our father was a hero to us boys, not less so was he to our darling mother, and to little Sister Flora as well. So it may be truthfully said that we were a happy family. The time sped by, the years flew on without, apparently, ever a bit of change from one Christmas Day to another. Mr. Townley, our tutor, seemed to have little ambition to 'better himself,' as it is termed. When challenged one morning at breakfast with his want of desire to push,

'Oh,' said Townley, 'I'm only a young man yet, and really I do not wish to be any happier than I am. It will be a grief to me when the boys grow older and go out into the world and need me no more.'

Mr. Townley was a strict and careful teacher, but by no means a hard taskmaster. Indoors during school hours he was the pedagogue all over. He carried etiquette even to the extent of wearing cap and gown, but these were thrown off with scholastic duties; he was then—out of doors—as jolly as a schoolboy going to play at his first cricket-match.

In the field father was our teacher. He taught us, and the 'grieve,' or bailiff, taught us everything one needs to know about a farm. Not in headwork alone. No; for, young as we were at this time, my brothers and I could wield axe, scythe, hoe, and rake.

We were Highland boys all over, in mind and body, blood and bone. I—Murdoch—was fifteen when the cloud gathered that finally changed our fortunes. Donald and Dugald were respectively fourteen and thirteen, and Sister Flora was eleven.

Big for our years we all were, and I do not think there was anything on dry land, or on the water either, that we feared. Mr. Townley used very often to accompany us to the hills, to the river and lake, but not invariably. We dearly loved our tutor. What a wonderful piece of muscularity and good-nature he was, to be sure, as I remember him! Of both his muscularity and good-nature I am afraid we often took advantage. Flora invariably did, for out on the hills she would turn to him with the utmost *sang-froid*, saying, 'Townley, I'm tired; take me on your back.' And for miles Townley would trudge along with her, feeling her weight no more than if she had been a moth that had got on his shoulders by accident. There was no tiring Townley.

To look at our tutor's fair young face, one would never have given him the credit of possessing a deal of romance, or believed it possible that he could have harboured any feeling akin to love. But he did. Now this is a story of stirring adventure and of struggle, and not a love tale; so the truth may be as well told in this place as further on—Townley loved my aunt. It should be remembered that at this time she was young, but little over twenty, and in every way she was worthy to be the heroine of a story.

Townley, however, was no fool. Although he was admitted to the companionship of every member of our family, and treated in every respect as an equal, he could not forget that there was a great gulf fixed between the humble tutor and the youngest sister of the chief of the M'Crimmans. If he loved, he kept the secret bound up in his own breast, content to live and be near the object of his adoration. Perhaps this hopeless passion of Townley's had much to do with the formation of his history.

Those dear old days of boyhood! Even as they were passing away we used to wish they would last for ever. Surely that is proof positive that we were very happy, for is it not common for boys to wish they were men? We never did.

For we had everything we could desire to make our little lives a pleasure long drawn out. Boys who were born in towns—and we knew many of these, and invited them occasionally to visit us at our Highland home—we used to pity from the bottom of our hearts. How little they knew about country sports and country life!

One part of our education alone was left to our darling mother—namely, Bible history. Oh, how delightful it used to be to listen to her voice as, seated by our bedside in the summer evenings, she told us tales from the Book of Books! Then she would pray with us, for us, and for father; and sweet and soft was the slumber that soon visited our pillows.

Looking back now to those dear old days, I cannot help thinking that the practice of religion as carried on in our house was more Puritanical in its character than any I have seen elsewhere. The Sabbath was a day of such solemn rest that one lived as it were in a dream. No food was cooked; even the tables in breakfast-room and dining-hall were laid on Saturday; no horse left the stables, the servants dressed in their sombrest and best, moved about on tiptoe, and talked in whispers. We children were taught to consider it sinful even to think our own thoughts on this holy day. If we boys ever forgot ourselves so far as to speak of things secular, there was Flora to lift a warning finger and with terrible earnestness remind us that this was God's day.

From early morn to dewy eve all throughout the Sabbath we felt as if our footsteps were on the boundaries of another world—that kind, loving angels were near watching all our doings.

I am drawing a true picture of Sunday life in many a Scottish family, but I would not have my readers mistake me. Let me say, then, that ours was not a religion of fear so much as of love. To grieve or vex the great Good Being who made us and gave us so much to be thankful for would have been a crime which would have brought its own punishment by the sorrow and repentance created in our hearts.

Just one other thing I must mention, because it has a bearing on events to be related in the next chapter. We were taught then never to forget that a day of reckoning was before us all, that after death should come the judgment. But mother's prayers and our religion brought us only the most unalloyed happiness.

CHAPTER III
A TERRIBLE RIDE

I have but to gaze from the window of the tower in which I am writing to see a whole fieldful of the daftest-looking long-tailed, long-maned ponies imaginable. These are the celebrated Castle Coila ponies, as full of mischief, fun, and fire as any British boy could wish, most difficult to catch, more difficult still to saddle, and requiring all the skill of a trained equestrian to manage after mounting. As these ponies are to-day, so they were when I was a boy. The very boys whom I mentioned in the last chapter would have gone anywhere and done anything rather than attempt to ride a Coila pony. Not that they ever refused, they were too courageous for that. But when Gilmore led a pony round, I know it needed all the pluck they could muster to put foot in stirrup. Flora's advice to them was not bad.

'There is plenty of room on the moors, boys,' she would say, laughing; and Flora always brought out the word 'boys' with an air of patronage and self-superiority that was quite refreshing. 'Plenty of room on the moors, so you keep the ponies hard at the gallop, till they are quite tired. Mind, don't let them trot. If you do, they will lie down and tumble.'

Poor Archie Bateman! I shall never forget his first wild scamper over the moorland. He would persist in riding in his best London clothes, spotless broad white collar, shining silk hat, gloves, and all. Before mounting he even bent down to flick a little tiny bit of dust off his boots.

The ponies were fresh that morning. In fact, the word 'fresh' hardly describes the feeling of buoyancy they gave proof of. For a time it was as difficult to mount one as it would be for a fly to alight on a top at full spin. We took them to the paddock, where the grass and moss were soft. Donald, Dugald, and I held Flora's fiery steed *vi et armis* till she got into the saddle.

'Mind to keep them at it, boys,' were her last words, as she flew out and away through the open gateway. Then we prepared to follow. Donald, Dugald, and I were used to tumbles, and for five minutes or more we amused ourselves by getting up only to get off again. But we were not hurt. Finally we mounted Archie. His brother was not going out that morning, and I do believe to this day that Archie hoped to curry favour with Flora by a little display of horsemanship, for he had been talking a deal to her the evening before of the delights of riding in London.

At all events, if he had meant to create a sensation he succeeded admirably, though at the expense of a portion of his dignity.

No sooner was he mounted than off he rode. Stay, though, I should rather say that no sooner did we mount him than off he was carried. That is a way of putting it which is more in accordance with facts, for we—Donald, Dugald, and I—mounted him, and the pony did the rest, he, Archie, being legally speaking *nolens volens*. When my brothers and I emerged at last, we could just distinguish Flora waiting on the horizon of a braeland, her figure well thrown out against the sky, her pony curveting round and round, which was Flora's pet pony's way of keeping still. Away at a tangent from the proper line of march, Archie on his steed was being rapidly whirled. As soon as we came within sight of our sister, we observed her making signs in Archie's direction and concluded to follow. Having duly signalled her wishes, Flora disappeared over the brow of the hill. Her intention was, we afterwards found out, to take a cross-cut and intercept, if possible, the mad career of Archie's Coila steed.

'Hurry up, Donald,' I shouted to my nearest brother; 'that pony is mad. It is making straight for the cliffs of Craigiemore.'

On we went at furious speed. It was in reality, or appeared to be, a race for life; but should we win? The terrible cliffs for which Archie's pony was heading away were perpendicular bluffs that rose from a dark slimy morass near the lake. Fifty feet high they were at the lowest, and pointed unmistakably to some terrible convulsion of Nature in ages long gone by. They looked like hills that had been sawn in half—one half taken, the other left.

Our ponies were gaining on Archie's. The boy had given his its head, but it was evident he was now aware of his danger and was trying to rein in. Trying, but trying in vain. The pony was in command of the situation.

On—on—on they rush. I can feel my heart beating wildly against my ribs as we all come nigher and nigher to the cliffs. Donald's pony and Dugald's both overtake me. Their saddles are empty. My brothers have both been unhorsed. I think not of that, all my attention is bent on the rider ahead. If he could but turn his pony's head even now, he would be saved.

But no, it is impossible. They are on the cliff. There! they are over it, and a wild scream of terror seems to rend the skies and turn my blood to water.

But lo! I, too, am now in danger. My pony has the bit fast between his teeth. He means to play at an awful game—follow my leader! I feel dizzy; I have forgotten that I might fling myself off even at the risk of broken bones. I am close to the cliff—I—hurrah! I am saved! Saved at the very moment when it seemed nothing could save me, for dear Flora has dashed in front of me—has cut across my bows, as sailors would say, striking my pony with all the strength of her arm as she is borne along. Saved, yes, but both on the ground. I extricate myself and get up. Our ponies are all panting; they appear now to realize the fearfulness of the danger, and stand together cowed and quiet. Poor Flora is very pale, and blood is trickling from a wound in her temple, while her habit is torn and soiled. We have little time to notice this; we must ride round and look for the body of poor Archie.

It was a ride of a good mile to reach the cliff foot, but it took us but a very short time to get round, albeit the road was rough and dangerous. We had taken our bearings aright, but for a time we could see no signs of those we had come to seek. But presently with her riding-whip Flora pointed to a deep black hole in the slimy bog.

'They are there!' she cried; then burst into a flood of tears.

We did the best we could to comfort our little sister, and were all returning slowly, leading our steeds along the cliff foot, when I stumbled against something lying behind a tussock of grass.

The something moved and spoke when I bent down. It was poor Archie, who had escaped from the morass as if by a miracle.

A little stream was near; it trickled in a half-cataract down the cliffs. Donald and Dugald hurried away to this and brought back Highland bonnetfuls of water. Then we washed Archie's face and made him drink. How we rejoiced to see him smile again! I believe the London accent of his voice was at that moment the sweetest music to Flora she had ever heard in her life.

'What a pwepostewous tumble I've had! How vewy, *vewy* stoopid of me to be wun away with!'

Poor Flora laughed one moment at her cousin and cried the next, so full was her heart. But presently she proved herself quite a little woman.

'I'll ride on to the castle,' she said, 'and get dry things ready. You'd better go to bed, Archie, when you come home; you are not like a Highland boy, you know. Oh, I'm so glad you're alive! But—ha, ha, ha! excuse me— but you do look *so* funny!' and away she rode.

We mounted Archie on Dugald's nag and rode straight away to the lake. Here we tied our ponies to the birch-trees, and, undressing, plunged in for a swim. When we came out we arranged matters thus: Dugald gave Archie his shirt, Donald gave him a pair of stockings, and I gave him a cap and my jacket, which was long enough to reach his knees. We tied the wet things, after washing the slime off, all in a bundle, and away the procession went to Coila. Everybody turned out to witness our home-coming. Well, we did look rather motley, but—Archie was saved.

My own adventures, however, had not ended yet. Neither my brothers nor Flora cared to go out again that day, so in the afternoon I shouldered my fishing rod and went off to enjoy a quiet hour's sport.

What took my footsteps towards the stream that made its exit from the loch, and went meandering down the glen, I never could tell. It was no favourite stream of mine, for though it contained plenty of trout, it passed through many woods and dark, gloomy defiles, with here and there a waterfall, and was on the whole so overhung with branches that there was difficulty in making a cast. I was far more successful than I expected to be, however, and the day wore so quickly away that on looking up I was surprised to find that the sun had set, and I must be quite seven miles from home. What did that matter? there would be a moon! I had Highland legs and a Highland heart, and knew all the cross-cuts in the country side. I would try for that big trout that had just leapt up to catch a moth. It took me half an hour to hook it. But I did, and after some pretty play I had the satisfaction of landing a lovely three-pounder. I now reeled up, put my rod in its canvas case, and prepared to make the best of my way to the castle.

It was nearly an hour since the sun had gone down like a huge crimson ball in the west, and now slowly over the hills a veritable facsimile of it was rising, and soon the stars came out as gloaming gave place to night, and moonlight flooded all the woods and glen.

The scene around me was lovely, but lonesome in the extreme, for there was not a house anywhere near, nor a sound to break the stillness except now and then the eerisome cry of the brown owl that flitted silently past overhead. Had I been very timid I could have imagined that figures were creeping here and there in the flickering shadows of the trees, or that ghosts and bogles had come out to keep me company. My nearest way home would be to cross a bit of heathery moor and pass by the neglected graveyard and ruined Catholic chapel; and, worse than all, the ancient manse where lived old Mawsie.

I never believed that Mawsie was a witch, though others did. She was said to creep about on moonlight nights like a dry aisk,[1] so people said, 'mooling' among heaps of rubbish and the mounds over the graves as she gathered herbs to concoct strange mixtures withal. Certainly Mawsie was no beauty; she walked 'two-fold,' leaning on a crutch; she was gray-bearded, wrinkled beyond conception; her head was swathed winter and summer in wraps of flannel, and altogether she looked uncanny. Nevertheless, the peasant people never hesitated to visit her to beg for herb-tea and oil to rub their joints. But they always chose the daylight in which to make their calls.

'Perhaps,' I thought, 'I'd better go round.' Then something whispered to me, 'What! you a M'Crimman, and confessing to fear!'

That decided me, and I went boldly on. For the life of me, however, I could not keep from mentally repeating those weird and awful lines in Burns' 'Tam o' Shanter,' descriptive of the hero's journey homewards on that unhallowed and awful night when he forgathered with the witches:

> 'By this time he was 'cross the ford
> Whare in the snaw the chapman smo'red;[2]
> And past the birks[3] and meikle stane
> Whare drunken Charlie brak's neck-bane;
> And through the furze and by the cairn

Where hunters found the murdered bairn,
And near the thorn, aboon the well,
Where Mungo's mither hanged hersel',
When glimmering through the groaning trees,
Kirk Alloway seemed in a bleeze.'

I almost shuddered as I said to myself, 'What if there be lights glimmering from the frameless windows of the ruined chapel? or what if old Mawsie's windows be "in a bleeze"?'

Tall, ghostly-looking elder-trees grew round the old manse, which people had told me always kept moving, even when no breath of wind was blowing.

If I had shuddered before, my heart stood still now with a nameless dread, for sure enough, from both the 'butt' and the 'ben' of the so-called witch's cottage lights were glancing.

What could it mean? She was too old to have company, almost an invalid, with age alone and its attendant infirmities—so, at least, people said. But it had also been rumoured lately that Mawsie was up to doings which were far from canny, that lights had been seen flitting about the old churchyard and ruin, and that something was sure to happen. Nobody in the parish could have been found hardy enough to cross the glen-foot where Mawsie lived long after dark. Well, had I thought of all this before, it is possible that I might have given her house a wide berth. It was now too late. I felt like one in a dream, impelled forward towards the cottage. I seemed to be walking on the air as I advanced.

To get to the windows, however, I must cross the graveyard yard and the ruin. This last was partly covered with tall rank ivy, and, hearing sounds inside, and seeing the glimmer of lanterns, I hid in the old porch, quite shaded by the greenery.

From my concealment I could notice that men were at work in a vault or pit on the floor of the old chapel, from which earth and rubbish were being dislodged, while another figure—not that of a workman—was bending over and addressing them in English. It was evident, therefore, those people below were not Highlanders, for in the face of the man who spoke I was able at a glance to distinguish the hard-set lineaments of the villain Duncan M'Rae. This man had been everything in his time—soldier, school-teacher, poacher, thief. He was abhorred by his own clan, and feared by every one.

Even the school children, if they met him on the road, would run back to avoid him.

Duncan had only recently come back to the glen after an absence of years, and every one said his presence boded no good. I shuddered as I gazed, almost spellbound, on his evil countenance, rendered doubly ugly in the uncertain light of the lantern. Suppose he should find me! I crept closer into my corner now, and tried to draw the ivy round me. I dared not run, for fear of being seen, for the moonlight was very bright indeed, and M'Rae held a gun in his hand.

After a time, which appeared to be interminable, I heard Duncan invite the men into supper, and slowly they clambered up out of the pit, and the three prepared to leave together.

All might have been well now, for they passed me without even a glance in my direction; but presently I heard one of the men stumble.

'Hullo!' he said; 'is this basket of fish yours, Mr. Mac?'

'No,' was the answer, with an imprecation that made me quake. 'We are watched!'

In another moment I was dragged from my place of concealment, and the light was held up to my face.

'A M'Crimman of Coila, by all that is furious! And so, youngster, you've come to watch? You know the family feud, don't you? Well, prepare to meet your doom. You'll never leave here alive.'

He pointed his gun at me as he spoke.

'Hold!' cried one of the men. 'We came from town to do a bit of honest work, but we will not witness murder.'

'I only wanted to frighten him,' said M'Rae, lowering his gun. 'Look you, sir,' he continued, addressing me once more, 'I don't want revenge, even on a M'Crimman of Coila. I'm a poacher; perhaps I'm a distiller in a quiet way. No matter, you know what an oath is. You'll swear ere you leave here, not to breathe a word of what you've seen. You hear?'

'I promise I won't,' I faltered.

He handled his fowling-piece threateningly once again. Verily, he had just then a terribly evil look.

'I swear,' I said, with trembling lips.

His gun was again lowered. He seemed to breathe more freely—less fiercely.

'Go, now,' he said, pointing across the moor. 'If a poor man like myself wants to hide either his game or his private still, what odds is it to a M'Crimman of Coila?'

How I got home I never knew. I remember that evening being in our front drawing-room with what seemed a sea of anxious faces round me, some of which were bathed in tears. Then all was a long blank, interspersed with fearful dreams.

It was weeks before I recovered consciousness. I was then lying in bed. In at the open window was wafted the odour of flowers, for it was a summer's evening, and outside were the green whispering trees. Townley sat beside the bed, book in hand, and almost started when I spoke.

'Mr. Townley!'

'Yes, dear boy.'

'Have I been long ill?'

'For weeks—four, I think. How glad I am you are better! But you must keep very, *very* quiet. I shall go and bring your mother now, and Flora.'

I put out my thin hand and detained him.

'Tell me, Mr. Townley,' I said, 'have I spoken much in my sleep, for I have been dreaming such foolish dreams?'

Townley looked at me long and earnestly. He seemed to look me through and through. Then he replied slowly, almost solemnly,

'Yes, dear boy, you have spoken *much.*'

I closed my eyes languidly. For now I knew that Townley was aware of more than ever I should have dared to reveal.

[1] Triton.

[2] Smothered.

[3] Birch-trees.

CHAPTER IV
THE RING AND THE BOOK

My return to health was a slow though not a painful one. My mind, however, was clear, and even before I could partake of food I enjoyed hearing sister play to me on her harp. Sometimes aunt, too, would play. My mother seldom left the room by day, and one of my chief delights was her stories from Bible life and tales of Bible lands.

At last I was permitted to get up and recline in fauteuil or on sofa.

'Mother,' I said one day, 'I feel getting stronger, but somehow I do not regain spirits. Is there some sorrow in your heart, mother, or do I only imagine it?'

She smiled, but there were tears in her eyes.

'I'm sure we are all very, *very* happy, Murdoch, to have you getting well again.'

'And, mother,' I persisted, 'father does not seem easy in mind either. He comes in and talks to me, but often I think his mind is wandering to other subjects.'

'Foolish child! nothing could make your father unhappy. He does his duty by us all, and his faith is fixed.'

One day they came and told me that the doctor had ordered me away to the seaside. Mother and Flora were to come, and one servant; the rest of our family were to follow.

It was far away south to Rothesay we went, and here, my cheeks fanned by the delicious sea-breezes, I soon began to grow well and strong again. But the sorrow in my mother's face was more marked than ever, though I had ceased to refer to it.

The rooms we had hired were very pleasant, but looked very small in comparison with the great halls I had been used to.

Well, on a beautiful afternoon father and my brothers arrived, and we all had tea out on the shady lawn, up to the very edge of which the waves were lapping and lisping.

I was reclining in a hammock chair, listening to the sea's soft, soothing murmur, when father brought his camp-stool and sat near me.

'Murdoch, boy,' he said, taking my hand gently, almost tenderly, in his, 'are you strong enough to bear bad news?'

My heart throbbed uneasily, but I replied, bravely enough, 'Yes, dear father; yes.'

'Then,' he said, speaking very slowly, as if to mark the effect of every word, 'we are—never—to return—to Castle Coila!'

I was calm now, for, strange to say, the news appeared to be no news at all.

'Well, father,' I answered, cheerfully, 'I can bear that—I could bear anything but separation.'

I went over and kissed my mother and sister.

'So this is the cloud that was in your faces, eh? Well, the worst is over. I have nothing to do now but get well. Father, I feel quite a man.'

'So do we both feel men,' said Donald and Dugald; 'and we are all going to work. Won't that be jolly?'

In a few brief words father then explained our position. There had arrived one day, some weeks after the worst and most dangerous part of my illness was over, an advocate from Aberdeen, in a hired carriage. He had, he said, a friend with him, who seemed, so he worded it, 'like one risen from the dead.'

His friend was helped down, and into father's private room off the hall.

His friend was the old beldame Mawsie, and a short but wonderful story she had to tell, and did tell, the Aberdeen advocate sitting quietly by the while with a bland smile on his face. She remembered, she said with many a sigh and groan, and many a doleful shake of head and hand, the marriage of Le Roi the dragoon with the Miss M'Crimman of Coila, although but a girl at the time; and she remembered, among many other things, that the priest's books were hidden for safety in a vault, where he also kept all the money he possessed. No one knew of the existence of this vault except her, and so on and so forth. So voluble did the old lady become that the advocate had to apply the *clôture* at last.

'It is strange—if true,' my father had muttered. 'Why,' he added, 'had the old lady not spoken of this before?'

'Ah, yes, to be sure,' said the Aberdonian. 'Well, that also is strange, but easily explained. The shock received on the night of the fire at the chapel had deprived the poor soul of memory. For years and years this deprivation continued, but one day, not long ago, the son of the present claimant, and probably rightful heir, to Coila walked into her room at the old manse, gun in hand. He had been down shooting at Strathtoul, and naturally came across to view the ruin so intimately connected with his father's fate and fortune. No sooner had he appeared than the good old dame rushed towards him, calling him by his grandfather's name. Her memory had returned as suddenly as it had gone. She had even told him of the vault. 'Perhaps,' continued he, with a meaning smile,

> '"'Tis the sunset of life gives her mystical lore,
> And coming events cast their shadow before."'

A fortnight after this visit a meeting of those concerned took place at the beldame's house. She herself pointed to the place where she thought the vault lay, and with all due legal formality digging was commenced, and the place was found not far off. At first glance the vault seemed empty. In one corner, however, was found, covered lightly over with withered ferns, many bottles of wine and—a box. The two men of law, Le Roi's solicitor and M'Crimman's, had a little laugh all to themselves over the wine. Legal men will laugh at anything.

'The priest must have kept a good cellar on the sly,' one said.

'That is evident,' replied the other.

The box was opened with some little difficulty. In it was a book—an old Latin Bible. But something else was in it too. Townley was the first to note it. Only a silver ring such as sailors wear—a ring with a little heart-shaped ruby stone in it. Book and ring were now sealed up in the box, and next day despatched to Edinburgh with all due formality. The best legal authorities the Scotch metropolis could boast of were consulted on both sides, but fate for once was against the M'Crimmans of Coila. The book told its tale. Half-carelessly written on fly-leaves, but each duly dated and signed by Stewart, the priest, were notes concerning many marriages, Le Roi's among the rest.

Even M'Crimman himself confessed that he was satisfied—as was every one else save Townley.

'The book has told one tale—or rather its binding has,' said Townley; 'but the ring may yet tell another.'

All this my father related to me that evening as we sat together on the lawn by the beach of Rothesay.

When he had finished I sat silently gazing seawards, but spoke not. My brothers told me afterwards that I looked as if turned to stone. And, indeed,

indeed, my heart felt so. When father first told me we should go back no more to Coila I felt almost happy that the bad news was no worse; but now that explanations had followed, my perplexity was extreme.

One thing was sure and certain—there was a conspiracy, and the events of that terrible night at the ruin had to do with it. The evil man Duncan M'Rae was in it. Townley suspected it from words I must have let fall in my delirium; but, worst of all, my mouth was sealed. Oh, why, why did I not rather die than be thus bound!

It must be remembered that I was very young, and knew not then that an oath so forced upon me could not be binding.

Come weal, come woe, however, I determined to keep my word.

The scene of our story changes now to Edinburgh itself. Here we had all gone to live in a house owned by aunt, not far from the Calton Hill. We were comparatively poor now, for father, with the honour and Christian feeling that ever characterized him, had even paid up back rent to the new owner of Coila Castle and Glen.

That parting from Coila had been a sad one. I was not there—luckily for me, perhaps; but Townley has told me of it often and often.

'Yes, Murdoch M'Crimman,' he said, 'I have been present at the funeral of many a Highland chief, but none of these impressed me half so much as the scene in Glen Coila, when the carriage containing your dear father and mother and Flora left the old castle and wound slowly down the glen. Men, women, and little ones joined in procession, and marched behind it, and so followed on and on till they reached the glen-foot, with the bagpipes playing "Farewell to Lochaber." This affected your father as much, I think, as anything else. As for your mother, she sat silently weeping, and Flora dared hardly trust herself to look up at all. Then the parting! The chief, your father, stood up and addressed his people—for "his people" he still would call them. There was not a tremor in his voice, nor was there, on the other hand, even a spice of bravado. He spoke to them calmly, logically. In the old days, he said, might had been right, and many a gallant corps of heroes had his forefathers led from the glen, but times had changed. They were governed by good laws, and good laws meant fair play, for they protected all alike, gentle and simple, poor as well as rich. He bade them love and honour the new chief of Coila, to whom, as his proven right, he not only heartily transferred his lands and castle, but even, as far as possible, the allegiance of his people. They must be of good cheer, he said; he would never forget the happy time he had spent in Coila, and if they should meet no more on this earth, there was a Happier Land beyond death and the grave. He ended his brief oration with that little word which means so much, "Good-bye." But scarcely would they let him go. Old, bare-headed, white-haired men crowded round the carriage to bless their chief and press his hand; tearful women held children up that he might but touch their hair, while some had thrown themselves on the heather in paroxysms of a grief which was uncontrollable. Then the pipes played once more as the carriage drove on, while the voices of the young men joined in chorus—

"Youth of the daring heart, bright be thy doom
As the bodings that light up thy bold spirit now.
But the fate of M'Crimman is closing in gloom,
And the breath of the grey wraith hath passed o'er his brow."

'When,' added Townley, 'a bend of the road and the drooping birch-trees shut out the mournful sight, I am sure we all felt relieved. Your father, smiling, extended his hand to your mother, and she fondled it and wept no more.'

For a time our life, to all outward seeming, was now a very quiet one. Although Donald and Dugald were sent to that splendid seminary which has given so many great men and heroes to the world, the 'High School of Edinburgh,' Townley still lived on with us as my tutor and Flora's.

What my father seemed to suffer most from was the want of something at which to employ his time, and what Townley called his 'talent for activity.' 'Doing nothing' was not father's form after leading so energetic a life for so many years at Coila. Like the city of Boston in America, Edinburgh prides itself on the selectness of its society. To this, albeit we had come down in the world, pecuniarily speaking, our family had free *entrée*. This would have satisfied some men; it did not satisfy father. He missed the bracing mountain air, he missed the freedom of the hills and the glorious exercise to which he had been accustomed.

He missed it, but he mourned it not. His was the most unselfish nature one could imagine. Whatever he may have felt in the privacy of his own apartment, however much he may have sorrowed in silence, among us he was ever cheerful and even gay. Perhaps, on the whole, it may seem to some that I write or speak in terms too eulogistic. But it should not be forgotten that the M'Crimman was my father, and that he is—gone. *De mortuis nil nisi bonum.*

The ex-chief of Coila was a gentleman. And what a deal there is in that one wee word! No one can ape the gentleman. True gentlemanliness must come from the heart; the heart is the well from which it must spring—constantly, always, in every position of life, and wherever the owner may be. No amount of exterior polish can make a true gentleman. The actor can play the part on the stage, but here he is but acting, after all. Off the stage he may or may not be the gentleman, for then he must not be judged by his dress, by his demeanour in company, his calmness, or his ducal bow, but by his actions, his words, or his spoken thoughts.

> 'Chesterfields and modes and rules
> For polished age and stilted youth.
> And high breeding's choicest school
> Need to learn this deeper truth:
> That to act, whate'er betide,
> Nobly on the Christian plan,
> This is still the surest guide
> How to be a gentleman.'

About a year after our arrival in Edinburgh, Townley was seated one day midway up the beautiful mountain called Arthur's Seat. It was early summer; the sky was blue and almost cloudless; far beneath, the city of palaces and monuments seemed to sleep in the sunshine; away to the east lay the sea, blue even as the sky itself, except where here and there a cloud shadow passed slowly over its surface. Studded, too, was the sea with many a white sail, and steamers with trailing wreaths of smoke.

The noise of city life, faint and far, fell on the ear with a hum hardly louder than the murmur of the insects and bees that sported among the wild flowers.

Townley would not have been sitting here had he been all by himself, for this Herculean young parson never yet set eye on a hill he meant to climb without going straight to the top of it.

'There is no tiring Townley.' I have often heard father make that remark; and, indeed, it gave in a few words a complete clue to Townley's character.

But to-day my aunt Cecilia was with him, and it was on her account he was resting. They had been sitting for some time in silence.

'It is almost too lovely a day for talking,' she said, at last.

'True; it is a day for thinking and dreaming.'

'I do not imagine, sir, that either thinking or dreaming is very much in your way.'

He turned to her almost sharply.

'Oh, indeed,' he said, 'you hardly gauge my character aright, Miss M'Crimman.'

'Do I not?'

'No, if you only knew how much I think at times; if you only knew how much I have even dared to dream—'

There was a strange meaning in his looks if not in his words. Did she interpret either aright, I wonder? I know not. Of one thing I am sure, and that is, my friend and tutor was far too noble to seem to take advantage of my aunt's altered circumstances in life to press his suit. He might be her equal some day, at present he was—her brother's guest and domestic.

'Tell me,' she said, interrupting him, 'some of your thoughts; dreams at best are silly.'

He heaved the faintest sigh, and for a few moments appeared bent only on forming an isosceles triangle of pebbles with his cane.

Then he put his fingers in his pocket.

'I wish to show you,' he said, 'a ring.'

'A ring, Mr. Townley! What a curious ring! Silver, set with a ruby heart. Why, this is the ring—the mysterious ring that belonged to the priest, and was found in his box in the vault.'

'No, that is not *the* ring. *The* ring is in a safe and under seal. That is but a facsimile. But, Miss M'Crimman, the ring in question did not, I have reason to believe, belong to the priest Stewart, nor was it ever worn by him.'

'How strangely you talk and look, Mr. Townley!'

'Whatever I say to you now, Miss M'Crimman, I wish you to consider sacred.'

The lady laughed, but not lightly.

'Do you think,' she said, 'I can keep a secret?'

'I do, Miss M'Crimman, and I want a friend and occasional adviser.'

'Go on, Mr. Townley. You may depend on me.'

'All we know, or at least all he will tell us of Murdoch's—your nephew's—illness, is that he was frightened at the ruin that night. He did not lead us to infer—for this boy is honest—that the terror partook of the supernatural, but he seemed pleased we did so infer.'

'Yes, Mr. Townley.'

'I watched by his bedside at night, when the fever was at its hottest. I alone listened to his ravings. Such ravings have always, so doctors tell us, a foundation in fact. He mentioned this ring over and over again. He mentioned a vault; he mentioned a name, and starting sometimes from uneasy slumber, prayed the owner of that name to spare him—to shoot him not.'

'And from this you deduce— —'

'From this,' said Townley, 'I deduce that poor Murdoch had seen that ring on the left hand of a villain who had threatened to shoot him, for some potent reason or another, that Murdoch had seen that vault open, and that he has been bound down by sacred oath not to reveal what he did see.'

'But oh, Mr. Townley, such oath could not, cannot be binding on the boy. We must— —'

'No, we must *not*, Miss M'Crimman. We must not put pressure on Murdoch at present. We must not treat lightly his honest scruples. *You* must leave *me* to work the matter out in my own way. Only, whenever I need your assistance or friendship to aid me, I may ask for it, may I not?'

'Indeed you may, Mr. Townley.'

Her hand lay for one brief moment in his; then they got up silently and resumed their walk.

Both were thinking now.

CHAPTER V
A NEW HOME IN THE WEST

To-night, before I entered my tower-room study and sat down to continue our strange story, I was leaning over the battlements and gazing admiringly at the beautiful sunset effects among the hills and on the lake, when my aunt came gliding to my side. She always comes in this spirit-like way.

'May I say one word,' she said, 'without interrupting the train of your thoughts?'

'Yes, dear aunt,' I replied; 'speak as you please—say what you will.'

'I have been reading your manuscript, Murdoch, and I think it is high time you should mention that the M'Raes of Strathtoul were in no degree connected with or voluntarily mixed up in the villainy that banished your poor father from Castle Coila.'

'It shall be as you wish,' I said, and then Aunt Cecilia disappeared as silently as she had come.

Aunt is right. Nor can I forget that—despite the long-lasting and unfortunate blood-feud—the Strathtouls were and are our kinsmen. It is due to them to add that they ever acted honourably, truthfully; that there was but one villain, and whatever of villainy was transacted was his. Need I say his name was Duncan M'Rae? A M'Rae of Strathtoul? No; I am glad and proud to say he was not. I even doubt if he had any right or title to the name at all. It may have been but an *alias*. An *alias* is often of the greatest use to such a man as this Duncan; so is an *alibi* at times!

I have already mentioned the school in the glen which my father the chief had built. M'Rae was one of its first teachers. He was undoubtedly clever, and, though he had not come to Coila without a little cloud on his character, his plausibility and his capability prevailed upon my father to give him a chance. There used at that time to be services held in the school on Sunday evenings, to which the most humbly dressed peasant could come. Humble though they were, they invariably brought their mite for the collection. It was dishonesty—even sacrilegious dishonesty—in Duncan to appropriate such moneys to his use, and to falsify the books. It is needless to say he was dismissed, and ever after he bore little good-will to the M'Crimmans of Coila.

He had now to live on his wits. His wits led him to dishonesty of a different sort—he became a noted poacher. His quarrels with the glen-keepers often led to ugly fights and to bloodshed, but never to Duncan's reform. He lived and lodged with old Mawsie. It suited him to do so for several reasons, one of which was that she had, as I have already said, an ill-name, and the keepers were superstitious; besides, her house was but half a mile from a high road, along which a carrier passed once a week on his way to a distant town, and Duncan nearly always had a mysterious parcel for him.

The poacher wanted a safe or store for his ill-gotten game. What better place than the floor of the ruined church? While digging there, to his surprise he had discovered a secret vault or cell; the roof and sides had fallen in, but masons could repair them. Such a place would be invaluable in his craft if it could be kept secret, and he determined it should be. After this, strange lights were said to be seen sometimes by belated travellers flitting among the old graves; twice also a ghost had been met on the hill adjoining— some *thing* at least that disappeared immediately with eldritch scream.

It was shortly after this that Duncan had imported two men to do what they called 'a bit of honest work.' Duncan had lodged and fed them at Mawsie's; they worked at night, and when they had done the 'honest work,' he took them to Invergowen and shipped them back to Aberdeen.

But the poacher's discovery of the priest's Bible turned his thoughts to a plan of enriching himself far more effectually and speedily than he ever could expect to do by dealing in game without a licence.

At the same time Duncan had found the poor priest's modest store of wine. A less scientific villain would have made short work with this, but the poacher knew better at present than to 'put an enemy in his mouth to steal away his brains;' besides, the vault would look more natural, when afterwards 'discovered,' with a collection of old bottles of wine in it.

To forge an entry on one of the fly-leaves of the book was no difficult task, nor was it difficult to deal with Mawsie so as to secure the end he had in view in the most natural way. Once again his villain-wit showed its ascendency. A person of little acumen would have sought to work upon the old lady's greed—would have tried to bribe her to say this or that, or to swear to anything. But well Duncan knew how treacherous is the aged memory, and yet how easily acted on. He began by talking much about the Le Roi marriage which had taken place when she was a girl. He put words in the old lady's mouth without seeming to do so; he manufactured an artificial memory for her, and neatly fitted it.

'Surely, mother,' he would say, 'you remember the marriage that took place in the chapel at midnight—the rich soldier, you know, Le Roi, and the bonnie M'Crimman lady? You're not so *very* old as to forget that.'

'Heigho! it's a long time ago, *ma yhillie og*, a long time ago, and I was young.'

'True, but old people remember things that happened when they were young better than more recent events.'

They talked in Gaelic, so I am not giving their exact words.

'Ay, ay, lad—ay, ay! And, now that you mention it, I do remember it well—the lassie M'Crimman and the bonnie, bonnie gentleman.'

'Gave you a guinea—don't you remember?'

'Ay, ay, the dear man!'

'Is this it?' continued Duncan, holding up a golden coin.

Her eyes gloated over the money, her birdlike claw clutched it; she 'crooned' over it, sang to it, rolled it in a morsel of flannel, and put it away in her bosom.

A course of this kind of tuition had a wonderful effect on Mawsie. After the marriage came the vault, and she soon remembered all that. But probably the guinea had more effect than anything else in fixing her mind on the supposed events of the past.

You see, Duncan was a psychologist, and a good one, too. Pity he did not turn his talents to better use.

The poacher's next move was to hurry up to London, and obtain an interview with the chief of Strathtoul's son. He seldom visited Scotland, being an officer of the Guards—a soldier, as his grandfather had been.

Is it any wonder that Duncan M'Rae's plausible story found a ready listener in young Le Roi, or that he was only too happy to pay the poacher a large but reasonable sum for proofs which should place his father in possession of fortune and a fine estate?

The rest was easy. A large coloured sketch was shown to old Mawsie as a portrait of the Le Roi who had been married in the old chapel in her girlhood. It was that of his grandson, who shortly after visited the manse and the ruin.

Duncan was successful beyond his utmost expectations. Only 'the wicked flee when no man pursueth' them, and this villain could not feel easy while he remained at home. Two things preyed on his mind—first, the meeting with myself at the ruin; secondly, the loss of his ring. Probably had the two men not interfered that night he would have made short work of me. As for the ring, he blamed his own carelessness for losing it. It was a dead man's ring; would it bring him ill-luck?

So he fled—or departed—put it as you please; but, singular to say, old Mawsie was found dead in her house the day *after* he had been seen to take his departure from the glen. It was said she had met her death by premeditated violence; but who could have slain the poor old crone, and for what reason? It was more charitable and more reasonable to believe that she had fallen and died where she was found. So the matter had been allowed to rest. What could it matter to Mawsie?

Townley alone had different and less charitable views about the matter. Meanwhile Townley's bird had flown. But everything comes to him who can wait, and—there was no tiring Townley.

A year or two flew by quickly enough. I know what that year or two did for me—*it made me a man!*

Not so much in stature, perhaps—I was young, barely seventeen—but a man in mind, in desire, in ambition, and in brave resolve. Do not imagine that I had been very happy since leaving Coila; my mind was racked by a thousand conflicting thoughts that often kept me awake at night when all others were sunk in slumber. Something told me that the doings of that night at the ruin had undone our fortunes, and I was bound by solemn promise never to divulge what I had seen or what I knew. A hundred times over I tried to force myself to the belief that the poacher was only a poacher, and not a villain of deeper dye, but all in vain.

Time, however, is the *edax rerum*—the devourer of all things, even of grief and sorrow. Well, I saw my father and mother and Flora happy in their new home, content with their new surroundings, and I began to take heart. But to work I must go. What should I do? What should I be? The questions were answered in a way I had little dreamt of.

One evening, about eight o'clock, while passing along a street in the new town, I noticed well-dressed mechanics and others filing into a hall, where, it was announced, a lecture was to be delivered—

'A New Home in the West.'

Such was the heading of the printed bills. Curiosity led me to enter with others.

I listened entranced. The lecture was a revelation to me. The 'New Home in the West' was the Argentine Republic, and the speaker was brimful of his subject, and brimful to overflowing with the rugged eloquence that goes straight to the heart.

There was wealth untold in the silver republic for those who were healthy, young, and willing to work—riches enough to be had for the digging to buy all Scotland up—riches of grain, of fruit, of spices, of skins and wool and meat—wealth all over the surface of the new home—wealth *in* the earth and bursting through it—wealth and riches everywhere.

And beauty everywhere too—beauty of scenery, beauty of woods and wild flowers; of forest stream and sunlit skies. Why stay in Scotland when wealth like this was to be had for the gathering? England was a glorious country, but its very over-population rendered it a poor one, and poorer it was growing every day.

> 'Hark! old Ocean's tongue of thunder,
> Hoarsely calling, bids you speed
> To the shores he held asunder
> Only for these times of need.
> Now, upon his friendly surges
> Ever, ever roaring "Come,"
> All the sons of hope he urges
> To a new, a richer home.
>
> There, instead of festering alleys,
> Noisome dirt and gnawing dearth,
> Sunny hills and smiling valleys
> Wait to yield the wealth of earth.
> All she seeks is human labour,
> Healthy in the open air;
> All she gives is—every neighbour
> Wealthy, hale, and happy There!'

Language like this was to me simply intoxicating. I talked all next day about what I had heard, and when evening came I once more visited the lecture-hall, this time in company with my brothers.

'Oh,' said Donald, as we were returning home, 'that is the sort of work we want.'

'Yes,' cried Dugald the younger; 'and that is the land to go to.'

'You are so young—sixteen and fifteen—I fear I cannot take you with me,' I put in.

Donald stopped short in the street and looked straight in my face.

'So *you* mean to go, then? And you think you can go without Dugald and me? Young, are we? But won't we grow out of that? We are not town-bred brats. Feel my arm; look at brother's lusty legs! And haven't we both got hearts—the M'Crimman heart? Ho, ho, Murdoch! big as you are, you don't go without Dugald and me!'

'That he sha'n't!' said Dugald, determinedly.

'Come on up to the top of the craig,' I said; 'I want a walk. It is only half-past nine.'

But it was well-nigh eleven before we three brothers had finished castle-building.

Remember, it was not castles in the air, either, we were piling up. We had health, strength, and determination, with a good share of honest ambition; and with these we believed we could gather wealth. The very thoughts of doing so filled me with a joy that was inexpressible. Not that I valued money for itself, but because wealth, if I could but gain it, would enable me to in some measure restore the fortunes of our fallen house.

We first consulted father. It was not difficult to secure his acquiescence to our scheme, and he even told mother that it was unnatural to expect birds to remain always in the parent nest.

I have no space to detail all the outs and ins of our arguments; suffice it to say they were successful, and preparations for our emigration were soon commenced. One stipulation of dear mother's we were obliged to give in to—namely, that Aunt Cecilia should go with us. Aunt was very wise, though very romantic withal—a strange mixture of poetry and common-sense. My father and mother, however, had very great faith in her. Moreover, she had already travelled all by herself half-way over the world. She had therefore the benefit of former experiences. But in every way we were fain to admit that aunt was eminently calculated to be our friend and mentor. She was and is clever. She could talk philosophy to us, even while darning our stockings or seeing after our linen; she could talk half a dozen languages, but she could talk common-sense to the cook as well; she was fitted to mix in the very best society, but she could also mix a salad. She played entrancingly on the harp, sang well, recited Ossian's poems by the league, had a beautiful face, and the heart of a lion, which well became the sister of a chief.

It is only fair to add that it was aunt who found the sinews of war—our war with fortune. She, however, made a sacrifice to our pride in promising to consider any and all moneys spent upon us as simply loans, to be repaid with interest when we grew rich, if not—and this was only an honest stipulation—worked off beforehand.

But poor dear aunt, her love of travel and adventure was quite wonderful, and she had a most childlike faith in the existence and reality of the El Dorado we were going in search of.

The parting with father, mother, and Flora was a terrible trial. I can hardly think of it yet without a feeling akin to melancholy. But we got away at last amid prayers and blessings and tears. A hundred times over Flora had begged us to write every week, and to make haste and get ready a place for her and mother and father and all in our new home in the West, for she would count the days until the summons came to follow.

Fain would honest, brawny Townley have gone with us. What an acquisition he would have proved! only, he told me somewhat significantly, he had work to do, and if he was successful he might follow on. I know, though, that parting with Aunt Cecilia almost broke his big brave heart.

There was so much to do when we arrived in London, from which port we were to sail, so much to buy, so much to be seen, and so many people to visit, that I and my brothers had little time to revert even to the grief of parting from all we held dear at home.

We did not forget to pay a visit to our forty-second cousins in their beautiful and aristocratic mansion at the West End. Archie Bateman was our favourite. My brothers and I were quite agreed as to that. The other cousin—who was also the elder—was far too much swamped in *bon ton* to please Highland lads such as we were.

But over and over again Archie made us tell him all we knew or had heard of the land we were going to. The first night Archie had said,

'Oh, I wish I were going too!'

The second evening his remark was,

'Why *can't* I go?'

But on the third and last day of our stay Archie took me boldly by the hand—

'Don't tell anybody,' he said, 'but I'm going to follow you very soon. Depend upon that. I'm only a younger son. Younger sons are nobodies in England. The eldest sons get all the pudding, and we have only the dish to scrape. They talk about making me a barrister. I don't mean to be made a barrister; I'd as soon be a bumbailiff. No, I'm going to follow you, cousin, so I sha'n't say good-bye—just *au revoir.*'

And when we drove away from the door, I really could not help admiring the handsome bold-looking English lad who stood in the porch waving his handkerchief and shouting,

'*Au revoir—au revoir.*'

CHAPTER VI
THE PROMISED LAND AT LAST

'There is nothing more annoyin' than a hitch at the hin'eren'. What think you, young sir?'

'I beg pardon,' I replied, 'but I'm afraid I did not quite understand you.'

I had been standing all alone watching our preparations for dropping down stream with the tide. What a wearisome time it had been, too!

The Canton was advertised to sail the day before, but did not. We were assured, however, she would positively start at midnight, and we had gone to bed expecting to awake at sea. I had fallen asleep brimful of all kinds of romantic thoughts. But lo! I had been awakened early on the dark morning of this almost wintry day with the shouting of men, the rattling of chains, and puff-puff-puffing of that dreadful donkey-engine.

'Oh yes, we'll be off, sure enough, about eight bells.'

This is what the steward told us after breakfast, but all the forenoon had slipped away, and here we still were. The few people on shore who had stayed on, maugre wind and sleet, to see the very, *very* last of friends on board, looked very worn and miserable.

But surely we were going at last, for everything was shipped and everything was comparatively still—far too still, indeed, as it turned out!

'I said I couldn't stand a hitch at the hin'eren', young sir—any trouble at the tail o' the chapter.'

I looked up—I *had* to look up, for the speaker was a head and shoulders bigger than I—a broad-shouldered, brawny, brown-bearded Scotchman. A Highlander evidently by his brogue, but one who had travelled south, and therefore only put a Scotch word in here and there when talking—just, he told me afterwards, to make better sense of the English language.

'Do I understand you to mean that something has happened to delay the voyage?'

'I dinna care whether you understand me or not,' he replied, with almost fierce independence, 'but we're broken down.'

It was only too true, and the news soon went all over the ship—spread like wild-fire, in fact. Something had gone wrong in the engine-room, and it would take a whole week to make good repairs.

I went below to report matters to aunt and my brothers, and make preparations for disembarking again.

When we reached the deck we found the big Scot walking up and down with rapid, sturdy strides; but he stopped in front of me, smiling. He had an immense plaid thrown Highland-fashion across his chest and left shoulder, and clutched a huge piece of timber in his hand, which by courtesy might have been called a cane.

'You'll doubtless go on shore for a spell?' he said. 'A vera judicious arrangement. I'll go myself, and take my mither with me. And are these your two brotheries, and your sister? How d'ye do, miss?'

He lifted his huge tam-o'-shanter as he made these remarks—or, in other words, he seized it by the top and raised it into the form of a huge pyramid.

'My aunt,' I said, smiling.

'A thousand parrdons, ma'am!' he pleaded, once more making a pyramid of his 'bonnet,' while the colour mounted to his brow. 'A thousand parrdons!'

Like most of his countrymen, he spoke broader when taken off his guard or when excited. At such times the r's were thundered or rolled out.

Aunt Cecilia smiled most graciously, and I feel sure she did not object to be mistaken for our sister.

'It seems,' he added, 'we are to be fellow-passengers. My name is Moncrieff, and if ever I can be of the slightest service to you, pray command me.'

'You mentioned your mother,' said aunt, by way of saying something. 'Is the old—I mean, is she going with you?'

'What else, what else? And you wouldn't be wrong in calling her "old" either. My mither's no' a spring chicken, but—she's a marvel. Ay, mither's a marvel.'

'I presume, sir, you've been out before?'

'I've lived for many years in the Silver West. I've made a bit of money, but I couldn't live a year longer without my mither, so I just came straight home to take her out. I think when you know my mither you'll agree with me—she's a marvel.'

On pausing here for a minute to review a few of the events of my past life, I cannot agree with those pessimists who tell us we are the victims of chance; that our fates and our fortunes have nothing more certain to guide them to a good or a bad end than yonder thistle-down which is the sport of the summer breeze.

When I went on board the good ship Canton, had any one told me that in a few days more I would be standing by the banks of Loch Coila, I would have laughed in his face.

Yet so it was. Aunt and Donald stayed in London, while I and Dugald formed the strange resolve of running down and having one farewell glance at Coila. I seemed impelled to do so, but how or by what I never could say.

No; we did not go near Edinburgh. Good-byes had been said, why should we rehearse again all the agony of parting?

Nor did we show ourselves to many of the villagers, and those who did see us hardly knew us in our English dress.

Just one look at the lake, one glance at the old castle, and we should be gone, never more to set foot in Coila.

And here we were close by the water, almost under shadow of our own old home. It was a forenoon in the end of February, but already the larch-trees were becoming tinged with tender green, a balmy air went whispering through the drooping silver birches, the sky was blue, flecked only here and there with fleecy clouds that cast shadow-patches on the lake. Up yonder a lark was singing, in adjoining spruce thickets we could hear the croodle of the ringdove, and in the swaying branches of the elms the solemn-looking rooks were already building their nests. Dugald and I were lying on the moss.

'Spring always comes early to dear Coila,' I was saying; 'and I'm so glad the ship broke down, just to give me a chance of saying "Good-bye" to the loch. You, Dugald, did say "Good-bye" to it, you know, but I never had a chance.

Ahem! We were startled by the sound of a little cough right behind us—a sort of made cough, such as people do when they want to attract attention.

Standing near us was a gentleman of soldierly bearing, but certainly not haughty in appearance, for he was smiling. He held a book in his hand, and on his arm leant a beautiful young girl, evidently his daughter, for both had blue eyes and fair hair.

Dugald and I had started to our feet, and for the life of me I could not help feeling awkward.

'I fear,' I stammered, 'we are trespassing. But—but my brother and I ran down from London to say good-bye to Coila. We will go at once.'

'Stay one moment,' said the gentleman. 'Do not run away without explaining. You have been here before?'

'We are the young M'Crimmans of Coila, sir.'

I spoke sadly—I trust not fiercely.

'Pardon me, but something seemed to tell me you were. We are pleased to meet you. Irene, my daughter. It is no fault of ours—at least, of mine—that your family and the M'Raes were not friendly long ago.'

'But my father *would* have made friends with the chief of Strathtoul,' I said.

'Yes, and mine had old Highland prejudices. But look, yonder comes a thunder-shower. You *must* stay till it is over.'

'I feel, sir,' I said, 'that I am doing wrong, and that I have done wrong. My father, even, does not know we are here. He has prejudices now, too,'

'Well,' said the officer, laughing, 'my father is in France. Let us both be naughty boys. You must come and dine with me and my daughter, anyhow. Bother old-fashioned blood-feuds! We must not forget that we are living in the nineteenth century.'

I hesitated a moment, then I glanced at the girl, and next minute we were all walking together towards the castle.

We did stop to dinner, nor did we think twice about leaving that night. The more I saw of these, our hereditary enemies, the more I liked them. Irene was very like Flora in appearance and manner, but she had a greater knowledge of the world and all its ways. She was very beautiful. Yes, I have said so already, but somehow I cannot help saying it again. She looked older than she really was, and taller than most girls of fourteen.

'Well,' I said in course of the evening, 'it *is* strange my being here.'

'It is only the fortune of war our both being here,' said M'Rae.

'I wonder,' I added, 'how it will all end!'

'If it would only end as I should wish, it would end very pleasantly indeed. But it will not. You will write filially and tell your good father of your visit. He will write cordially, but somewhat haughtily, to thank us. That will be all. Oh, Highland blood is very red, and Highland pride is very high. Well, at all events, Murdoch M'Crimman—if you will let me call you by your name without the "Mr."—we shall never forget your visit, shall we, darling?'

I looked towards Miss M'Rae. Her answer was a simple 'No'; but I was much surprised to notice that her eyes were full of tears, which she tried in vain to conceal.

I saw tears in her eyes next morning as we parted. Her father said 'Good-bye' so kindly that my whole heart went out to him on the spot.

'I'm not sorry I came,' I said; 'and, sir,' I added, 'as far as you and I are concerned, the feud is at an end?'

'Yes, yes; and better so. And,' he continued, 'my daughter bids me say that she is happy to have seen you, that she is going to think about you very often, and is so sorrowful you poor lads should have to go away to a foreign land to seek your fortune while we remain at Coila. That is the drift of it, but I fear I have not said it prettily enough to please Irene. Good-bye.'

We had found fine weather at Coila, and we brought it back with us to London. There was no hitch this time in starting. The Canton got away early in the morning, even before breakfast. The last person to come on board was the Scot, Moncrieff. He came thundering across the plank gangway with strides like a camel, bearing something or somebody rolled in a tartan plaid.

Dugald and I soon noticed two little legs dangling from one end of the bundle and a little old face peeping out of the other. It was his mother undoubtedly.

He put her gently down when he gained the deck, and led her away amidships somewhere, and there the two disappeared. Presently Moncrieff came back alone and shook hands with us in the most friendly way.

'I've just disposed of my mither,' he said, as if she had been a piece of goods and he had sold her. 'I've just disposed of the poor dear creature, and maybe she won't appear again till we're across the bay.'

'You did not take the lady below?'

'There's no' much of the lady about my mither, though I'm doing all I can to make her one. No; I didn't take her below. Fact is, we have state apartments, as you might say, for I've rented the second lieutenant's and purser's cabins. There they are, cheek-by-jowl, as cosy as wrens'-nests, just abaft the cook's galley amidships yonder.'

'Well,' I said, 'I hope your mother will be happy and enjoy the voyage.'

'Hurrah!' shouted the Scot; 'we're off at last! Now for a fair wind and a clear sea to the shores of the Silver West. I'll run and tell my mither we're off.'

That evening the sun sank on the western waves with a crimson glory that spoke of fine weather to follow. We were steaming down channel with just enough sail set to give us some degree of steadiness.

Though my brothers and I had never been to sea before, we had been used to roughing it in storms around the coast and on Loch Coila, and probably this may account for our immunity from that terror of the ocean, *mal-de-mer*. As for aunt, she was an excellent sailor. The saloon, when we went below to dinner, was most gay, beautifully lighted, and very home-like. The officers present were the captain, the surgeon, and one lieutenant. The captain was president, while the doctor occupied the chair of *vice*. Both looked thorough sailors, and both appeared as happy as kings. There seemed also to exist a perfect understanding between the pair, and their remarks and anecdotes kept the passengers in excellent good humour during dinner.

The doctor had been the first to enter, and he came sailing in with aunt, whom he seated on his right hand. Now aunt was the only young lady among the passengers, and she certainly had dressed most becomingly. I could not help admiring her—so did the doctor, but so also did the captain.

When he entered he gave his surgeon a comical kind of a look and shook his head.

'Walked to windward of me, I see!' he said. 'Miss M'Crimman,' he added, 'we don't, as a rule, keep particular seats at table in this ship.'

'Don't believe a word he says, Miss M'Crimman!' cried the doctor. 'Look, he's laughing! He never is serious when he smiles like that. Steward, what is the number of this chair?'

'Fifteen, sir.'

'Fifteen, Miss M'Crimman, and you won't forget it; and this table-napkin ring, observe, is Gordon tartan, green and black and orange.'

'Miss M'Crimman,' the captain put in, as if the doctor had not said a word, 'to-morrow evening, for example, you will have the honour to sit on my right.'

'Honour, indeed!' laughed the doctor.

'The honour to sit on my right. You will find I can tell much better stories than old Conserve-of-roses there; and I feel certain you will not sit anywhere else all the voyage!'

'Ah, stay one moments!' cried a merry-looking little Spaniard, who had just entered and seated himself quietly at the table; 'the young lady weel not always sit dere, or dere, for sometime she weel have de honour to sit at my right hand, for example, eh, capitan?'

There was a hearty laugh at these words, and after this, every one seemed on the most friendly terms with every one else, and willing to serve every one else first and himself last. This is one good result that accrues from travelling, and I have hardly ever yet known a citizen of the world who could be called selfish.

There were three other ladies at table to-night, each of whom sat by her husband's side. Though they were all in what Dr. Spinks afterwards termed the sere and yellow leaf, both he and the good captain really vied with each other in paying kindly attention to their wants.

So pleasantly did this our first dinner on board pass over that by the time we had risen from our seats we felt, one and all, as if we had known each other for a very long time indeed.

Next came our evening concert. One of the married ladies played exceedingly well, and the little Spanish gentleman sang like a minor Sims Reeves.

'Your sister sings, I feel sure,' he said to me.

'My aunt plays the harp and sings,' I answered.

'And the harp—you have him?'

'Yes.'

'Oh, bring him—bring him! I do love de harp!'

While my aunt played and sang, it would have been difficult to say which of her audience listened with the most delighted attention. The doctor's face was a study; the captain looked tenderly serious; Captain Bombazo, the black-moustachioed Spaniard, was animation personified; his dark eyes sparkled like diamonds, his very eyelids appeared to snap with pleasure. Even the stewards and stewardess lingered in the passage to listen with respectful attention, so that it is no wonder we boys were proud of our clever aunt.

When she ceased at last there was that deep silence which is far more eloquent than applause. The first to break it was Moncrieff.

'Well,' he said, with a deep sigh, 'I never heard the like o' that afore!'

The friendly relations thus established in the saloon lasted all the voyage long—so did the captain's, the doctor's, and little Spanish officer's attentions to my aunt. She had made a triple conquest; three hearts, to speak figuratively, lay at her feet.

Our voyage was by no means a very eventful one, and but little different from thousands of others that take place every month.

Some degree of merriment was caused among the men, when, on the fourth day, big Moncrieff led his mother out to walk the quarter-deck leaning on his arm. She was indeed a marvel. It would have been impossible even to guess at her age; for though her face was as yellow as a withered lemon, and as wrinkled as a Malaga rasin, she walked erect and firm, and was altogether as straight as a rush. She was dressed with an eye to comfort, for, warm though the weather was getting, her cloak was trimmed with fur. On her head she wore a neat old-fashioned cap, and in her hand carried a huge green umbrella, which evening and morning she never laid down except at meals.

This umbrella was a weapon of offence as well as defence. We had proof of that on the very first day, for as he passed along the deck the second steward had the bad manners to titter. Next moment the umbrella had descended with crushing force on his head, and he lay sprawling in the lee scuppers.

'I'll teach ye,' she said, 'to laugh at an auld wife, you gang-the-gate swinger.'

'Mither! mither!' pleaded Moncrieff, 'will you never be able to behave like a lady?'

The steward crawled forward crestfallen, and the men did not let him forget his adventure in a hurry.

'Mither's a marrvel,' Moncrieff whispered to me more than once that evening, for at table no 'laird's lady' could have behaved so well, albeit her droll remarks and repartee kept us all laughing. After dinner it was just the same—there were no bounds to her good-nature, her excellent spirits and comicality. Even when asked to sing she was by no means taken aback, but treated us to a ballad of five-and-twenty verses, with a chorus to each; but as it told a story of love and war, of battle and siege, of villainy for a time in the ascendant, and virtue triumphant at the end, it really was not a bit wearisome; and when Moncrieff told us that she could sing a hundred more as good, we all agreed that his mother was indeed a marvel.

I have said the voyage was uneventful, but this is talking as one who has been across the wide ocean many times and oft. No long voyage can be uneventful; but nothing very dreadful happened to mar our passage to Rio de Janeiro. We were not caught in a tornado; we were not chased by a pirate; we saw no suspicious sail; no ghostly voice hailed us from aloft at the midnight hour; no shadowy form beckoned us from a fog. We did not even spring a leak, nor did the mainyard come tumbling down. But we *did* have foul weather off Finisterre; a man *did* fall overboard, and was duly picked up again; a shark *did* follow the ship for a week, but got no corpse to devour, only the contents of the cook's pail, sundry bullets from sundry revolvers, and, finally, a red-hot brick rolled in a bit of blanket. Well, of course, a man fell from aloft and knocked his shoulder out—a man always does—and Mother Carey's chickens flew around our stern, boding bad weather, which never came, and shoals of porpoises danced around us at sunset, and we saw huge whales pursuing their solitary path through the bosom of the great deep, and we breakfasted off flying fish, and caught Cape pigeons, and wondered at the majestic flight of the albatross; and we often saw lightning without hearing thunder, and heard thunder without seeing lightning; and in due course we heard the thrilling shout from aloft of 'Land ho!' and heard the officer of the watch sing out, 'Where away?'

And lo and behold! three or four hours afterwards we were all on deck marvelling at the rugged grandeur of the shores of Rio, and the wondrous steeple-shaped mountain that stands sentry for ever and ever and ever at the entrance to the marvellous haven.

When this was in sight, Moncrieff rushed off into the cabin and bore his mother out.

He held the old lady aloft, on one arm, shouting, as he pointed landwards—

'Look, mither, look! the Promised Land! Our new home in the Silver West!'

CHAPTER VII
ON SHORE AT RIO

It was well on in the afternoon when land was sighted, but so accurately had the ship been navigated for all the long, pleasant weeks of our voyage that both the captain and his first officer might easily have been excused for showing a little pride in their seamanship. Your British sailor, however, is always a modest man, and there was not the slightest approach to bombast. The ship was now slowed, for we could not cross the bar that night.

At the dinner-table we were all as merry as schoolboys on the eve of a holiday. Old Jenny, as Moncrieff's mother had come to be called, was in excellent spirits, and her droll remarks not only made us laugh, but rendered it very difficult indeed for the stewards to wait with anything approaching to *sang-froid*. Moncrieff was quietly happy. He seemed pleased his mother was so great a favourite. Aunt, in her tropical toilet, looked angelic. The adjective was applied by our mutual friend Captain Roderigo de Bombazo, and my brothers and I agreed that he had spoken the truth for once in a way. Did he not always speak the truth? it may be asked. I am not prepared to accuse the worthy Spaniard of deliberate falsehood, but if everything he told us was true, then he must indeed have come through more wild and terrible adventures, and done more travelling and more fighting, than any lion-hunter that ever lived and breathed.

He was highly amusing nevertheless, and as no one, with the exception of Jenny, ever gave any evidence of doubting what he said and related concerning his strange career, he was encouraged to carry on; and even the exploits of Baron Munchausen could not have been compared to some of his. I think it used to hurt his feelings somewhat that old Jenny listened so stolidly to his relations, for he used to cater for her opinion at times.

'Ah!' Jenny would say, 'you're a wonderful mannie wi' your way o't! And what a lot you've come through! I wonder you have a hair in your heed!'

'But the señora believes vot I say?'

'Believe ye? If a' stories be true, yours are no lees, and I'm not goin' ahint your back to tell ye, sir.'

Once, on deck, he was drawing the long-bow, as the Yankees call it, at a prodigious rate. He was telling how, once upon a time, he had caught a young alligator; how he had tamed it and fed it till it grew a monster twenty feet long; how he used to saddle it and bridle it, and ride through the streets of Tulcora on its back—men, women, and children screaming and flying in all directions; how, armed only with his good sabre, he rode it into a lake which was infested with these dread saurians; how he was attacked in force by the awful reptiles, and how he had killed and wounded so many that they lay dead in dozens next day along the banks.

'Humph!' grunted old Jenny when he had finished.

The little captain put the questions,

'Ah! de aged señora not believe! De aged señora not have seen much of de world?'

Jenny had grasped her umbrella.

'Look here, my mannie,' she said, 'I'll gie ye a caution; dinna you refer to my age again, or I'll "aged-snorer" you. If ye get the weight o' my gingham on your shou'ders, ye'll think a coo has kick't ye—so mind.'

And the Spanish captain had slunk away very unlike a lion-hunter, but he never called Jenny old again.

To-night, however, even before we had gone below, Jenny had given proofs that she was in an extra good temper, for being a little way behind Bombazo—as if impelled by some sudden and joyous impulse—she lifted that everlasting umbrella and hit him a friendly thwack that could be heard from bowsprit to binnacle.

'Tell as mony lees the nicht as ye like, my mannie,' she cried, 'and I'll never contradict ye, for I've seen the promised land!'

'And so, captain, you must stay at Rio a whole week?' said my aunt at dessert.

'Yes, Miss M'Crimman,' replied the captain. 'Are you pleased?'

'I'm delighted. And I propose that we get up a grand picnic in "the promised land," as good old Jenny calls it.'

And so it was arranged. Bombazo and Dr. Spinks, having been at Rio de Janeiro before, were entrusted with the organization of the 'pig-neeg,' as Bombazo called it, and held their first consultation on ways and means that very evening. Neither I nor my brothers were admitted to this meeting, though aunt was. Nevertheless, we felt confident the picnic would be a grand success, for, to a late hour, men were hurrying fore and aft, and the stewards were up to their eyes packing baskets and making preparations, while from the cook's gally gleams of rosy light shot out every time the door was opened, to say nothing of odours so appetising that they would have awakened Van Winkle himself.

Before we turned in, we went on deck to have a look at the night. It was certainly full of promise. We were not far from the shore—near enough to see a long line of white which we knew was breakers, and to hear their deep sullen boom as they spent their fury on the rocks. The sky was studded with brilliant stars—far more bright, we thought them, than any we ever see in our own cold climate. Looking aloft, the tall masts seemed to mix and mingle with the stars at every roll of the ship. The moon, too, was as bright as silver in the east, its beams making strange quivering lines and crescents in each approaching wave. And somewhere—yonder among those wondrous cone-shaped hills, now bathed in this purple moonlight—lay the promised land, the romantic town of Rio, which to-morrow we should visit.

We went below, and, as if by one accord, my brothers and I knelt down together to thank the Great Power on high who had guided us safely over the wide illimitable ocean, and to implore His blessing on those at home, and His guidance on all our future wanderings.

Early next morning we were awakened by a great noise on deck, and the dash and turmoil of breaking water. The rudder-chains, too, were constantly rattling as the men at the wheel obeyed the shouts of the officer of the watch.

'Starboard a little!'

'Starboard it is, sir!'

'Easy as you go! Steady!'

'Steady it is, sir!'

'Port a little! Steady!'

Then came a crash that almost flung us out of our beds. Before we gained the deck of our cabin there was another, and still another. Had we run on shore? We dreaded to ask each other.

But just then the steward, with kindly thought, drew back our curtain and reassured us.

'We're only bumping over the bar, young gentlemen—we'll be in smooth water in a jiffey.'

We were soon all dressed and on deck. We were passing the giant hill called Sugar Loaf, and the mountains seemed to grow taller and taller, and to frown over us as we got nearer.

Once through the entrance, the splendid bay itself lay spread out before us in all its silver beauty. Full twenty miles across it is, and everywhere surrounded by the grandest hills imaginable. Not even in our dreams could we have conceived of such a noble harbour, for here not only could all the fleets in the world lie snug, but even cruise and manœuvre. Away to the west lay the picturesque town itself, its houses and public buildings shining clear in the morning sun, those nearest nestling in a beauty of tropical foliage I have never seen surpassed.

My brothers and I felt burning to land at once, but regulations must be carried out, and before we had cleared the customs, and got a clean bill of health, the day was far spent. Our picnic must be deferred till to-morrow.

However, we could land.

As they took their seats in the boat and she was rowed shoreward, I noticed that Donald and Dugald seemed both speechless with delight and admiration; as for me, I felt as if suddenly transported to a new world. And such a world—beauty and loveliness everywhere around us! How should I ever be able to describe it, I kept wondering—how give dear old mother and Flora any notion, even the most remote, of the delight instilled into our souls by all we saw and felt in this strange, strange land! Without doubt, the beauty of our surroundings constitutes one great factor in our happiness, wherever we are.

When we landed—indeed, before we landed—while the boat was still skimming over the purple waters, the green mountains appearing to mingle and change places every moment as we were borne along, I felt conquered, if I may so express it, by the enchantment of my situation. I gave in my allegiance to the spirit of the scene, I abandoned all thoughts of being able to describe anything, I abandoned myself to enjoyment. *Laisser faire*, I said to my soul, is to live. Every creature, every being here seems happy. To partake of the *dolce far niente* appears the whole aim and object of their lives.

And so I stepped on shore, regretting somewhat that Flora was not here, feeling how utterly impossible it would be to write that 'good letter' home descriptive of this wondrous medley of tropical life and loveliness, but somewhat reckless withal, and filled with a determination to give full rein to my sense of pleasure. I could not help wondering, however, if everything I saw was real. Was I in a dream, from which I should presently be rudely awakened by the rattle and clatter of the men hauling up ashes, and find myself in bed on board the Canton? Never mind, I would enjoy it were it even a dream.

What a motley crowd of people of every colour! How jolly those negroes look! How gaily the black ladies are dressed! How the black men laugh! What piles of fruit and green stuff! What a rich, delicious, warm aroma hovers everywhere!

An interpreter? You needn't ask *me*. I'm not in charge. Ask my aunt here; but she herself can talk many languages. Or ask that tall brawny Scot, who is hustling the darkies about as if South America all belonged to him.

'A carriage, Moncrieff? Oh, this is delightful! Auntie, dear, let me help you on board. Hop in, Dugald. Jump, Donald. No, no, Moncrieff, I mean to have the privilege of sitting beside the driver. Off we go. Hurrah! Do you like it, Donald? But aren't the streets rough! I won't talk any more; I want to watch things.'

I wonder, though, if Paradise itself was a bit more lovely than the gardens we catch glimpses of as we drive along?

How cool they look, though the sun is shining in a blue and cloudless sky! What dark shadows those gently waving palm-trees throw! Look at those cottage verandahs! Look, oh, look at the wealth of gorgeous flowers—the climbing, creeping, wreathing flowers! What colours! What fantastic shapes! What a merry mood Nature must have been in when she framed them so! And the perfume from those fairy gardens hangs heavy on the air; the delicious balmy breeze that blows through the green, green palm-leaves is not sufficient to waft away the odour of that orange blossom. Behold those beautiful children in groups, on terraces and lawns, at windows, or in verandahs—so gaily are they dressed that they themselves might be mistaken for bouquets of lovely flowers!

I wonder what the names of all those strange blossom-bearing shrubs are. But, bah! who would bother about names of flowers on a day like this? The butterflies do not, and the bees do not. Are those really butterflies, though—really and truly? Are they not gorgeously painted fans, waved and wafted by fairies, themselves unseen?

The people we meet chatter gaily as we pass, but they do not appear to possess a deal of curiosity; they are too contented for anything. All life here must be one delicious round of enjoyment. And nobody surely ever dies here; I do not see how they could.

'Is this a cave we are coming to, Moncrieff? What is that long row of columns and that high, green, vaulted roof, through which hardly a ray of sunshine can struggle? Palm-trees! Oh, Moncrieff, what glorious palms! And there is life upon life there, for the gorgeous trees, not apparently satisfied with their own magnificence of shape and foliage, must array themselves in wreaths of dazzling orchids and festoons of trailing flowers. The fairies *must* have hung those flowers there? Do not deny it, Moncrieff!'

And here, in the Botanical Gardens, imagination must itself be dumb— such a wild wealth of all that is charming in the vegetable and animal creation.

'Donald, go your own road. Dugald, go yours; let us wander alone. We may meet again some day. It hardly matters whether we do or not. I'm in a dream, and I don't think I want to awaken for many a long year.'

I go wandering away from my brothers, away from every one.

A fountain is sending its spray aloft till the green drooping branches of the bananas and those feathery tree-ferns are everywhere spangled with diamonds. I will rest here. I wish I could catch a few of those wondrous butterflies, or even one of those fairylike humming-birds—mere sparks of light and colour that flit and buzz from flower to flower. I wish I could— that I—I mean—I—wish—'

'Hullo! Murdoch. Where are you? Why, here he is at last, sound asleep under an orange-tree!'

It is my wild Highland brothers. They have both been shaking me by the shoulders. I sit up and rub my eyes.

'Do you know we've been looking for you for over an hour?'

'Ah, Dugald!' I reply, 'what is an hour, one wee hour, in a place like this?'

We must now go to visit the market-place, and then we are going to the hotel to dine and sleep.

The market is a wondrously mixed one, and as wondrously foreign and strange as it is possible to conceive. The gay dresses of the women—some of whom are as black as an ebony ball; their gaudy head-gear; their glittering but tinselled ornaments; their round laughing faces, in which shine rows of teeth as white perhaps as alabaster; the jaunty men folks; the world of birds and beasts, all on the best of terms with themselves, especially the former, arrayed in all the colours of the rainbow; the world of fruit, tempting in shape, in beauty, and in odour; the world of fish, some of them beautiful enough to have dwelt in the coral caves of fairyland beneath the glittering sea—some ugly, even hideous enough to be the creatures of a demon's dream, and some, again, so odd-looking or so grotesque as to make one smile or laugh outright;—the whole made up a picture that even now I have but to close my eyes to see again!

When night falls the streets get for a time more crowded; side-paths hardly exist—at all events, the inhabitants show their independence by crowding along the centre of the streets. Not much light to guide them, though, except where from open doors or windows the rays from lamps shoot out into the darkness.

Away to the hotel. A dinner in a delightfully cool, large room, a punkah waving overhead, brilliant lights, joy on all our faces, a dessert fit to set before a king. Now we shall know how those strange fruits taste, whose perfume hung around the market to-day. To bed at last in a room scented with orange-blossoms, and around the windows of which the sweet stephanotis clusters in beauty—to bed, to sleep, and dream of all we have done and seen.

We awaken—at least, I do—in the morning with a glad sensation of anticipated pleasure. What is it? Oh yes, the picnic!

But it is no ordinary picnic. It lasts for three long days and nights, during which we drive by day through scenes of enchantment apparently, and sleep by night under canvas, wooed to slumber by the wind whispering in the waving trees.

'Moncrieff,' I say on the second day, 'I should like to live here for ever and ever and ever.'

'Man!' replies Moncrieff, 'I'm glad ye enjoy it, and so does my mither here. But dinna forget, lads, that hard work is all before us when we reach Buenos Ayres.'

'But I will, and I *shall* forget, Moncrieff,' I cry. 'This country is full of forgetfulness. Away with all thoughts of work; let us revel in the sunshine like the bees, and the birds, and the butterflies.'

'Revel away, then,' says Moncrieff; and dear aunt smiles languidly.

On the last day of 'the show,' as Dugald called it, and while our mule team is yet five good miles from town, clouds dark and threatening bank rapidly up in the west. The driver lashes the beasts and encourages them with shout and cry to do their speedy utmost; but the storm breaks over us in all its fury, the thunder seems to rend the very mountains, the rain pours down in white sheets, the lightning runs along the ground and looks as if it would set the world on fire; the wind goes tearing through the trees, bending the palms like reeds, rending the broad banana-leaves to ribbons; branches crack and fall down, and the whole air is filled with whirling fronds and foliage.

Moncrieff hastily envelopes his mother in that Highland plaid till nought is visible of the old lady save the nose and one twinkling eye. We laugh in spite of the storm. Louder and louder roars the thunder, faster and faster fly the mules, and at last we are tearing along the deserted streets, and hastily draw up our steaming steeds at the hotel door. And that is almost all I remember of Rio; and to-morrow we are off to sea once more.

CHAPTER VIII
MONCRIEFF RELATES HIS EXPERIENCES

Our life at sea had been like one long happy dream. That, at all events, is how it had felt to me. 'A dream I could have wished to last for aye.' I was enamoured of the ocean, and more than once I caught myself yearning to be a sailor. There are people who are born with strange longings, strange desires, which only a life on the ever-changing, ever-restless waves appears to suit and soothe. To such natures the sea seems like a mother—a wild, hard, harsh mother at times, perhaps, but a mother who, if she smiles but an hour, makes them forget her stormy anger of days or weeks.

But the dream was past and gone. And here we had settled down for a spell at Buenos Ayres. We had parted with the kindly captain and surgeon of the Canton, with many a heartily expressed hope of meeting again another day, with prayers on their side for our success in the new land, with kindliest wishes on ours for a pleasant voyage and every joy for them.

Dear me! What a very long time it felt to look back to, since we had bidden them 'good-bye' at home! How very old I was beginning to feel! I asked my brothers if their feelings were the same, and found them identical. Time had been apparently playing tricks on us.

And yet we did not look any older in each other's eyes, only just a little more serious. Yes, that was it—*serious*. Even Dugald, who was usually the most light-hearted and merry of the three of us, looked as if he fully appreciated the magnitude of what we had undertaken.

Here we were, three—well, young men say, though some would have called us boys—landed on a foreign shore, without an iota of experience, without much knowledge of the country apart from that we had gleaned from books or gathered from the conversations of Bombazo and Moncrieff. And yet we had landed with the intention, nay, even the determination, to make our way in the new land—not only to seek our fortunes, but to find them.

Oh, we were not afraid! We had the glorious inheritance of courage, perseverance, and self-reliance. Here is how Donald, my brother, argued one night:

'Look, here, Murdo,' he said. 'This *is* a land of milk and honey, isn't it? Well, we're going to be the busy bees to gather it. It *is* a silver land, isn't it? Well, we're the boys to tap it. Fortunes *are* made here, and *have* been made. What is done once can be done five hundred times. Whatever men dare they can do. *Quod erat demonstrandum.*'

'*Et nil desperandum,*' added Dugald.

'I'm not joking, I can tell you, Dugald, I'm serious now, and I mean to remain so, and stick to work—aren't you, Murdo?'

'I am, Donald.'

Then we three brothers, standing there, one might say, on the confines of an unknown country, with all the world before us, shook hands, and our looks, as we gazed into each other's eyes, said—if they said anything— 'We'll do the right thing one by the other, come weal, come woe.'

Aunt entered soon after.

'What are you boys so serious about?' she said, laughing merrily, as she seated herself on the couch. 'You look like three conspirators.'

'So we are, aunt. We're conspiring together to make our fortunes.'

'What! building castles in the air?'

'Oh, no, no, *no,*' cried Donald, 'not in the air, but on the earth. And our idols are not going to have feet of clay, I assure you, auntie, but of solid silver.'

'Well, we shall hope for the best. I have just parted with Mr. Moncrieff, whom I met down town. We have had a long walk together and quite a nice chat. He has made me his confidant—think of that!'

'What! you, auntie?'

'Yes, me. Who else? And that sober, honest, decent, Scot is going to take a wife. It was so good of him to tell *me.* We are all going to the wedding next week, and I'm sure I wish the dear man every happiness and joy.'

'So do we, aunt.'

'And oh, by the way, he is coming to dine here to-night, and I feel sure he wants to give you good advice, and that means me too, of course.'

'Of course, auntie, you're one of us.'

Moncrieff arrived in good time, and brought his mother with him.

'Ye didn't include my mither in the invitation, Miss M'Crimman,' said the Scot; 'but I knew you meant her to come. I've been so long without the poor old creature, that I hardly care to move about without her now.'

'Poor old creature, indeed!' Mrs. Moncrieff was heard to mumble. 'Where,' she said to a nattily dressed waiter, 'will you put my umbrella?'

'I'll take the greatest care of it, madam,' the man replied.

'Do, then,' said the little old dame, 'and I may gi'e ye a penny, though I dinna mak' ony promises, mind.'

A nicer little dinner was never served, nor could a snugger room for such a *tête-à-tête* meal be easily imagined. It was on the ground floor, the great casement windows opening on to a verandah in a shady garden, where grass was kept green and smooth as velvet, where rare ferns grew in luxurious freedom with dwarf palms and drooping bananas, and where stephanotis and the charming lilac bougainvillea were still in bloom.

When the dessert was finished, and old Jenny was quite tired talking, it seemed so natural that she should curl up in an easy-chair and go off to sleep.

'I hope my umbrella's safe, laddie,' were her last words as her son wrapped her in his plaid.

'As safe as the Union Bank,' he replied.

So we left her there, for the waiter had taken coffee into the verandah.

Aunt, somewhat to our astonishment, ordered cigars, and explained to Moncrieff that she did not object to smoking, but *did* like to see men happy.

Moncrieff smiled.

'You're a marvel as well as my mither,' he said.

He smoked on in silence for fully five minutes, but he often took the cigar from his mouth and looked at it thoughtfully; then he would allow his eyes to follow the curling smoke, watching it with a smile on his face as it faded into invisibility, as they say ghosts do.

'Mr. Moncrieff,' said aunt, archly, 'I know what you are thinking about.'

Moncrieff waved his hand through a wreath of smoke as if to clear his sight.

'If you were a man,' he answered, 'I'd offer to bet you couldn't guess my thoughts. I was not thinking about my Dulcinea, nor even about my mither; I was thinking about you and your britheries—I mean your nephews.'

'You are very kind, Mr. Moncrieff.'

'I'm a man of the worrrld, though I wasn't aye a man of the worrrld. I had to pay deep and dear for my experience, Miss M'Crimman.'

'I can easily believe that; but you have benefited by it.'

'Doubtless, doubtless; only it was concerning yourselves I was about to make an observation or two.'

'Oh, thanks, do. You are so kind.'

'Never a bit. This is a weary worrrld at best. Where would any of us land if the one didn't help the other? Well then, there you sit, and woman of the worrrld though you be, you're in a strange corner of it. You're in a foreign land now if ever you were. You have few friends. Bah! what are all your letters of introduction worth? What do they bring you in? A few invitations to dinner, or to spend a week up country by a wealthy *estanciero*, advice from this friend and the next friend, and from a dozen friends maybe, but all different. You are already getting puzzled. You don't know what to do for the best. You're stopping here to look about you, as the saying is. You might well ask me what right have I to advise you. The right of brotherhood, I may answer. By birth and station you may be far above me, but—you are friends—you are from dear auld Scotland. Boys, you are my brothers!'

'And I your sister!' Aunt extended her hand as she spoke, and the worthy fellow 'coralled' it, so to speak, in his big brown fist, and tears sprang to his eyes.

He pulled himself up sharp, however, and surrounded himself with smoke, as the cuttle-fish does with black water, and probably for the same reason—to escape observation.

'Now,' he said, 'this is no time for sentiment; it is no land for sentiment, but for hard work. Well, what are you going to do? Simply to say you're going to make your fortune is all fiddlesticks and folly. How are you going to begin?'

'We were thinking—' I began, but paused.

'*I* was thinking—' said my aunt; then she paused also.

Moncrieff laughed, but not unmannerly.

'I was thinking,' he said. '*You* were thinking; *he, she*, or *it* was thinking. Well, my good people, you may stop all your life in Buenos Ayres and conjugate the verb "to think"; but if you'll take my advice you will put a shoulder to the wheel of life, and try to conjugate the verb "to do".'

'We all want to *do* and act,' said Donald, energetically.

'Right. Well, you see, you have one thing already in your favour. You have a wee bit o' siller in your pouch. It is a nest egg, though; it is not to be spent—it is there to bring more beside it. Now, will I tell you how I got on in the world? I'm not rich, but I am in a fair way to be independent. I am very fond of work, for work's sake, and I'm thirty years of age. Been in this country now for over fourteen years. Had I had a nest egg when I started, I'd have been half a millionaire by now. But, wae's me! I left the old country with nothing belonging to me but my crook and my plaid.'

'You were a shepherd before you came out, then?' said aunt.

'Yes; and that was the beauty of it. You've maybe heard o' Foudland, in Aberdeenshire? Well, I came fra far ayant the braes o' Foudland. That's, maybe, the way my mither's sae auldfarrent. There, ye see, I'm talkin' Scotch, for the very thought of Foudland brings back my Scotch tongue. Ay, dear lady, dear lady, my father was an honest crofter there. He owned a bit farm and everything, and things went pretty well with us till death tirled at the door-sneck and took poor father away to the mools. I was only a callan o' some thirteen summers then, and when we had to leave the wee croft and sell the cows we were fain to live in a lonely shieling on the bare brae side, just a butt and a ben with a wee kailyard, and barely enough land to grow potatoes and keep a little Shetland cowie. But, young though I was, I could herd sheep—under a shepherd at first, but finally all by myself. I'm not saying that wasn't a happy time. Oh, it was, lady! it was! And many a night since then have I lain awake thinking about it, till every scene of my boyhood's days rose up before me. I could see the hills, green with the tints of spring, or crimson with the glorious heather of autumn; see the braes yellow-tasselled with the golden broom and fragrant with the blooming whins; see the glens and dells, the silver, drooping birch-trees, the grand old waving pines, the wimpling burns, the roaring linns and lochs asleep in the evening sunset. And see my mither's shieling, too; and many a night have I lain awake to pray I might have her near me once again.'

'And a kind God has answered that prayer!'

'Ay, Miss M'Crimman, and I'll have the sad satisfaction of one day closing her een. Never mind, we do our duty here, and we'll all meet again in the great "Up-bye." But, dear boys, to continue my story—if story I dare call it. Not far from the hills where I used to follow Laird Glennie's sheep, and down beside a bonnie wood and stream, was a house, of not much pretension, but tenanted every year by a gentleman who used to paint the hills and glens and country all round. They say he got great praise for his pictures, and big prices as well. I used often to arrange my sheep and dogs for him into what he would call picturesque groups and attitudes. Then he painted them and me and dogs and all. He used to delight to listen to my boyish story of adventure, and in return would tell me tales of far-off lands he had been in, and about the Silver Land in particular. Such stories actually fired my blood. He had sown the seeds of ambition in my soul, and I began to long for a chance of getting away out into the wide, wide world, and seeing all its wonders, and, maybe, becoming a great man myself. But how could a penniless laddie work his way abroad? Impossible.

'Well, one autumn a terrible storm swept over the country. It began with a perfect hurricane of wind, then it settled down to rain, till it became a perfect "spate." I had never seen such rain, nor such tearing floods as came down from the hills.

'Our shieling was a good mile lower down the stream than the artist's summer hut. It was set well up the brae, and was safe. But on looking out next day a sight met my eyes that quite appalled me. All the lowlands and haughs were covered with a sea of water, down the centre of which a mighty river was chafing and roaring, carrying on its bosom trees up-torn from their roots, pieces of green bank, "stooks" of corn and "coles" of hay, and, saddest of all, the swollen bodies of sheep and oxen. My first thought was for the artist. I ran along the bank till opposite his house. Yes, there it was flooded to the roof, to which poor Mr. Power was clinging in desperation, expecting, doubtless, that every moment would be his last, for great trees were surging round the house and dashing against the tiles.

'Hardly knowing what I did, I waved my plaid and shouted. He saw me, and waved his arm in response. Then I remembered that far down stream a man kept a boat, and I rushed away, my feet hardly seeming to touch the ground, till I reached—not the dwelling, that was covered, but the bank opposite; and here, to my delight, I found old M'Kenzie seated in his coble. He laughed at me when I proposed going to the rescue of Mr. Power.

'"Impossible!" he said. "Look at the force of the stream."

'"But we have not to cross. We can paddle up the edge," I insisted.

'He ventured at last, much to my joy. It was hard, dangerous work, and often we found it safest to land and haul up the boat along the side.

'We were opposite the artist's hut at length, hardly even the chimney of which was now visible. But Power was safe as yet.

'At the very moment our boat reached him the chimney disappeared, and with it the artist. The turmoil was terrible, for the whole house had collapsed. For a time I saw nothing, then only a head and arm raised above the foaming torrent, far down stream. I dashed in, in spite of M'Kenzie's remonstrances, and in a minute more I had caught the drowning man. I must have been struck on the head by the advancing boat. That mattered little—the sturdy old ferryman saved us both; and for a few days the artist had the best room in mither's shieling.

'And this, dear lady, turned out to be—as I dare say you have guessed—my fairy godfather. He went back to Buenos Ayres, taking me as servant. He is here now. I saw him but yesterday, and we are still the fastest friends.

'But, boys, do not let me deceive you. Mr. Power was not rich; all he could do for me was to pay my passage out, and let me trust to Providence for the rest.

'I worked at anything I could get to do for a time, principally holding horses in the street, for you know everybody rides here. But I felt sure enough that one day, or some day, a settler would come who could value the services of an honest, earnest Scottish boy.

'And come the settler did. He took me away, far away to the west, to a wild country, but one that was far too flat and level to please me, who had been bred and born among the grand old hills of Scotland.

'Never mind, I worked hard, and this settler—a Welshman he was—appreciated my value, and paid me fairly well. The best of it was that I could save every penny of my earnings.

'Yes, boys, I roughed it more than ever you'll have to do, though remember you'll have to rough it too for a time. You don't mind that, you say. Bravely spoken, boys. Success in the Silver Land rarely fails to fall to him who deserves it.

'Well, in course of time I knew far more about sheep and cattle-raising than my master, so he took me as a partner, and since then I have done well. We changed our quarters, my partner and I. We have now an excellent steading of houses, and a grand place for the beasts.'

'And to what qualities do you chiefly attribute your success?' said my aunt.

'Chiefly,' replied Moncrieff, 'to good common-sense, to honest work and perseverance. I'm going back home in a week or two, as soon as I get married and my mither gets the "swimming" out of her head. She says she still feels the earth moving up and down with her; and I don't wonder, an auld body like her doesn't stand much codging about.

'Well, you see, boys, that I, like yourselves, had one advantage to begin with. You have a bit o' siller—I got a fairy godfather. But if I had a year to spare I'd go back to Scotland and lecture. I'd tell them all my own ups and downs, and I'd end by saying that lads or young men, with plenty of go in them and willingness to work, will get on up country here if they can once manage to get landed. Ay, even if they have hardly one penny to rattle against another.

'Now, boys, do you care to go home with me? Mind it is a wild border-land I live on. There are wild beasts in the hill jungles yet, and there are wilder men—the Indians. Yes, I've fought them before, and hope to live to fight them once again.'

'I don't think *we'll* fear the Indians *very* much,' said my bold brother Donald.

'And,' I added, 'we are so glad you have helped us to solve the problem that we stood face to face with—namely, how to begin to do something.'

'Well, if that is all, I'll give you plenty to do. I've taken out with me waggon-loads of wire fencing as well as a wife. Next week, too, I expect a ship from Glasgow to bring me seven sturdy Scotch servant men that I picked myself. Every one of them has legs like pillar post-offices, hands as broad as spades, and a heart like a lion's. And, more than all this, we are trying to form a little colony out yonder, then we'll be able to hold our own against all the reeving Indians that ever strode a horse. Ah! boys, this Silver Land has a mighty future before it! We have just to settle down a bit and work with a will and a steady purpose, then we'll fear competition neither with Australia nor the United States of America either.

'But you'll come. That's right. And now I have you face to face with fate and fortune.

"Now's the day and now's the hour,

See the front of battle lower."

Yes, boys, the battle of life, and I would not give a fig for any lad who feared to face it.

'Coming, mither, coming. That's the auld lady waking up, and she'll want a cup o' tea.'

CHAPTER IX
SHOPPING AND SHOOTING

We all went to Moncrieff's wedding, and it passed off much the same way as do weddings in other parts of the world. The new Mrs. Moncrieff was a very modest and charming young person indeed, and a native of our sister island—Ireland. I dare say Moncrieff loved his wife very much, though there was no extra amount of romance about his character, else he would hardly have spoken about his wife and a truck-load of wire fencing in the self-same sentence. But I dare say this honest Scot believed that wire fencing was quite as much a matter of necessity in the Silver West as a wife was.

As for my brothers and me, and even aunt, we were impatient now—'burning' bold Donald called it—to get away to this same Silver West and begin the very new life that was before us.

But ships do not always arrive from England exactly to a day; the vessel in which Moncrieff's men, dogs, goods, and chattels were coming was delayed by contrary winds, and was a whole fortnight behind her time.

Meanwhile we restrained ourselves as well as we could, and aunt went shopping. She had set her heart upon guanaco robes or ponchos for each of us; and though they cost a deal of money, and were, according to Moncrieff, a quite unnecessary expense, she bought them all the same.

'They will last for ever, you know,' was aunt's excuse for the extravagance.

'Yes,' he said, 'but we won't. Besides,' he added, 'these ponchos may bring the Gaucho malo (the bad Gaucho) round us.'

'All the better,' persisted aunt. 'I've heard such a deal about this Gaucho malo that I should very much like to see a live specimen.'

Moncrieff laughed.

'I much prefer *dead* specimens,' he said, with that canny twinkle in his eye. 'That's the way I like to see them served up. It is far the safest plan.'

We were very fond of aunt's company, for she really was more of a sister to us than our auntie; but for all that we preferred going shopping with Moncrieff. The sort of stores he was laying in gave such earnest of future sport and wild adventure.

Strange places he took us to sometimes—the shop of a half-caste Indian, for instance, a fellow from the far south of Patagonia. Here Moncrieff bought quite a quantity of ordinary ponchos, belts, and linen trousers of great width with hats enough of the sombrero type to thatch a rick. This mild and gentle savage also sold Moncrieff some dozen of excellent lassoes and bolas as well. From the way our friend examined the former, and tried the thong-strength of the latter, it was evident he was an expert in the use of both. Bolas may be briefly described as three long leather thongs tied together at one end, and having a ball at the free end of each. On the pampas, these balls are as often as not simply stones tied up in bits of skin; but the bolas now bought by Moncrieff were composed of shining metal, to prevent their being lost on the pampas. These bolas are waved round the heads of the horsemen hunters when chasing ostriches, or even pumas. As soon as the circular motion has given them impetus they are dexterously permitted to leave the hand at a tangent, and if well thrown go circling round the legs, or probably neck of the animal, and bring it to the ground by tripping it up, or strangling it.

The lasso hardly needs any description.

'Can you throw that thing well?' said Dugald, his eyes sparkling with delight.

'I think I can,' replied Moncrieff. 'Come to the door and see me lasso a dog or something.'

Out we all went.

'Oh!' cried Dugald, exultingly, 'here comes little Captain Bombazo, walking on the other side of the street with my aunt. Can you lasso him without hurting auntie?'

'I believe I can,' said Moncrieff. 'Stand by, and let's have a good try. Whatever a man dares he can do. Hoop là!'

The cord left the Scotchman's hand like a flash of lightning, and next moment Bombazo, who at the time was smiling and talking most volubly, was fairly noosed.

The boys in the street got up a cheer. Bombazo jumped and struggled, but Moncrieff stood his ground.

'He must come,' he said, and sure enough, greatly to the delight of the town urchins, Moncrieff rounded in the slack of the rope and landed the captain most beautifully.

'Ah! you beeg Scot,' said Bombazo, laughing good-humouredly. 'I would not care so mooch, if it were not for de lady.'

'Oh, she won't miss you, Bombazo.'

'On the contraire, she veel be inconsolabeel.'

'Ha, ha, ha!' laughed Moncrieff. 'What a tall opinion of yourself you have, my little friend!'

Bombazo drew himself up, but it hardly added an inch to his height, and nothing to his importance.

Saddles of the pampas pattern the semi-savage had also plenty of, and bridles too, and Moncrieff gave a handsome order.

A more respectable and highly civilized saddler's store was next visited, and real English gear was bought, including two charming ladies' saddles of the newest pattern, and a variety of rugs of various kinds.

Off we went next to a wholesale grocer's place. Out came Moncrieff's great note-book, and he soon gave evidence that he possessed a wondrous memory, and was a thorough man of business. He kept the shopman hard at it for half an hour, by which time one of the pyramids of Egypt, on a small scale, was built upon the counter.

'Now for the draper's, and then the chemist's,' said our friend. From the former—a Scot, like himself—he bought a pile of goods of the better sort, but from their appearance all warranted to wear a hundred years.

His visit to the druggist was of brief duration.

'Is my medicine chest filled?'

'Yes, sir, all according to your orders.'

'Thanks; send it, and send the bill.'

'Never mind about the bill, Mr. Moncrieff. You'll be down here again.'

'Send the bill, all the same. And I say, Mr. Squills—'

'Yes, sir.'

'Don't forget to deduct the discount.'

But Moncrieff's shopping was not quite all over yet, and the last place he went to was a gunsmith's shop.

And here I and my brothers learned a little about Silver West shooting, and witnessed an exhibition that made us marvel.

Moncrieff, after most careful examination, bought half a dozen good rifles, and a dozen fowling pieces. It took him quite a long time to select these and the ammunition.

'You have good judgment, sir,' said the proprietor.

'I require it all,' said Moncrieff. 'But now I'd look at some revolvers.'

He was shown some specimens.

'Toys—take them away.'

He was shown others.

'Toys again. Have you nothing better?'

'There is nothing better made.'

'Very well. Your bill please. Thanks.'

'If you'll wait one minute,' the shopkeeper said, 'I should feel obliged. My man has gone across the way to a neighbour gunsmith.'

'Couldn't I go across the way myself?'

'No,' and the man smiled. 'I don't want to lose your custom.'

'Your candour is charming. I'll wait.'

In a few minutes the man returned with a big basket.

'Ah! these are beauties,' cried Moncrieff. 'Now, can I try one or two?'

'Certainly.'

The man led the way to the back garden of the premises. Against a wall a target was placed, and Moncrieff loaded and took up his position. I noticed that he kept his elbow pretty near his side. Then he slowly raised the weapon.

Crack—crack—crack! six times in all.

'Bravo!' cried the shopkeeper. 'Why, almost every shot has hit the spot.'

Moncrieff threw the revolver towards the man as if it had been a cricket-ball.

'Take off the trigger,' he said.

'Off the trigger, sir?'

'Yes,' said Moncrieff, quietly; 'I seldom use the trigger.'

The man obeyed. Then he handed back the weapon, which he had loaded.

Moncrieff looked one moment at the target, then the action of his arm was for all the world like that of throwing stones or cracking a whip.

He seemed to bring the revolver down from his ear each time.

Bang—bang—bang! and not a bullet missed the bull's-eye.

'How is it done?' cried Dugald, excitedly.

'I lift the hammer a little way with my thumb and let it go again as I get my aim—that is all. It is a rapid way of firing, but I don't advise you laddies to try it, or you may blow off your heads. Besides, the aim, except in practised hands like mine, is not so accurate. To hit well it is better to raise the weapon. First fix your eye on your man's breast-button—if he has one—then elevate till you have your sight straight, and there you are, and there your Indian is, or your "Gaucho malo."'

Moncrieff pointed grimly towards the ground with his pistol as he spoke, and Dugald gave a little shudder, as if in reality a dead man lay there.

'It is very simple, you see.'

'Oh, Mr. Moncrieff,' said Dugald, 'I never thought you were so terrible a man!'

Moncrieff laughed heartily, finished his purchases, ordering better cartridges, as these, he said, had been badly loaded, and made the weapon kick, and then we left the shop.

'Now then, boys, I'm ready, and in two days' time hurrah for the Silver West! Between you and me, I'm sick of civilization.'

And in two days' time, sure enough, we had all started.

The train we were in was more like an American than an English one. We were in a very comfortable saloon, in which we could move about with freedom.

Moncrieff, as soon as we had rattled through the streets and found ourselves out in the green, cool country, was brimful of joy and spirits. Aunt said he reminded her of a boy going off on a holiday. His wife, too, looked 'blithe' and cheerful, and nothing could keep his mother's tongue from wagging.

Bombazo made the old lady a capital second, while several other settlers who were going out with us—all Scotch, by the way—did nothing but smile and wonder at all they saw. We soon passed away for a time beyond the region of trees into a rich green rolling country, which gave evidence of vast wealth, and sport too. Of this latter fact Dugald took good notice.

'Oh, look!' he would cry, pointing to some wild wee lake. 'Murdoch! Donald! wouldn't you like to be at the lochside yonder, gun in hand?'

And, sure enough, all kinds of feathered game were very plentiful.

But after a journey of five hours we left the train, and now embarked on a passenger steamer, and so commenced our journey up the Paraná. Does not the very name sound musical? But I may be wrong, according to some, in calling the Paraná beautiful, for the banks are not high; there are no wild and rugged mountains, nor even great forests; nevertheless, its very width, its silent moving power, and its majesticness give it a beauty in my eye that few rivers I know of possess. We gazed on it as the sunset lit up its wondrous waters till an island we were passing appeared to rise into the sky and float along in the crimson haze. We gazed on it again ere we retired for the night. The stars were now all out, and the river's dark bosom was studded here and there with ripples and buttons of light; but still it was silent, as if it hid some dark mysterious secret which it must tell only to the distant ocean.

We slept very soundly this night, for the monotonous throb-throb of the engine's great pulse and the churning rush of the screw not only wooed us to slumber, but seemed to mingle even with our dreams.

All night long, then, we were on the river, and nearly all next day as well. But the voyage appeared to my brothers and me to be all too short. We neared Rosario about sunset, and at last cast anchor. But we did not land. We were too snug where we were, and the hotel would have had far fewer charms.

To-night we had a little impromptu concert, for several of Moncrieff's friends came on board, and, strange to say, they were nearly all Scotch. So Scotch was spoken, Scotch songs were sung, and on deck, to the wild notes of the great bagpipes, Scotch reels and strathspeys were danced. After that,

'The nicht drave on wi' songs and clatter,'

till it was well into the wee short hours of the morning.

At Rosario we stopped for a day—more, I think, because Moncrieff wished to give aunt and his young wife a chance of seeing the place than for any business reason. Neither my brothers nor I were very much impressed by it, though it is a large and flourishing town, built somewhat on Philadelphia principles, in blocks, and, like Philadelphia, gridironed all over with tramway lines. It is a good thing one is able to get off the marble pavements into the cars without having far to go, for the streets are at times mere sloughs of despond. It is the same in all new countries.

Rosario lies in the midst of a flat but fertile country, on the banks of the Paraná. The hotel where we lodged was quite Oriental in its appearance, being built round a beautiful square, paved with marble, and adorned with the most lovely tropical shrubs, flowers, and climbing plants.

There seems to be a flea in Rosario, however—just one flea; but he is a most ubiquitous and a most insatiably blood-thirsty little person. The worst of it is that, night or day, you are never perfectly sure where he may be. It is no use killing him either—that is simply labour thrown away, for he appears to come to life again, and resumes his evil courses as merrily as before.

Fifty times a day did I kill that flea, and Dugald said he had slain him twice as often; but even as Dugald spoke I could have vowed the lively *pulex* was thoroughly enjoying a draught of my Highland blood inside my right sock.

Although none of our party shed tears as we mounted into the train, still the kindly hand-shakings and the hearty good-byes were affecting enough; and just as the train went puffing and groaning away from the station they culminated in one wild Highland hurrah! repeated three times thrice, and augmented by the dissonance of a half-ragged crew of urchins, who must needs wave their arms aloft and shout, without the faintest notion what it was all about.

We were now *en route* for Cordoba, westward ho! by Frayle Muerto and Villa Neuva.

CHAPTER X
A JOURNEY THAT SEEMS LIKE A DREAM

It was towards sunset on the day we had left Rosario, and we had made what our guard called a grand run, though to us it was a somewhat tedious one. Moncrieff had tucked his mother up in the plaid, and she had gone off to sleep on the seat 'as gentle as "ewe lammie,"' according to her son. My aunt and the young bride were quietly talking together, and I myself was in that delightful condition called "twixt sleeping and waking,' when suddenly Dugald, who had been watching everything from the window, cried, 'Oh, Donald, look here. What a lovely changing cloud!'

Had Moncrieff not been busy just then—very earnestly busy indeed—discussing the merits of some sample packets of seeds with one of his new men, he might have come at once and explained the mystery.

It was indeed a lovely cloud, and it lay low on the north-western horizon. But we had never before seen so strange a cloud, for not only did it increase in length and breadth more rapidly than do most clouds, but it caught the sun's parting rays in quite a marvellous manner. When first we looked at it the colour throughout was a bluish purple; suddenly it changed to a red with resplendent border of fiery orange. Next it collapsed, getting broader and rounder, and becoming a dark blue, almost approaching to black, while the border beneath was orange-red. But the glowing magnificence of the colour it is impossible to describe in words; and the best artist would have failed to reproduce it even were he ten times a Turner.

At this moment, and just as the cloud was becoming elongated again, Moncrieff came to our side. His usually bright face fell at once as soon as he glanced at it.

'Locusts!' He almost gasped the word out.

'Locusts!' was re-echoed from every corner of the carriage; and immediately all eyes were strained in the direction of our 'lofty golden cloud.'

As we approached nearer to it, and it came nearer to us, even the light from the setting sun was obscured, and in a short time we were in the cloud, and apparently part of it. It had become almost too dark to see anything inside our carriage, owing to that dense and awful fog of insect life. We quickly closed the windows, for the loathsome insects were now pattering against the glass, and many had already obtained admittance, much to the horror of young Mrs. Moncrieff, though aunt took matters easy enough, having seen such sights before.

The train now slowly came to a standstill. Something—no one appeared to know what—had happened on ahead of us, and here we must wait till the line was clear. Even Moncrieff's mother had awakened, and was looking out with the rest of us.

'Dearie me! Dearie me!' she exclaimed. 'A shower o' golochs! The very licht o' day darkened wi' the fu'some craiters. Ca' you this a land o' milk and honey? Egyptian darkness and showers o' golochs!'

We descended and walked some little distance into the country, and the sight presented to our astonished gaze I, for one, will not forget to my dying day. The locusts were still around us, but were bearing away southward, having already devastated the fields in this vicinity. But they fell in hundreds and thousands around us; they struck against our hands, our faces, and hats; they got into our sleeves, and even into our pockets; and we could not take a step without squashing them under foot.

Only an hour before we had been passing through a country whose green fertility was something to behold once and dream about for ever. Evidence of wealth and contentment had been visible on all sides. Beautiful, home-looking, comfortable *estancias* and out-buildings, fat, sleek cattle and horses, and flocks of beautiful sheep, with feathered fowls of every description. But here, though there were not wanting good farmsteadings, all was desolation and threatened famine; hardly a green blade or leaf was left, and the woebegone looks of some of the people we met wandering aimlessly about, dazed and almost distracted, were pitiful to behold. I was not sorry when a shriek from the engine warned us that it was time to retrace our slippery footsteps.

'Is this a common occurrence?' I could not help asking our friend Moncrieff.

He took me kindly by the arm as he replied,

'It's a depressing sight to a youngster, I must allow; but we should not let our thoughts dwell on it. Sometimes the locusts are a terrible plague, but they manage to get over even that. Come in, and we'll light up the saloon.'

For hours after this the pattering continued at the closed windows, showing that the shower of golochs had not yet ceased to fall. But with lights inside, the carriage looked comfortable and cheerful enough, and when presently Moncrieff got out Bombazo's guitar and handed it to him, and that gentleman began to sing, we soon got happy again, and forgot even the locusts—at least, all but Moncrieff's mother did. She had gone to sleep in a corner, but sometimes we heard her muttering to herself, in her dreams, about the 'land o' promise,' 'showers of golochs,' and 'Egyptian darkness.'

The last thing I remember as I curled up on the floor of the saloon, with a saddle for a pillow and a rug round me—for the night had grown bitterly cold—was Bombazo's merry face as he strummed on his sweet guitar and sang of tresses dark, and love-lit eyes, and sunny Spain. This was a delightful way of going to sleep; the awakening was not quite so pleasant, however, for I opened my eyes only to see a dozen of the ugly 'golochs' on my rug, and others asquat on the saddle, washing their faces as flies do. I got up and went away to wash mine.

The sun was already high in the heavens, and on opening a window and looking out, I found we were passing through a woodland country, and that far away in the west were rugged hills. Surely, then, we were nearing the end of our journey.

I asked our mentor Moncrieff, and right cheerily he replied,

'Yes, my lad, and we'll soon be in Cordoba now.'

This visit of ours to Cordoba was in reality a little pleasure trip, got up for the special delectation of our aunt and young Mrs. Moncrieff. It formed part and parcel of the Scotchman's honeymoon, which, it must be allowed, was a very chequered one.

If the reader has a map handy he will find the name Villa Maria thereon, a place lying between Rosario and Cordoba. This was our station, and there we had left all heavy baggage, including Moncrieff's people. On our return we should once more resume travelling together westward still by Mercedes. And thence to our destination would be by far and away the most eventful portion of the journey.

'Look out,' continued Moncrieff, 'and behold the rugged summits of the grand old hills.'

'And these are the Sierras?'

'These are the Sierras; and doesn't the very sight of mountains once again fill your heart with joy? Don't you want to sing and jump—'

'And call aloud for joy,' said his mother, who had come up to have a peep over our shoulders. 'Dearie me,' she added, 'they're no half so bonny and green as the braes o' Foudland.'

'Ah! mither, wait till you get to our beautiful home in Mendoza. Ye'll be charmed wi' a' you see.'

'I wish,' I said, 'I was half as enthusiastic as you are, Moncrieff.'

'You haven't been many days in the Silver Land. Wait, lad, wait! When once you've fairly settled and can feel at home, man, you'll think the time as short as pleasure itself. Days and weeks flee by like winking, and every day and every week brings its own round o' duty to perform. And all the time you'll be makin' money as easy as makin' slates.'

'Money isn't everything,' I said.

'No, lad, money isn't everything; but money is a deal in this worrrld, and we mustn't forget that money puts the power in our hands to do others good, and that I think is the greatest pleasure of a'. And you know, Murdoch, that if God does put talents in our hands He expects us to make use of them.'

'True enough, Moncrieff,' I said.

'See, see! that is Cordoba down in the hollow yonder, among the hills. Look, mither! see how the domes and steeples sparkle in the mornin's sunshine. Yonder dome is the cathedral, and further off you see the observatory, and maybe, mither, you'll have a peep through a telescope that will bring the moon so near to you that you'll be able to see the good folks thereon ploughin' fields and milkin' kye.'

We stayed at Cordoba for four days. I felt something of the old pleasant languor of Rio stealing over me again as I lounged about the handsome streets, gazed on the ancient churches and convent, and its world-renowned University, or climbed its *barranca*, or wandered by the Rio Balmeiro, and through the lovely and romantic suburbs. In good sooth, Cordoba is a dreamy old place, and I felt better for being in it. The weather was all in our favour also, being dry, and neither hot nor cold, although it was now winter in these regions. I was sorry to leave Cordoba, and so I feel sure was aunt, and even old Jenny.

Then came the journey back to Villa Maria, and thence away westward to Villa Mercedes. The railway to the latter place had not long been opened.

It seems all like a beautiful halo—that railway ride to the *Ultima Thule* of the iron horse—and, like a dream, it is but indistinctly remembered. Let me briefly catch the salient points of this pleasant journey.

Villa Maria we reach in the evening. The sun is setting in a golden haze; too golden, for it bodes rain, and presently down it comes in a steady pour, changing the dust of the roads into the stickiest of mud, and presently into rivers. Moncrieff is here, there, and everywhere, seeing after his manifold goods and chattels; but just as the short twilight is deepening into night, he returns 'dressed and dry,' as he calls it, to the snug little room of the inn, where a capital dinner is spread for us, and we are all hungry. Even old Jenny, forgetting her troubles and travels, makes merry music with knife and fork, and Bombazo is all smiles and chatter. It rains still; what of that? It will drown the mosquitoes and other flying 'jerlies.' It is even pleasant to listen to the rattle of the rain-drops during the few lulls there were in the conversation. The sound makes the room inside seem ever so much more cosy. Besides, there is a fire in the grate, and, to add to our enjoyment, Bombazo has his guitar.

Even the landlord takes the liberty of lingering in the room, standing modestly beside the door, to listen. It is long, he tells us, since he has had so cheerful a party at his house.

Aileen, as Moncrieff calls his pretty bride, is not long in discovering that the innkeeper hails from her own sweet Isle of Sorrow, and many friendly questions are asked on both sides.

Bed at last. A bright morning, the sun coming up red and rosy through an ocean of clouds more gorgeous than ever yet was seen in tame old England.

We are all astir very early. We are all merry and hungry. Farewells are said, and by and by off we rattle. The train moves very slowly at first, but presently warms to her work and settles down to it. We catch a glimpse of a town some distance off, and nearer still the silver gleam of a river reflecting the morning sun. By and by we are on the river bridge, and over it, and so on and away through an open pampa. Such, at least, I call it. Green swelling land all around, with now and then a lake or loch swarming with web-footed fowl, the sight of which makes Dugald's eyes water.

We pass station after station, stopping at all. More woods, more pampa; thriving fields and fertile lands; *estancias*, flocks of sheep, herds of happy cattle. A busy, bustling railway station, with as much noise around it as we find at Clapham Junction; another river—the Rio Cuarto, if my memory does not play me false; pampas again, with hills in the distance. Wine and water-melons at a station; more wine and more water-melons at another.

After this I think I fall asleep, and I wonder now if the wine and the water-melons had anything to do with that. I awake at last and rub my eyes. Bombazo is also dozing; so is old Jenny. Old Jenny is a marvel to sleep. Dugald is as bright as a humming bird; he says I have lost a sight.

'What was the sight?'

'Oh, droves upon droves of real wild horses, wilder far than our ponies at Coila.'

I close my eyes again. Dear old Coila! I wish Dugald had not mentioned the word. It takes me back again in one moment across the vast and mighty ocean we have crossed to our home, to father, mother, and Flora.

Before long we are safe at Villa Mercedes. Not much to see here, and the wind blows cold from west and south.

We are not going to lodge in the town, however. We are independent of inns, if there are any, and independent of everything. We are going under canvas.

Already our pioneers have the camp ready in a piece of ground sheltered by a row of lordly poplars; and to-morrow morning we start by road for the far interior.

Another glorious morning! There is a freshness in the air which almost amounts to positive cold, and reminds one of a November day in Scotland. Bombazo calls it bitterly cold, and my aunt has distributed guanaco ponchos to us, and has adorned herself with her own. Yes, adorned is the right word to apply to auntie's own travelling toilet; but we brothers think we look funny in ours, and laugh at each other in turn. Moncrieff sticks to the Highland plaid, but the sight of a guanaco poncho to old Jenny does, I verily believe, make her the happiest old lady in all the Silver Land. She is mounted in the great canvas-covered waggon, which is quite a caravan in every respect. It has even windows in the sides and real doorways, and is furnished inside with real sofas and Indian-made chairs, to say nothing of hammocks and tables and a stove. This caravan is drawn by four beautiful horses, and will be our sitting-room and dining-room by day, and the ladies' boudoir and bedroom for some time to come.

Away we rattle westwards, dozens of soldiers, half-bred Chilians, Gauchos, and a crowd of dark-eyed but dirty children, giving us a ringing cheer as we start.

What a cavalcade it is, to be sure! Waggons, drays, carts, mules, and horses. All our imported Scotchmen are riding, and glorious fellows they look. Each has a rifle slung across his shoulder, belts and sheath knives, and broad sombrero hat. The giant Moncrieff himself is riding, and looks to me the bravest of the brave. I and each of my brothers have undertaken to drive a cart or waggon, and we feel men from hat to boots, and as proud all over as a cock with silver spurs.

We soon leave behind us those tall, mysterious-looking poplar trees. So tall are they that, although when we turned out not a breath of wind was blowing on the surface of the ground, away aloft their summits were waving gently to and fro, with a whispering sound, as if they were talking to unseen spirits in the sky.

We leave even the *estancias* behind. We are out now on the lonesome rolling plain. Here and there are woods; away, far away, behind us are the jagged summits of the everlasting hills. By and by the diligence, a strange-looking rattle-trap of a coach—a ghost of a coach, I might call it—goes rattling and swaying past us. Its occupants raise a feeble cheer, to which we respond with a three times three; for we seem to like to hear our voices.

After this we feel more alone than ever. On and on and on we jog. The road is broad and fairly good; our waggons have broad wheels; this retards our speed, but adds to our comfort and that of the mules and horses.

Before very long we reach a broad river, and in we plunge, the horsemen leading the van, with the water up to their saddle-girths. I give the reins of my team to my attendant Gaucho, and, running forward, jump on board the caravan to keep the ladies company while we fight the ford. But the ladies are in no way afraid; they are enjoying themselves in the front of the carriage, which is open. Old Jenny is in an easy-chair and buried to the nose in her guanaco robe. She is muttering something to herself, and as I bend down to listen I can catch the words: 'Dearie me! Dearie me! When'll ever we reach the Land o' Promise? Egyptian darkness! Showers of golochs! Chariots and horsemen! Dearie me! Dearie me!'

But we are over at last, and our whole cavalcade looks sweeter and fresher for the bath.

Presently we reach a corral, where two men beckon to Moncrieff. They are wild and uncouth enough in all conscience; their baggy breeches and ponchos are in sad need of repair, and a visit to a barber would add to the respectability of their appearance. They look excited, wave their arms, and point southwards. But they talk in a strange jargon, and there are but two words intelligible to me. These, however, are enough to set my heart throbbing with a strange feeling of uneasiness I never felt before.

'*Los Indios! Los Indios!*'

Moncrieff points significantly to his armed men and smiles. The Gauchos wave their arms in the air, rapidly opening and shutting their hands in a way that to me is very mysterious. And so they disappear.

CHAPTER XI
THE TRAGEDY AT THE FONDA

I could not help wondering, as I glanced at aunt whether she had heard and understood the meaning of those wild Gauchos' warning. If she did she made no sign. But aunt is a M'Crimman, and the sister of a bold Highland chief. She would not *show* fear even if she *felt* it. Yes, the brave may feel fear, but the coward alone is influenced by it.

Old Jenny had gone to sleep, so I said good-bye to aunt, nodded to Aileen, and went back to my waggon once more.

We made good progress that day, though we did not hurry. We stopped to feed our cattle, and to rest and feed ourselves. The jolting had been terrible on some parts of the road. But now the sun was getting very low indeed, and as we soon came to a piece of high, hard ground, with a view of the country round us for miles, we determined to bivouac for the night.

The horses and mules were hobbled and turned off to graze under the charge of sentry Gauchos. No fear of their wandering off far. They were watered not an hour ago, and would be fresh by daybreak.

Now, Moncrieff had been too long in the wilds to neglect precautions while camping out. I had taken an early opportunity to-day to interview our leader concerning the report that Indians were abroad.

'Ah!' he answered, 'you heard and understood what that half-breed said, then?'

'Just a word or two. He appeared to give us a warning of some kind. Is it of any account?'

'Well, there's always some water where the stirkie drowns; there's always some fire where you see smoke; and it is better to be sure than sorry.'

I could elicit no more information from my canny countryman than that. I said nothing to any one, not even my brothers. Why should I cause them the slightest alarm, and speak a word that might tend to make them sleep less soundly?

However, as soon as the halt was made, I was glad to see that Moncrieff took every precaution against a surprise. The caravan was made the centre of a square, the waggons being 'laggered' around it. The fire was lit and the dinner cooked close beside a sheltering *barranca*, and as soon as this meal was discussed the fire was extinguished.

'Then came still evening on,'

and we all gathered together for prayer. Even the Gauchos were summoned, though I fear paid but little attention, while Moncrieff, standing bare-headed in the midst of us, read a chapter from the Book by the pale yellow light of the western sky. Then, still standing—

'Brothers, let us pray,' he said.

Erect there, with the twilight shadows falling around him, with open eyes and face turned skywards, with the sunset's after-glow falling on his hard but comely features, his plaid depending from his broad shoulders, I could not help admiring the man. His prayer—and it was but brief—had all the trusting simplicity of a little child's, yet it was in every way the prayer of a man communing with his God; in every tone thereof was breathed belief, reliance, gratitude, and faith in the Father.

As he finished, Dugald pressed my arm and pointed eastwards, smiling. A star had shone out from behind a little cloud, and somehow it seemed to me as if it were an angel's eye, and that it would watch over us all the live-long night. Our evening service concluded with that loveliest of hymns, commencing—

'O God of Bethel, by whose hand
Thy children still are fed;
Who through this weary wilderness
Hath all our fathers led.'

He gave it out in the old Scotch way, two lines at a time, and to the tune 'Martyrdom.'

It was surely appropriate to our position and our surroundings, especially that beautiful verse—

'Oh, spread Thy covering wings around,
Till all our wanderings cease,
And at our Father's loved abode
Our souls arrive in peace.'

We now prepared for rest. The sentries were set, and in a short time all was peace and silence within our camp. More than once during the night the collies—dogs brought out by Moncrieff's men—gave an uneasy bark or two, their slumbers being probably disturbed by the cry of some night bird, or the passing of a prowling fox.

So, wrapped in our guanaco robes—the benefit of which we felt now—my brothers and I slept sweetly and deeply till the sun once more rose in the east.

Soon all was bustle and stir again.

Thus were our days spent on the road, thus our evenings, and eke our nights. And at the end of some days we were still safe and sound, and happy. No one sick in the camp; no horse or mule even lame; while we were all hardening to travel already.

So far, hardly anything had happened to break the even tenour of our journey. Our progress, however, with so much goods and chattels, and over such roads, was necessarily slow; yet we never envied the lumbering diligence that now and then went rattling past us.

We saw many herds of wild horses. Some of these, led by beautiful stallions, came quite close to us. They appeared to pity our horses and mules, condemned to the shafts and harness, and compelled to work their weary lives away day after day. Our beasts were slaves. They were free—free as the breezes that blew over the pampas and played with their long manes, as they went thundering over the plains. We had seen several ostriches, and my brothers and I had enjoyed a wild ride or two after them. Once we encountered a puma, and once we saw an armadillo. We had never clapped eyes on a living specimen before, but there could be no mistaking the gentleman in armour. Not that he gave us much time for study, however. Probably the creature had been asleep as we rounded the corner of a gravel bank, but in one moment he became alive to his danger. Next moment we saw nothing but a rising cloud of dust and sand; lo! the armadillo was gone to the Antipodes, or somewhere in that direction—buried alive. Probably the speed with which an armadillo—there are several different species in the Silver West—disappears at the scent of any one belonging to the *genus homo*, is caused by the decided objection he has to be served up as a side-dish. He is excellent eating—tender as a chicken, juicy as a sucking-pig, but the honour of being roasted whole and garnished is one he does not crave.

Riding on ahead one day—I had soon got tired of the monotony of driving, and preferred the saddle—at a bend of the road I came suddenly upon two horsemen, who had dismounted and were lying on a patch of sward by the roadside. Their horses stood near. Both sprang up as I appeared, and quick as lightning their hands sought the handles of the ugly knives that depended in sheaths from their girdles. At this moment there was a look in the swarthy face of each that I can only describe as diabolical. Hatred, ferocity, and cunning were combined in that glance; but it vanished in a moment, and the air assumed by them now was one of cringing humility.

'The Gaucho malo,' I said to myself as soon as I saw them. Their horses were there the nobler animals. Bitted, bridled, and saddled, the latter were in the manner usual to the country, the saddle looking like a huge hillock of skins and rags; but rifles were slung alongside, to say nothing of bolas and lasso. The dress of the men was a kind of nondescript garb. Shawls round the loins, tucked up between their legs and fastened with a girdle, did duty as breeches; their feet were encased in *potro* boots, made of the hock-skin of horses, while over their half-naked shoulders hung ponchos of skin, not without a certain amount of wild grace.

Something else as well as his rifle was lashed to the saddle of one of these desert gipsies, and being new to the country, I could not help wondering at this—namely, a guitar in a case of skin.

With smiles that I knew were false one now beckoned me to alight, while the other unslung the instrument and began to tune it. The caravan must have been fully two miles behind me, so that to some extent I was at the mercy of these Gauchos, had they meant mischief. This was not their plan of campaign, however.

Having neighed in recognition of the other horses, my good nag stood as still as a statue; while, with my eyes upon the men and my hand within easy distance of my revolver, I listened to their music. One sang while the other played, and I must confess that the song had a certain fascination about it, and only the thought that I was far from safe prevented me from thoroughly enjoying it. I knew, as if by instinct, however, that the very fingers that were eliciting those sweet sad tones were itching to clutch my throat, and that the voice that thrilled my senses could in a moment be changed into a tiger yell, with which men like these spring upon their human prey.

On the whole I felt relieved when the rumble of the waggon wheels fell once more on my ears. I rode back to meet my people, and presently a halt was made for the midday feed.

If aunt desired to feast her eyes on the Gaucho malo she had now a chance. They played to her, sang to her, and went through a kind of wild dance for her especial delectation.

'What romantic and beautiful blackguards they are!' was the remark she made to Moncrieff.

Moncrieff smiled, somewhat grimly, I thought.

'It's no' for nought the cland[4] whistles,' he said in his broadest, canniest accents.

These Gauchos were hunting, they told Moncrieff. Had they seen any Indians about? No, no, not an Indian. The Indians were far, far south.

Aunt gave them some garments, food, and money; and, with many bows and salaams, they mounted their steeds and went off like the wind.

I noticed that throughout the remainder of the day Moncrieff was unusually silent, and appeared to wish to be alone. Towards evening he beckoned to me.

'We'll ride on ahead,' he said, 'and look for a good bit of camping-ground.'

Then away we both went at a canter, but in silence.

We rode on and on, the ground rising gently but steadily, until we stopped at last on a high plateau, and gazed around us at the scene. A more bleak and desolate country it would be impossible to imagine. One vast and semi-desert plain, the eye relieved only by patches of algarrobo bushes, or little lakes of water. Far ahead of us the cone of a solitary mountain rose on the horizon, and towards this the sun was slowly declining. Away miles in our rear were the waggons and horses struggling up the hill. But silence as deep as death was everywhere. Moncrieff stretched his arm southwards.

'What do you see yonder, Murdo?' he said.

'I see,' I replied, after carefully scanning the rolling plain, 'two ostriches hurrying over the pampas.'

'Those are not ostriches, boy. They are those same villain Gauchos, and they are after no good. I tell you this, that you may be prepared for anything that may happen to-night. But look,' he added, turning his horse's head; 'down here is a corral, and we are sure to find water.'

We soon reached it. Somewhat to our surprise we found no horses anywhere about, and no sign of life around the little inn or *fonda* except one wretched-looking dog.

As we drew up at the door and listened the stillness felt oppressive. Moncrieff shouted. No human voice responded; but the dog, seated on his haunches, gave vent to a melancholy howl.

'Look,' I said, 'the dog's paws are red with blood. He is wounded.'

'It isn't *his* blood, boy.'

The words thrilled me. I felt a sudden fear at my heart, born perhaps of the death-like stillness. Ah! it was indeed a death-like stillness, and the stillness of death itself as well.

Moncrieff dismounted. I followed his example, and together we entered the *fonda*.

We had not advanced a yard when we came on an awesome sight—the dead body of a Gaucho! It lay on its back with the arms spread out, the face hacked to pieces, and gashes in the neck. The interior of the hut was a chaos of wild confusion, the little furniture there was smashed, and evidently everything of value had been carried away. Half buried in the *débris* was the body of a woman, and near it that of a child. Both were slashed and disfigured, while pools of blood lay everywhere about. Young though I was, I had seen death before in several shapes, but never anything so ghastly and awful as this.

A cold shudder ran through my frame and seemed to pierce to the very marrow of my bones. I felt for a few moments as if in some dreadful nightmare, and I do not hesitate to confess that, M'Crimman and all as I am, had those Gauchos suddenly appeared now in the doorway, I could not have made the slightest resistance to their attack. I should have taken my death by almost rushing on the point of their terrible knives. But Moncrieff's calm earnest voice restored me in a moment. At its tones I felt raised up out of my coward self, and prepared to face anything.

'Murdoch,' he said, 'this is a time for calm thought and action.'

'Yes,' I answered; 'bid me do anything, and I will do it. But come out of this awful place. I—I feel a little faint.'

Together we left the blood-stained *fonda*, Moncrieff shutting the door behind him.

'No other eye must look in there,' he said. 'Now, Murdoch, listen.'

He paused, and I waited; his steadfast eyes bent on my face.

'You are better now? You are calm, and no longer afraid?'

'I am no longer afraid.'

'Well, I can trust *you*, and no one else. Led by those evil fiends whom we saw to-day, the Indians will be on us to-night in force. I will prepare to give them a warm reception—'

'And I will assist,' I hastened to say.

'No, Murdoch, you will not be here to help us at the commencement. I said the Indians would attack in *force*, because they know our numbers.

Those *malo* men have been spying on us when we little thought it. They know our strength to a gun, and they will come in a cloud that nothing can withstand, or that nothing could withstand in the open. But we will entrench and defend ourselves till your return.'

'My return!'

'Twelve miles from here,' he went on, 'is a fort. It contains two officers and over a score soldiers. In two hours it will be dusk, in an hour after that the moon rises. 'Twixt twilight and moonrise you must ride to that fort and bring assistance. Depend upon it, we can defend ourselves till you come with your men, and you must attack the savages in the rear. You understand?'

'Perfectly. But had I not better ride away at once?'

'No, the Indians would waylay you. You never would reach the frontier fort. Even if you did escape from the chase, the knowledge that the troops were coming would prevent them from attacking to-night.'

'And you want them to attack to-night?'

'I wish them to attack to-night. We may never be able to give a good account of them again, but all depends on your success.'

In a short time the first waggons came up. They would have stopped, but Moncrieff beckoned them onwards. When the last waggon had gone we mounted our horses and slowly followed. At a stream not far distant we watered, and once more continued our journey.

The road now rose rapidly, till in half an hour we were on high ground, and here the halt was made. I could breathe more easily now we had left that blood-stained hollow, though well I knew the sight I had witnessed would not leave my thoughts for years to come.

Everything was done as quietly and orderly as if no cloud were hovering over us, so soon to burst. The big fire was lit as usual, supper cooked, prayers said, and the fire also lit in the ladies' caravan, for the nights were cold and raw now.

The night began to fall. Moncrieff and I had kept our secret to ourselves hitherto, but we could no longer conceal from any one that there was danger in the air. Yet the news seemed to astonish no one, not even aunt.

'Dear brother,' she said to our leader, 'I read it in your face all the afternoon.'

It was almost dusk now, and work was commenced in earnest. Spades were got out, and every man worked like a slave to entrench the whole position. The strength that I was to leave behind me was seven-and-twenty men all told, but this included ten Gauchos. Nevertheless, behind trenches, with plenty of guns, revolvers, and ammunition, they were powerful enough to defend the position against hundreds of badly-armed Indians. Not far off was a patch of wood which stretched downwards into a rocky ravine. Luckily it lay on the north side of the road, and hither, as soon as it was dark enough, every horse and mule was led and secured to the trees. Nor even in this extremity of danger were their wants forgotten, for grass mixed with grains was placed in front of each.

My horse was now led round. Each hoof was encased in a new and strong *potro* boot, secured by thongs around the legs.

'You must neither be heard nor seen,' said Moncrieff, as he pointed to these. 'Now, good-night, boy; God be wi' ye, and with us all!'

'Amen!' I responded, earnestly.

Then away I rode in silence, through the starlight; but as I looked back to the camp my heart gave an uneasy throb. Should I ever see them alive again?

[4] Cland, a kind of hawk.

CHAPTER XII
ATTACK BY PAMPA INDIANS

So lonesome a ride in the darkness of night, through a country wild and bleak, with danger lurking perhaps on either side of me, might easily have daunted a bolder heart than mine.

Something of the unspeakable feeling of dread I had experienced in the *fonda* while surrounded by those awful corpses came back to me now. I tried to banish it, but failed. My nervousness became extreme, and appeared to increase rather than diminish as I left the camp farther and farther behind me. It was almost a superstitious fear that had gotten possession of my soul. It was fear of the unseen; and even at this distance of time I can only say I would willingly face death in open day a hundred times over rather than endure for an hour the terrors I suffered that night. Every bush I saw I took for a figure lurking by the roadside, while solitary trees I had to pass assumed the form and shape and even movement of an enemy on horseback riding silently down to meet me. Again and again I clutched my revolver, and even now I cannot tell what power prevented me from firing at my phantom foes. Over and over again I reined up to listen, and at such times the wind whispering through the tall grass sounded to me like human voices, while the cry of birds that now and then rose startlingly close to me, made my heart beat with a violence that in itself was painful.

Sometimes I closed my eyes, and gave the horse his head, trying to carry my thoughts back to the lights of the camp, or forward to the fort which I hoped soon to reach.

I had ridden thus probably five good miles, when I ventured to look behind me, and so great had been the strain on my nerves that the sight I now witnessed almost paralyzed me.

It was the reflection as of a great fire on the brow of the hill where my people were beleaguered.

'The camp is already attacked, and in flames,' I muttered. Whither should I ride now—backwards or forwards?

While I yet hesitated the flames appeared to wax fiercer and fiercer, till presently—oh, joy!—a big round moon gradually shook itself clear of a cloud and began slowly to climb the eastern sky.

All fear fled now. I muttered a prayer of thankfulness, dashed the spurs into my good horse's sides, and went on at the gallop.

The time seemed short after this, and almost before I knew I came right upon the fort, and was challenged by the sentry.

'*Amigo!*' I yelled. '*Amigo! Angleese!*'

I dare say I was understood, for soon after lights appeared on the ramparts, and I was hailed again, this time in English, or for what passed as English. I rode up under the ramparts, and quickly told my tale.

In ten minutes more I was received within the fort. A tumble-down place I found it, but I was overjoyed to be in it, nevertheless. In the principal room most of the men were playing games, and smoking and talking, while the commandant himself lounged about with a cigarette in his mouth.

He considered for a minute or two—an age it appeared to me—ere he answered. Yes; he would come, and take with him fifteen soldiers, leaving the rest to guard the fort. I could have embraced him, so joyful did I feel on hearing these words.

How long would he be? One hour, no more. For arms had to be cleaned, and ammunition to be got ready; and the men must feed.

A whole hour! No wonder I sighed and looked anxious. Why, every minute was precious to my poor beleaguered friends. It would be long past midnight ere I reached the camp again, for these men would not be mounted. Yet I saw the good little commander was doing his best, not only to expedite matters, but to treat me with kindness and hospitality. He brought forth food and wine, and forced me to eat and drink. I did so to please him; but when he proposed a game to pass the time, I began to think the man was crazed. He was not. No; but possessed a soldierly virtue which I could not boast of—namely, patience.

The work of entrenchment was soon completed after my departure; then there was nothing more to be done except to appoint the men to their quarters, place sentinels on the highest of the waggons, and wait.

Ah, but this waiting is a weary thing under circumstances like the present—waiting and watching, not knowing from what quarter the attack will come, what form it will take, or when it will commence.

Except in the chief caravan itself, where Moncrieff and Donald sat for a time to keep up the hearts of the ladies, no lights were lit.

There was no singing to-night, hardly a smile on any face, and no one spoke much above a whisper. Poor old Jenny had gone to sleep, as usual.

'Wake me,' had been her last words. 'Wake me, laddie, when the Philistines are upon us.'

'The old lady's a marvel!' Moncrieff had whispered to aunt.

Moncrieff was doing all he could to keep conversation alive, though, strange to say, Bombazo seldom spoke. Surely he could not be afraid. Moncrieff had his suspicions. Brave as my aunt was, the waiting made her nervous.

'Hark!' she would say every now and then; or, 'Listen! What was that?'

'Only the cry of a burrowing owl,' Moncrieff might have to answer; or, 'Only the yap of a prowling fox.' Oh, the waiting, the weary waiting!

The moon rose at last, and presently it was almost as light as day.

'Will they come soon, think you?' whispered poor Aileen.

'No, darling; not for hours yet. Believe me there is no danger. We are well prepared.'

'Oh, Alec, Alec!' she answered, bursting into tears; 'it is you I fear for, not myself. Let me go with you when they come. I would not then be afraid; but waiting here—oh, it is the waiting that takes all the heart out of me.'

'Egyptian darkness!' murmured the old lady in her sleep. Then in louder, wilder key, 'Smite them!' she exclaimed. 'Smite this host of the Philistines from Gideon to Gaza.'

'Dear old mither, she's dreaming,' said Moncrieff. 'But, oh, we'll laugh at all this by to-morrow night, Aileen, my darling.'

One hour, two hours went slowly, painfully past. The moon mounted higher and higher, and shone clearer and clearer, but not yet on all the plains were there signs of a mounted Indian.

Yet even at that moment, little though our people knew it, swarthy forms were creeping stealthily through the pampas grass, with spears and guns at trail, pausing often to glance towards the camp they meant so soon to surprise and capture.

The moon gets yet brighter. Moncrieff is watching. Shading his eyes from the light, he is gazing across the marsh and listening to every sound. Not a quarter of a mile away is a little marshy lake. From behind it for several minutes he has heard mournful cries. They proceed from the burrowing owls; but they must have been startled! They even fly towards the camp, as if to give warning of the approach of the swarthy foe.

Suddenly from the edge of the lake a sound like the blast of a trumpet is heard; another and another, and finally a chorus of trumpet notes; and shortly after a flock of huge flamingoes are seen wheeling in the moonlit air.

'It is as I thought,' says Moncrieff; 'they are creeping through the grass. Hurry round, Dugald, and call the men quietly to quarters.'

Moncrieff himself, rifle in hand, climbs up to the top of the waggon.

'Go down now,' he tells the sentry. 'I mean to fire the first shot.'

He lies down to wait and watch. No bloodhound could have a better eye. Presently he sees a dark form raise itself near a tussock of grass. There is a sharp report, and the figure springs into the air, then falls dead on the pampas.

No need for the foe to conceal themselves any longer. With a wild and unearthly scream, that the very earth itself seems to re-echo, they spring from their hiding and advance at the double towards the fort—for fort it is now. As they come yelling on they fire recklessly towards it. They might as well fire in the air.

Moncrieff's bold Doric is heard, and to some purpose, at this juncture.

'Keep weel down, men! Keep weel to coverrr! Fire never a shot till he has the orrder. Let every bullet have its billet. Ready! Fire-r-r-r!'

Moncrieff rattled out the r's indefinitely, and the rifles rattled out at the same time. So well aimed was the volley that the dark cloud seemed staggered. The savages wavered for a time, but on they came again, redoubling their yells. They fired again, then, dropping their guns, rushed on towards the breastwork spears in hand. It was thus that the conflict commenced in dread earnest, and the revolvers now did fearful execution. The Indians were hurled back again and again, and finally they broke and sought cover in the bush. Their wounded lay writhing and crying out close beneath the rampart, and among these were also many who would never move more in this world.

On seeing the savages take to the bush, Moncrieff's anxiety knew no bounds. The danger of their discovering the horses was extreme. And if they did so, revenge would speedily follow defeat. They would either drive them away across the pampas, or in their wrath slaughter them where they stood.

What was to be done to avert so great a catastrophe? A forlorn hope was speedily formed, and this my two brothers volunteered to lead. On the first shout heard down in the hollow—indicating the finding of our horses—Donald, Dugald, and fifteen men were to rush out and turn the flank of the swarthy army if they could, or die in the attempt.

Meanwhile, however, the enemy appeared bent on trying cunning and desperate tactics. They were heard cutting down the bushes and smaller trees, and not long afterwards it looked as if the whole wood was advancing bodily up towards the breastwork on that side.

A rapid and no doubt effective fire was now kept up by Moncrieff and his men. This delayed the terrible *dénoûment*, but it was soon apparent that if some more strategic movement was not made on our part it could not wholly thwart it.

At all hazards that advancing wood must be checked, else the horrors of fire would be the prelude to one of the most awful massacres that ever took place on the lonely pampas.

'How is the wind?' asked Moncrieff, as if speaking to himself.

'It blows from the wood towards the camp,' said Dugald, 'but not quite in a line. See, I am ready to rush out and fire that pile.'

'No, Dugald,' cried Donald; 'I am the elder—I will go.'

'Brother, I spoke first.'

'Yes,' said Moncrieff, quietly, 'Dugald must go, and go now. Take five men, ten if you want them.'

'Five will do—five Gauchos,' said Dugald.

It was wise of Dugald to choose Gauchos. If the truth must be told, however, he did so to spare more valuable lives. But these wild plainsmen are the bravest of the brave, and are far better versed in the tactics of Indian warfare than any white man could be.

Dugald's plan would have been to issue out and make a bold rush across the open space of seventy and odd yards that intervened between the moving pile of brushwood and the camp. Had this been done, every man would have been speared ere he got half across.

The preparations for the sally were speedily made. Each man had a revolver and knife in his belt, and carried in his hands matches, a bundle of *pob* (or tarred yarn), and a small cask of petroleum oil. They issued from the side of the camp farthest from the wood, and, crawling on their faces, took advantage of every tussock of grass, waving thistle, or hemlock bush in their way. Meanwhile a persistent fire was kept up from behind the breastwork, which, from the screams and yells proceeding from the savages, must have been doing execution.

Presently, close behind the bush and near the ground, Moncrieff could see Dugald's signal, the waving of a white handkerchief, and firing immediately ceased.

Almost immediately afterwards smoke and flames ran all along the wood and increased every moment. There was a smart volley of revolver firing, and in a minute more Dugald and his Gauchos were safe again within the fort.

'Stand by now, lads, to defend the ramparts!' cried Moncrieff; 'the worst is yet to come.'

The worst was indeed to come. For under cover of the smoke the Indians now made ready for their final assault. In the few minutes of silence that elapsed before the attack, the voice of a Gaucho malo was heard haranguing his men in language that could not but inflame their blood and passions. He spoke of the riches, the wealth of the camp, of the revenge they were going to have on the hated white man who had stolen their hunting fields, and driven them to the barren plains and mountains to seek for food with the puma and the snake, and finally began to talk of the pale-face prisoners that would become their possession.

'Give them another volley, men,' said Moncrieff, grimly. 'Fire low through the smoke.'

It would have been better, probably, had our leader waited.

Little need to precipitate an onslaught that could have but one ending—unless indeed assistance arrived from the fort.

The long, long hour of waiting came to an end at last, and the commander and myself left the frontier fort at the head of the men.

How terribly tedious the march back seemed! The officer would keep talking as cheerfully as if going to a concert or evening party. I hardly answered, I hardly heard him. I felt ashamed of my anxiety, but still I could not help it. I was but a young soldier.

At last we are within sight, ay, and hearing, of the camp, and the events of the next hour float before my memory now as I write, like the shadowy pantomime of some terrible dream.

First we see smoke and fire, but hear no sound. All must be over, I think—tragedy and massacre, all—and the camp is on fire.

Even the commander of our little force takes a serious view of the case now. He draws his sword, looks to his revolver, and speaks to his men in calm, determined tones.

For long minutes the silence round the camp is unbroken, but suddenly rifles ring out in the still air, and I breathe more freely once again. Then the firing ceases, and is succeeded by the wild war-cries of the attacking savages, and the hoarse, defiant slogan of the defending Scots.

'Hurrah!' I shout, 'we are yet in time. Oh, good sir, hurry on! Listen!'

Well might I say listen, for now high above the yell of savages and ring of revolvers rises the shriek of frightened women.

I can stand this no longer. I set spur to my horse, and go dashing on towards the camp.

CHAPTER XIII
THE FLIGHT AND THE CHASE

The very last thing I had seen that cool Argentine commander do, was to light a fresh cigarette with the stump of the old one. The next time I saw him, he was standing by his wounded horse, in the moonlight, with a spear wound in his brow, but smoking still.

The onslaught of the savages had been for a while a terrible one, but the soldiers came in time, and the camp was saved.

Hardly knowing what I did—not knowing till this day how I did it—I had put my good steed at the breastwork, and, tired though he was, he fairly cleared it. Next I remember hewing my way, sword in hand, through a crowd of spear-armed savages, finding myself close to the ladies' caravan, and next minute inside it.

A single glance showed me all were safe. Aileen lay pale and motionless on the sofa. Near her, revolver in hand, stood my brave aunt, and by the stove was old Jenny herself.

'Oh, bless you, dear boy!' cried auntie. 'How glad we are to see you!'

"Deed are we, laddie!' chimed old Jenny; 'but—' and she grinned as she spoke, 'they rievin' Philistines will be fools if they come this road again. I've gi'en some o' them het [hot] hurdies. Ha, ha! I'm makin' a drap mair for them in case they come again.'

'Poor thing!' I think; 'she has gone demented.'

There was no time now, however, to ask for explanation; for although the Indians had really been driven off, the chase, and, woe is me, the slaughter, had commenced.

And I shudder even yet when I think of that night's awful work on the moonlit pampas. Still, the sacrifice of so many redskins was calculated to insure our safety. Moreover, had our camp fallen into the hands of those terrible Indians, what a blood-blotted page would have been added to the history of the Silver West!

It is but just and fair to Moncrieff, however, to say that he did all in his power to stay the pursuit; but in vain. The soldiers were just returning, tired and breathless, from a fruitless chase after the now panic-stricken enemy, when a wild shout was heard, and our Gauchos were seen riding up from the woods, brandishing the very spears they had captured from the Indians, and each one leading a spare horse.

The *soldados* welcomed them with a shout. Next minute each was mounted and galloping across the pampas in one long extended line.

They were going to treat the Indians to a taste of their own tactics, for between each horse a lasso rope was fastened.

All our men who were safe and unwounded now clambered into the waggon to witness the pursuit. Nothing could exceed the mad grandeur of that charge—nothing could withstand that wild rash. The Indians were mowed down by the lasso lines, then all we could see was a dark commingled mass of rearing horses, of waving swords and spears, and struggling, writhing men.

Yells and screams died away at last, and no sound was now heard on the pampas except the thunder of the horses' hoofs, as our people returned to the camp, and occasionally the trumpet-like notes of the startled flamingoes.

As soon as daylight began to appear in the east the ramparts were razed, and soon after we were once more on the move, glad to leave the scene of battle and carnage.

From higher ground, at some distance, I turned and looked back. Already the air was darkened by flocks of pampas kites, among them many slow-winged vultures, and I knew the awful feast that ever follows slaughter had already commenced.

We had several Gauchos killed and one of our own countrymen, but many more were wounded, some severely enough, so that our victory had cost us dear, and yet we had reason to be thankful, and my only surprise to this day is that we escaped utter annihilation.

It would be anything but fair to pass on to other scenes without mentioning the part poor old Jenny played in the defence of the caravan.

Jenny was not demented—not she. Neither the fatigue of the journey, the many wonders she had witnessed, including the shower of golochs, nor the raid upon the camp had deprived Moncrieff's wonderful mither of her wits. I have said there was a stove burning in the caravan. As soon, then, as Jenny found out that they were fortifying or entrenching the camp, and that the Philistines, as she called them, might be expected at any moment, she awoke to a true sense of the situation. The first thing she did was to replenish the fire, then she put the biggest saucepan on top of the stove, and as soon as it commenced to boil she began 'mealing in,' as she called it.

'Oatmeal would have been best,' she told my aunt; 'but, after a',' she added, 'Indian meal, though it be but feckless stuff, is the kind o' kail they blackamoors are maist used to.'

Aunt wondered what she meant, but was silent, and, indeed, she had other things to think about than Jenny and her strange doings, for Aileen required all her attention.

When, however, the fight had reached its very fiercest, when the camp itself was enveloped in smoke, and the constant cracking of revolvers, the shrieks of the wounded men and clashing of weapons would have daunted a less bold heart than Jenny's—the old lady took her saucepan from the stove and stationed herself by the front door of the caravan. She had not long to wait. Three of the fiercest of the Indian warriors had sprung to the *coupé* and were half up,

> 'But little kenned they Jenny's mettle,
> Or dreamt what lay in Jenny's kettle.'

With eyes that seemed to flash living fire, her grey hair streaming over her shoulders, she must have looked a perfect fury as she rushed out and deluged the up-turned faces and shoulders of the savages with the boiling mess. They dropped yelling to the ground, and Jenny at once turned her attention to the back door of the van, where already one of the leading Gaucho malos—aunt's beautiful blackguards of the day before—had gained footing. This villain she fairly bonneted with the saucepan.

'Your brithers have gotten the big half o' the kail,' she cried, 'and ye can claw the pat.'

It was not till next evening that aunt told Moncrieff the brave part old Jenny had played. He smiled in his quiet way as he patted his mother's hand.

'Just as I told ye, Miss M'Crimman,' he said; 'mither's a marrrvel!'

But where had the bold Bombazo been during the conflict? Sword and revolver in hand, in the foremost ranks, and wherever the battle raged the fiercest? Nay, reader, nay. The stern truth remains to be told. During all the terrible tulzie Bombazo had never once been either seen or heard. Nor could he be anywhere found after the fight, nor even after the camp was struck, though search was made for him high and low.

Some one suggested that he might have been overcome by fear, and might have hidden himself. Moncrieff looked incredulous. What! the bold Bombazo be afraid—the hero of a hundred fights, the slayer of lions, the terror of the redskins, the brave hunter of pampas and prairie? Captain Rodrigo de Bombazo hide himself? Yet where could he be? Among the slain? No. Taken prisoner? Alas! for the noble redman. Those who had escaped would hardly have thought of taking prisoners. Bombazo's name was shouted, the wood was searched, the waggons overhauled, not a stone was left unturned, figuratively speaking, yet all in vain.

But, wonderful to relate, what *men* failed to do a *dog* accomplished. An honest collie found Bombazo—actually scraped him up out of the sand, where he lay buried, with his head in a tussock of grass. It would be unfair to judge him too harshly, wrong not to listen to his vouchsafed explanation; yet, sooth to say, to this very day I believe the little man had hidden himself after the manner of the armadillos.

'Where is my sword?' he shouted, staggering to his feet. 'Where is the foe?'

The Scotchmen and even the Gauchos laughed in his face. He turned from them scornfully on his heel and addressed Moncrieff.

'Dey tried to keel me,' he cried. 'Dey stunned me and covered me up wit' sand. But here I am, and now I seek revenge. Ha! ha! I will seek revenge!'

Old Jenny could stand it no longer.

'Oh, ye shameless sinner!' she roared. 'Oh, ye feckless fusionless winner! Let me at him. *I'll* gie him revenge.'

There was no restraining Jenny. With a yell like the war cry of a clucking hen, she waved her umbrella aloft, and went straight for the hero.

The blow intended for his head alighted lower down. Bombazo turned and fled, pursued by the remorseless Jenny; and not even once did she miss her aim till the terror of the redskins, to save his own skin, had taken refuge beneath the caravan.

As at sea, so in travelling. Day after day, amid scenes that are for ever new, the constantly recurring adventure and incident suffice to banish even thoughts of the dead themselves. But neither seafarers nor travellers need be ashamed of this; it is only natural. God never condemns His creatures to constant sorrow. The brave fellows, the honest Scot and the Gauchos, that we had laid side by side in one grave in the little burying-place at the frontier fort, were gone beyond recall. No amount of sorrowing could bring them back. We but hoped they were happier now than even we were, and so we spoke of them no more; and in a week's time everything about our caravan and camp resumed its wonted appearance, and we no longer feared the Indians.

One Gaucho, however, had escaped, and there was still the probability he might seek for revenge some other day.

We have left the bleak pampas land, although now and then we come to bare prairie land but scantily furnished with even bushes, and destitute of grass; houses and *estancias* become more frequent, and *fondas* too, but nothing like that fearful *fonda* in the prairie—the scene of the massacre.

We have passed through San Lui—too wretched a place to say much about; and even La Paz and Santa Rosa; and on taking her usual seat one forenoon in front of the caravan, old Jenny's eyes grew bright and sparkling with very delight.

'Saw anybody ever the like o' that?' she cried, as she raised both her hands and eyes cloudwards. But it was not the clouds old Jenny was marvelling at—for here we were in the Province of Mendoza, and a measurable distance from the beautiful city itself; and instead of the barren lands we had recently emerged from, beheld a scene of such natural loveliness and fertility, that we seemed to have suddenly dropped into a new world.

The sky was blue and almost cloudless; winter though it was, the fields were clad in emerald green; the trees, the vineyards, the verandahed houses, the comfortable dwellings, the cattle, the sheep, and flocks of poultry—all testified to the fact that in summer this must indeed be a paradise.

'What do you think of all this, mither?' said Moncrieff, with a happy smile. He was riding close to the caravan *coupé*.

'Think o' it, laddie! Loshie me, laddie! it beats the braes o' Foudlan'! It is surely the garden o' Eden we're coming to at last.'

It was shortly after this that Moncrieff went galloping on ahead. We could see him miles and miles away, for the road was as straight as one of the avenues in some English lord's domains. Suddenly he disappeared. Had the earth swallowed him up? Not quite. He had merely struck into a side path, and here we too turned with our whole cavalcade; and our road now lay away across a still fertile but far more open country. After keeping to this road for miles, we turned off once more and headed for the distant mountains, whose snow-clad, rugged tops formed so grand a horizon to the landscape.

On we journey for many a long hour, and the sun goes down and down in the west, and sinks at last behind the hills; and oh, with what ineffably sweet tints and shades of pink and blue and purple his farewell rays paint the summits!

Twilight is beginning to fall, and great bats are flitting about. We come within sight of a wide and well-watered valley; and in the very centre thereof, and near a broad lagoon which reminds us somewhat of dear old Coila, stands a handsome *estancia* and farmyard. There are rows and rows of gigantic poplar-trees everywhere in this glen, and the house itself—mansion, I might almost say—lies in the midst of a cloud of trees the names of which we cannot even guess. There was altogether such a home-like look about the valley, that I knew at once our long, long journey was over, and our weary wanderings finished for a time. There was not a very great deal of romance in honest Moncrieff's nature, but as he pointed with outstretched arm to the beautiful *estancia* by the lake, and said, briefly, 'Mither, there's your hame!' I felt sure and certain those blue eyes of his were moist with tears, and that there was the slightest perceptible waver in his manly voice.

But, behold! they have seen us already at the *estancia*.

There is a hurrying and scurrying to and fro, and out and in. We notice this, although the figures we see look no larger than ants, so clear and transparent is even the gloaming air in this wonderful new land of ours.

By and by we see these same figures on horseback, coming away from the farm, and hurrying down the road towards us. One, two, three, six! Why, there must be well-nigh a score of them altogether. Nearer and nearer they come, and now we see their arms wave. Nearer still, and we hear them shout; and now at length they are on us, with us, and around us, waving their caps, laughing, talking, and shaking hands over and over again—as often as not twice or thrice with the same person. Verily they are half delirious with joy and wholly hysterical.

What volleys of questions have to be asked and answered! What volumes of news to get and to give! What hurrying here and there and up and down to admire the new horses and mules, the new waggons and caravan—to admire everything! while the half-frightened looks those sturdy, sun-browned, bearded men cast at auntie and Aileen were positively comical to witness!

Then, when the first wave of joyous excitement had partially expended itself—

'Stand back, boys!' shouted Moncrieff's partner, a bold-faced little Welshman, with hair and beard just on the turn; 'stand back, my lads, and give them one more little cheer.'

But was it a little cheer? Nay, but a mighty rattling cheer—a cheer that could have issued only from brave British throats; a cheer that I almost expected to hear re-echoed back from the distant mountains.

Ah! but it *was* echoed back. Echoed by us, the new-comers, and with interest too, our faithful Gauchos swelling the chorus with their shrill but not unmusical voices.

But look! more people are coming down the road. The welcome home is not half over yet. Yonder are the lads and lasses, English, Irish, Castilian and Scotch, who have no horses to ride. Foremost among them is a Highlander in tartan trews and bagpipes. And if the welcome these give us is not altogether so boisterous it is none the less sincere.

In another hour we are all safe at home. All and everything appears to us very strange at first, but we soon settle down, and if we marvelled at the outside of Moncrieff's mansion, the interior of it excites our wonder to even a greater degree. Who could have credited the brawny Scot with so much refinement of taste? The rooms were large, the windows were bowers, and bowers of beauty too, around which climbed and trailed—winter though it was—flowers of such strange shapes and lovely colours that the best of our floral favourites in this country would look tame beside them. None of the walls were papered, but all were painted, and many had pictures in light, airy and elegant frames. The furniture too was all light and elegant, and quite Oriental in appearance. Oriental did I say? Nay, but even better; it was Occidental. One room in particular took my aunt's fancy. This was to be the boudoir, and everything in it was the work of Indian hands. It opened on to a charming trellised verandah, and thence was a beautiful garden which to-night was lit up with coloured lanterns, and on the whole looked like a scene in some Eastern fairy tale.

'And would you believe it, Aileen,' said Moncrieff, when he was done showing us round the rooms; 'would you believe it, auntie, when I came here first my good partner and I had no place to live in for years but a reed shanty, a butt and a ben, mither mine, with never a stick of furniture in it, and neither a chair nor stool nor table worth the name?'

'That is so, Miss M'Crimman,' said the partner, Mr. Jones. 'And I think my dear friend Moncrieff will let the ladies see the sort of place we lived in.'

'This way, then, ladies,' said the big Scot. He seized a huge naphtha lamp as he spoke, and strode before them through the garden. Arrived at the end of it they came to a strange little hut built apparently of mud and straw.

With little ceremony he kicked open the rickety door, and made them enter. Both aunt and Aileen did so, marvelling much to find themselves in a room not ten feet wide, and neither round nor square. The roof was blackened rafters and straw, the floor was hardened clay. A bed—a very rude one—stood in one corner. It was supported by horses' bones; the table in the centre was but a barrel lid raised on crossed bones.

'Won't you sit down, ladies?' said Moncrieff, smiling.

He pointed to a seat as he spoke. It was formed of horses' skulls.

Aunt smiled too, but immediately after looked suddenly serious, gathered her dress round her with a little shudder, and backed towards the door.

'Come away,' she said; 'I've seen enough.'

What she had seen more particularly was an awful-looking crimson and grey spider as big as a soft-shell crab. He was squatting on a bone in one corner, glaring at her with his little evil eyes, and moving his horizontal mandibles as if he would dearly like to eat her.

CHAPTER XIV
LIFE ON AN ARGENTINE ESTANCIA

I verily believe that Britons, whether English, Irish, or Scotch, are all born to wander, and born colonists. There really seems to be something in the very air of a new land, be it Australia, America, or the Silver West, that brings all their very best and noblest qualities to the surface, and oftentimes makes men—bold, hardy, persevering men—of individuals who, had they stayed in this old cut-and-dry country, would never have been anything better than louts or Johnnie Raws. I assure the reader that I speak from long experience when I make these remarks, and on any Saturday evening when I happen to be in London, and see poor young fellows coming home to garrets, perhaps with their pittance in their pockets, I feel for them from the very depths of my soul. And sometimes I sigh and murmur to myself——

'Oh dear me!' I say, 'if my purse were only half as big as my heart, wouldn't I quickly gather together a thousand of these white slaves and sail merrily off with them to the Land of the Silver West! And men would learn to laugh there who hardly ever smiled before, and tendons would wax wiry, and muscles hard, and pale faces grow brown with the tints of health. And health would mean work, and work would mean wealth, and—but, heigho! what is the good of dreaming? Only some day—yes, *some* day—and what a glorious sunrise it will be for this empire—Government will see its way to grant free passages to far-off lands, in which there is peace and plenty, work and food for all, and where the bread one eats is never damped by falling tears. God send that happy day! And send it soon!

It is the memory of our first months and years of a downright pleasant life that makes me write like this. We poor lads—my brothers and I—poor, but determined, found everything so enjoyable at our new home in the Silver West that oftentimes we could not help wishing that thousands of toiling mortals from Glasgow and other great overcrowded cities would only come out somehow and share our posy. For really, to put it in plain and simple language, next to the delight of enjoying anything oneself, should it only be an apple, is the pleasure of seeing one's neighbour have a bite.

Now here is a funny thing, but it is a fact. The air of Mendoza is so wonderfully dry and strong and bracing that it makes men of boys in a very short time, and makes old people young again. It might not smooth away wrinkles from the face, or turn grey hair brown, or even make two hairs grow where only one grew before; but it does most assuredly rejuvenate the heart, and shakes all the wrinkles out of that. Out here it is no uncommon thing for the once rheumatic to learn to dance, while stiff-jointed individuals who immigrated with crutches under their arms, pitch these crutches into the irrigation canals, and take to spades and guns instead.

It is something in the air, I think, that works these wondrous changes, though I am sure I could not say what. It may be oxygen in double doses, or it may be ozone, or even laughing gas; but there it is, and whosoever reads these lines and doubts what I say, has only to take flight for the beautiful province of Mendoza, and he shall remain a sceptic no longer.

Well, as soon as we got over the fatigues of our long journey, and began to realize the fact that we were no longer children of the desert, no longer nomads and gipsies, my brothers and I set to work with a hearty good-will that astonished even ourselves. In preparing our new homes we, and all the other settlers of this infant colony as well, enjoyed the same kind of pleasure that Robinson Crusoe must have done when he and his man Friday set up house for themselves in the island of Juan Fernandez.

Even the labourers or 'hands' whom Moncrieff had imported had their own dwellings to erect, but instead of looking upon this as a hardship, they said that this was the fun of the thing, and that it was precisely here where the laugh came in.

Moreover they worked for themselves out of hours, and I dare say that is more than any of them would have done in the old country.

Never once was the labour of the *estancia* neglected, nor the state of the aqueducts, nor Moncrieff's flocks and herds, nor his fences.

Some of these men had been ploughmen, others shepherds, but every one of them was an artisan more or less, and it is just such men that do well—men who know a good deal about country life, and can deftly use the spade, the hoe, the rake, the fork, as well as the hammer, the axe, the saw, and the plane. Thanks to the way dear father had brought us up, my brothers and I were handy with all sorts of tools, and we were rather proud than otherwise of our handicraft.

I remember that Dugald one day, as we sat at table, after looking at his hands—they had become awfully brown—suddenly said to Moncrieff,

'Oh, by the by, Brother Moncrieff, there is one thing that I'm ready to wager you forgot to bring out with you from England.'

'What was that?' said Moncrieff, looking quite serious.

'Why, a supply of kid gloves, white and coloured.'

We all laughed.

'My dear boy,' said this huge brother of ours, 'the sun supplies the kid gloves, and it strikes me, lad, you've a pair of coloured ones already.'

'Yes,' said Dugald, 'black-and-tan.'

'But, dear laddies,' old Jenny put in, 'if ye really wad like mittens, I'll shortly shank a curn for ye.'

'Just listen to the old braid Scotch tongue o' that mither o' moine— "shortly shank a curn."[5] Who but an Aberdonian could understand that?'

But indeed poor old Jenny was a marvel with her 'shank,' as she called her knitting, and almost every third day she turned off a splendid pair of rough woollen stockings for one or other of her bairns, as she termed us generically. And useful weather-defiant articles of hosiery they were too. When our legs were encased in these, our feet protected by a pair of double-soled boots, and our ankles further fortified by leather gaiters, there were few snakes even we were afraid to tackle.

The very word 'snake,' or 'serpent,' makes some people shudder, and it is as well to say a word or two about these ophidians here, and have done with them. I have, then, no very wild adventures to record concerning those we encountered on our *estancias*. Nor were either my brothers or myself much afraid of them, for a snake—this is my firm belief—will never strike a human being except in self-defence; and, of all the thousands killed annually in India itself by ophidians, most of the victims have been tramping about with naked feet, or naked legs at least.

Independent of the pure, wholesome, bracing air, there appeared to us to be another peculiarity in the climate which is worthy of note. It is *calmative*. There is more in that simple sentence than might at first be imagined, and the effect upon settlers might be best explained by giving an example: A young man, then, comes to this glorious country fresh from all the excitement and fever of Europe, where people are, as a rule, overcrowded and elbowing each other for a share of the bread that is not sufficient to feed all; he settles down, either to steady work under a master, or to till his own farm and mind his own flocks. In either case, while feeling labour to be not only a pleasure, but actually a luxury, there is no heat of blood and brain; there is no occasion to either chase or hurry. Life now is not like a game of football on Rugby lines—all scurry, push, and perspiration. The new-comer's prospects are everything that could be desired, and—mark this—*he does not live for the future any more than the present.* There is enough of everything around him *now*, so that his happiness does not consist in building upon the far-off *then*, which strugglers in this Britain of ours think so much about. The settler then, I say, be he young or old, can afford to enjoy himself to-day, certain in his own mind that to-morrow will provide for itself.

But this calmness of mind, which really is a symptom of glorious health, never merges into the dreamy laziness and ignoble activity exhibited by Brazilians in the east and north of him.

My brothers and I were happily saved a good deal of business worry in connection with the purchase of our *estancia*, so, too, were the new settlers, for Moncrieff, with that long Scotch head of his, had everything cut and dry, as he called it, so that the signing of a few papers and the writing of a cheque or two made us as proud as any Scottish laird in the old country.

'You must creep before you walk,' Moncrieff told us; 'you mustn't go like a bull at a gate. Just look before you "loup."'

So we consulted him in everything.

Suppose, for instance, we wanted another mule or horse, we went to Moncrieff for advice.

'Can you do without it?' he would say. 'Go home and settle that question between you, and if you find you can't, come and tell me, and I'll let you have the beast as cheap as you can buy it anywhere.'

Well, we started building our houses. Unlike the pampas, Mendoza *can* boast of stone and brick, and even wood, though round our district a deal of this had been planted. The woods that lay on Moncrieff's colony had been reared more for shelter to the flocks against the storms and tempests that often sweep over the country.

In the more immediate vicinity of the dwelling-houses, with the exception of some splendid elms and plane-trees, and the steeple-high solemn-looking poplar, no great growth of wood was encouraged. For it must be remembered we were living in what Moncrieff called uncanny times. The Indians[6] were still a power in the country, and their invasions were looked for periodically. The State did not then give the protection against this foe it does now. True, there existed what were called by courtesy frontier forts; they were supposed to billet soldiers there, too, but as these men were often destitute of a supply of ammunition, and spent much of their time playing cards and drinking the cheap wines of the country, the settlers put but little faith in them, and the wandering pampa Indians treated them with disdain.

Our houses, then, for safety's sake, were all built pretty close together, and on high ground, so that we had a good view all over the beautiful valley. They could thus be more easily defended.

Here and there over the *estancias*, *puestos*, as they were called, were erected for the convenience of the shepherds. They were mere huts, but, nevertheless, they were far more comfortable in every way than many a crofter's cottage in the Scottish Highlands.

Round the dwellings of the new settlers, which were built in the form of a square, each square, three in all, having a communication, a rampart and ditch were constructed. The making of these was mere pastime to these hardy Scots, and they took great delight in the work, for not only would it enable them to sleep in peace and safety, but the keeping of it in thorough decorative repair, as house agents say, would always form a pleasant occupation for spare time.

The mansion, as Moncrieff's beautiful house came to be called, was similarly fortified, but as it stood high in its grounds the rampart did not hide the building. Moreover, the latter was partially decorated inside with flowers, and the external embankment always kept as green as an English lawn in June.

The ditches were wide and deep, and were so arranged that in case of invasion they could be filled with water from a natural lake high up on the brae lands. For that matter they might have been filled at any time, or kept filled, but Moncrieff had an idea—and probably he was right—that too much stagnant, or even semi-stagnant water near a house rendered it unhealthy.

As soon as we had bought our claims and marked them out, each settler's distinct from the other, but ours—my brothers' and mine—all in one lot, we commenced work in earnest. There was room and to spare for us all about the Moncrieff mansion and farmyard, we—the M'Crimmans—being guests for a time, and living indoors, the others roughing it as best they could in the out-houses, some of which were turned into temporary huts.

Nothing could exceed the beauty of Moncrieff's *estancia*. It was miles and miles in extent, and more like a lovely garden than anything else. The fields were all square. Round each, in tasteful rows, waved noble trees, the weird and ghostly poplar, whose topmost branches touched the clouds apparently, the wide-spreading elm, the shapely chestnut, the dark, mysterious cypress, the fairy-leaved acacia, the waving willow and sturdy oak. These trees had been planted with great taste and judgment around the fields, and between all stretched hedges of laurel, willow, and various kinds of shrubs. The fields themselves were not without trees; in fact, trees were dotted over most of them, notably chestnuts, and many species of fruit trees.

But something else added to the extreme beauty of these fields, namely, the irrigation canals—I prefer the word canals to ditches. The highest of all was very deep and wide, and was supplied with water from the distant hills and river, while in its turn it supplied the whole irrigation system of the *estancia*. The plan for irrigating the fields was the simplest that could be thought of, but it was quite as perfect as it was simple.

Add to the beauty of the trees and hedges the brilliancy of trailing flowers of gorgeous hues and strange, fantastic shapes; let some of those trees be actually hanging gardens of beauty; let flowers float ever on the waters around the fields, and the fields themselves be emerald green—then imagine sunshine, balmy air, and perfume everywhere, and you will have some idea of the charm spread from end to end of Moncrieff's great *estancia*.

But there was another kind of beauty about it which I have not yet mentioned—namely, its flocks and herds and poultry.

A feature of the strath, or valley, occupied by this little Scoto-Welsh colony was the sandhills or dunes.

'Do you call those sandhills?' I said to Moncrieff one day, shortly after our arrival. 'Why, they are as green and bonnie as the Broad Hill on the links of Aberdeen.'

Moncrieff smiled, but looked pleased.

'Man!' he replied, 'did you ever hear of the proverb that speaks about making mountains of mole-hills? Well, that's what I've done up yonder. When my partner and I began serious work on these fields of ours, those bits of hills were a constant trouble and menace to us. They were just as big then, maybe, as they are now—about fifty feet high at the highest, perhaps, but they were bare sandy hillocks, constantly changing shape and even position with every big storm, till a happy thought struck my partner, and we chose just the right season for acting on it. We got the Gauchos to gather for us pecks and bushels of all kinds of wild seed, especially that of the long-rooted grasses, and these we sowed all over the mole-hills, as we called them, and we planted bushes here and there, and also in the hollows, and, lo! the mole-hills were changed into fairy little mountains, and the bits o' glens between into bosky dells.'

'Dear Brother Moncrieff,' I said, 'you are a genius, and I'm so glad I met you. What would I have been without you?'

'Twaddle, man! nonsensical havers and twaddle! If you hadn't met me you would have met somebody else; and if you hadn't met him, you would have foregathered wi' experience; and, man, experience is the best teacher in a' the wide worruld.'

In laying out and planning our farm, my brothers and I determined, however, not to wait for experience of our own, but just take advantage of Moncrieff's. That would sustain us, as the oak sustains the ivy.

[5] 'Shortly shank a curn'—speedily knit a few pairs.

[6] Since then the Indians have been swept far to the south, and so hemmed in that the provinces north of their territory are as safe from invasion as England itself.—G. S.

CHAPTER XV
WE BUILD OUR HOUSE AND LAY OUT GARDENS

About a hundred yards to the left of the buildings erected for the new colony and down near the lake, or laguna, was an elevated piece of ground about an acre in extent. It was bounded on two sides by water, which would thus form for it a kind of natural protection in case of Indian invasion. It really was part and parcel of Moncrieff's claim or land, and at an early date in his career, thinking probably it might come in handy some day for a site on which to build, he had taken considerable pains to plant it with rows of beautiful trees, especially on the sides next the water and facing the west.

My brothers and I arranged to have this, and Moncrieff was well pleased to have us so near to him. A more excellent position for a house could hardly be, and we determined it should be a good substantial one, and of as great architectural beauty as possible.

Having therefore laid out our farm proper, and stocked it with sheep and cattle, positioned our shepherds, and installed our labourers and general servants under the charge of a *capataz*, or working bailiff, we turned our attention to the erection of our house, or mansion, as Dugald grandly called it.

'Of course you will cut your coat according to your cloth,' said Moncrieff, as he came one evening into the room we had set apart for our private study. He had found us to-night with our heads all together over a huge sheet of paper on which we were planning out our house.

'Oh yes,' said Donald, 'that we must do.'

'But,' said Dugald, 'we do not expect to remain all our lives downright poor settlers.'

'That I am sure you won't.'

'Well, I propose building a much bigger house than we really want, so that when we do get a bit rich we can furnish it and set up—set up—'

'Set up a carriage and pair, eh?' said Donald, who was very matter of fact—'a carriage and pair, Dugald, a billiard-room, Turkey carpets, woven

all in one piece, a cellar of old wine, a butler in black and flunkeys in plush—
is that your notion?'

Donald and I laughed, and Dugald looked cross.

Moncrieff did not laugh: he had too much tact, and was far too kind-hearted to throw cold water over our young brother's ambitions and aspirations.

'And what sort of a house do you propose?' he said to us.

As he spoke he took a chair at Dugald's side of the table and put his arm gently across the boy's shoulders. There was very much in this simple act, and I feel sure Dugald loved him for it, and felt he had some one to assist his schemes.

'Oh,' replied Donald, 'a small tasteful cottage. That would suit well for the present, I think. What do you think, Murdoch?'

'I think with you,' I replied.

After having heard Moncrieff speaking so much about cutting coats according to cloth and looking before 'louping,' and all the rest of it, we were hardly prepared to hear him on the present occasion say boldly,

'And *I* think with Dugald.'

'Bravo, Moncrieff!' cried Dugald. 'I felt sure—'

'Bide a wee, though, lad. Ca' canny.[7] Now listen, the lot o' ye. Ye see, Murdoch man, your proposed cottage would cost a good bit of money and time and trouble, and when you thought of a bigger place, down that cottage must come, with an expense of more time and more trouble, even allowing that money was of little object. Besides, where are you going to live after your cottage is knocked down and while your mansion is building? So I say Dugald is right to some extent. Begin building your big house bit by bit.'

'In wings?'

'Preeesely, sirs; ye can add and add as you like, and as you can afford it.'

It was now our time to cry, 'Bravo, Moncrieff!'

'I wonder, Donald, we didn't think of this plan.'

'Ah,' said Moncrieff, 'ye canna put young he'ds on auld shoulders, as my mither says.'

So Moncrieff's plan was finally adopted—we would build our house wing by wing.

It took us weeks, however, to decide in what particular style of architecture it should be built. Among the literature which Moncrieff had brought out from England with him was a whole library in itself of the bound volumes of good magazines; and it was from a picture in one of these that we finally decided what our Coila Villa should be like, though, of course, the plan would be slightly altered to suit circumstances of climate, &c. It was to be—briefly stated—a winged bungalow of only one story, with a handsome square tower and portico in the centre, and verandahs nearly all round. So one wing and the tower was commenced at once. But bricks were to be made, and timber cut and dried and fashioned, and no end of other things were to be accomplished before we actually set about the erection.

To do all these things we appointed a little army of Gauchos, with two or three handy men-of-all-work from Scotland.

Meanwhile our villa gardens were planned and our bushes and trees were planted.

Terraces, too, were contrived to face the lake, and Dugald one evening proposed a boat-house and boat, and this was carried without a dissentient voice.

Dugald was extremely fond of our sister Flora. We only wondered that he now spoke about her so seldom. But if he spoke but little of her he thought the more, and we could see that all his plans for the beautification and adornment of the villa had but one end and object—the delight and gratification of its future little mistress.

Dear old Dugald! he had such a kind lump of a heart of his own, and never took any of our chaff and banter unpleasantly. But I am quite sure that as far as he himself was concerned he never would have troubled himself about even the boat-house or the terraced gardens either, for every idle hour that he could spare he spent on the hill, as he called it, with his dog—a lovely Irish setter—and his gun.

I met him one morning going off as usual with Dash, the setter, close beside the little mule he rode, and with his gun slung over his back.

'Where away, old man?' I said.

'Only to a little laguna I've found among the hills, and I mean to have a grand bag to-day.'

'Well, you're off early!'

'Yes; there is little to be done at home, and there are some rare fine ducks up yonder.'

'You'll be back to luncheon?'

'I'll try. If not, don't wait.'

'Not likely; ta-ta! Good luck to you! But you really ought to have a Gaucho with you.'

'Nonsense, Murdoch! I don't need a groom. Dash and old Tootsie, the mule, are all I want.'

It was the end of winter, or rather beginning of spring, but Moncrieff had not yet declared close time, and Dugald managed to supply the larder with more species of game than we could tell the names of. Birds, especially, he brought home on his saddle and in his bag; birds of all sizes, from the little luscious dove to the black swan itself; and one day he actually came along up the avenue with a dead ostrich. He could ride that mule of his anywhere. I believe he could have ridden along the parapet of London Bridge, so we were never surprised to see Dugald draw rein at the lower sitting-room window, within the verandah. He was always laughing and merry and mischievous-looking when he had had extra good luck; but the day he landed that ostrich he was fairly wild with excitement. The body of it was given to the Gauchos, and they made very merry over it: invited their friends, in fact, and roasted the huge bird whole out of doors. They did so in true Patagonian fashion—to wit, the ostrich was first trussed and cleaned, a roaring fire of wood having been made, round stones were made almost red-hot. The stones were for stuffing, though this kind of stuffing is not very eatable, but it helps to cook the bird. The fire was then raked away, and the dinner laid down and covered up. Meanwhile the Gauchos, male and female, girls and boys, had a dance. The ubiquitous guitars, of course, were the instruments, and two of these made not a bad little band. After dinner they danced again, and wound up by wishing Dugald all the good luck in the world, and plenty more ostriches. The feathers of this big game-bird were carefully packed and sent home to mother and Flora.

Well, we had got so used to Dugald's solitary ways that we never thought anything of even his somewhat prolonged absence on the hill, for he usually dropped round when luncheon was pretty nearly done. There was always something kept warm for 'old Dugald,' as we all called him, and I declare it did every one of us good to see him eat. His appetite was certainly the proverbial appetite of a hunter.

On this particular day, however, old Dugald did not return to luncheon.

'Perhaps,' said Donald, 'he is dining with some of the shepherds, or having "a pick at a priest's," as he calls it.'

'Perhaps,' I said musingly. The afternoon wore away, and there were no signs of our brother coming, so I began to get rather uneasy, and spoke to Donald about it.

'He may have met with an accident,' I said, 'or fifty things may have happened.'

'Well,' replied Donald, 'I don't suppose fifty things have happened; but as you seem a bit anxious, suppose we mount our mules, take a Gaucho with us, and institute a search expedition?'

'I'm willing,' I cried, jumping up, 'and here's for off!'

There was going to be an extra good dinner that day, because we expected letters from home, and our runner would be back from the distant post-office in good time to let us read our epistles before the gong sounded and so discuss them at table.

'Hurry up, boys; don't be late, mind!' cried aunt, as our mules were brought round to the portico, and we were mounted.

'All right, auntie dear!' replied Donald, waving his hand; 'and mind those partridges are done to a turn; we'll be all delightfully hungry.'

The Gaucho knew all Dugald's trails well, and when we mentioned the small distant laguna, he set out at once in the direction of the glen. He made so many windings, however, and took so many different turns through bush and grass and scrub, that we began to wonder however Dugald could have found the road.

But Dugald had a way of his own of getting back through even a cactus labyrinth. It was a very simple one, too. He never 'loaded up,' as he termed it; that is, he did not hang his game to his saddle till he meant to start for home; then he mounted, whistled to Dash, who capered and barked in front of the mule, permitted the reins to lie loosely on the animal's neck, and — there he was! For not only did the good beast take him safely back to Coila, as we called our *estancia*, but he took him by the best roads; and even when he seemed to Dugald's human sense to be going absolutely and entirely wrong, he never argued with him.

> 'Reason raise o'er instinct, if you can;
> In this 'tis God directs, in that 'tis man.'

'You are certain he will come this way, Zambo?' I said to our Gaucho.

'Plenty certain, señor. I follow de trail now.'

I looked over my saddle-bow; so did Donald, but no trail could we see — only the hard, yellow, sandy gravel.

We came at last to the hilly regions. It was exceedingly quiet and still here; hardly a creature of any kind to be seen except now and then a kite, or even condor, the latter winging his silent way to the distant mountains.

At times we passed a biscacha village. The biscacha is not a tribe of Indians, but, like the coney, a very feeble people, who dwell in caves or burrow underground, but all day long may be seen playing about the mounds they raise, or sitting on their hind legs on top of them. They are really a species of prairie-dog. With them invariably live a tribe of little owls—the burrowing owls—and it seems to be a mutual understanding that the owls have the principal possession of these residential chambers by day, while the biscachas occupy them by night. This arrangement answers wonderfully well, and I have proved over and over again that they are exceedingly fond of each other. The biscachas themselves are not very demonstrative, either in their fun or affection, but if one of them be killed, and is lying dead outside the burrow, the poor owl often exhibits the most frantic grief for the murder of his little housekeeper, and will even show signs of a desire to attack the animal—especially if a dog—which has caused his affliction.

Donald and I, with our guide, now reached the land of the giant cacti. We all at home here in Britain know something of the beauty of the common prickly cactus that grows in window-gardens or in hot-houses, and surprises us with the crimson glory of its flowers, which grow from such odd parts of the plant; but here we were in the land of the cacti. Dugald knew it well, and used to tell us all about them; so tall, so stately, so strange and weird, that we felt as if in another planet. Already the bloom was on some of them—for in this country flowers soon hear the voice of spring—but in the proper season nothing that ever I beheld can surpass the gorgeous beauty of these giant cacti.

The sun began to sink uncomfortably low down on the horizon, and my anxiety increased every minute. Why did not Dugald meet us? Why did we not even hear the sound of his gun, for the Gaucho told us we were close to the laguna?

Presently the cacti disappeared behind us, and we found ourselves in open ground, with here and there a tall, weird-looking tree. How those trees—they were not natives—had come there we were at first at a loss to understand, but when we reached the foot of a grass-grown hill or sand dune, and came suddenly on the ruins of what appeared a Jesuit hermitage or monastery, the mystery was explained.

On rounding a spur of this hill, lo! the lake; and not far from the foot of a tree, behold! our truant brother. Beside him was Dash, and not a great way off, tied to a dwarf algaroba tree, stood the mule. Dugald was sitting on the ground, with his gun over his arm, gazing up into the tree.

'Dugald! Dugald!' I cried.

But Dugald never moved his head. Was he dead, or were these green sand dunes fairy hillocks, and my brother enchanted?

I leapt off my mule, and, rifle in hand, went on by myself, never taking my eyes off my brother, and with my heart playing pit-a-pat against my ribs.

'Dugald!' I said again.

He never moved.

'Dugald, speak!'

He spoke now almost in a stage whisper:

'A lion in the tree. Have you your rifle?'

I beckoned to my brother to come on, and at the same moment the monster gave voice. I was near enough now to take aim at the puma; he was lying in a cat-like attitude on one of the highest limbs. But the angry growl and the moving tail told me plainly enough he was preparing to spring, and spring on Dugald. It was the first wild beast I had ever drawn bead upon, and I confess it was a supreme moment; oh, not of joy, but,—shall I say it?—fear.

What if I should miss!

But there was no time for cogitation. I raised my rifle. At the self-same moment, as if knowing his danger, the brute sprang off the bough. The bullet met him in mid-air, and—*he fell dead at Dugald's feet.*

The ball had entered the neck and gone right on and through the heart. One coughing roar, an opening and shutting of the terrible jaws—which were covered with blood and froth—and a few convulsive movements of the hind legs, and all was over.

'Thank Heaven, you are saved, dear old Dugald!' I cried.

'Yes,' said Dugald, getting up and coolly stretching himself; 'but you've been a precious long time in coming.'

'And you were waiting for us?'

'I couldn't get away. I was sitting here when I noticed the lion. Dash and I were having a bit of lunch. My cartridges are all on the mule, so I've been staring fixedly at that monster ever since. I knew it was my only chance. If I had moved away, or even turned my head, he would have had me as sure as—'

'But, I say,' he added, touching the dead puma with his foot, '*isn't* he a fine fellow? What a splendid skin to send home to Flora!'

This shows what sort of a boy Brother Dugald was; and now that all danger was past and gone, although I pretended to be angry with him for his rashness, I really could not help smiling.

'But what a crack shot you are, Murdoch!' he added; 'I had no idea—I—I really couldn't have done much better myself.'

'Well, Dugald,' I replied, 'I may do better next time, but to tell the truth I aimed at the beast *when he was on the branch*.'

'And hit him ten feet below it. Ha! ha! ha!'

We all laughed now. We could afford it.

The Gaucho whipped the puma out of his skin in less than a minute, and off we started for home.

I was the hero of the evening; though Dugald never told them of my funny aim. Bombazo, who had long since recovered his spirits, was well to the front with stories of his own personal prowess and narrow escapes; but while relating these he never addressed old Jenny, for the ancient and humorsome dame had told him one day that 'big lees were thrown awa' upon her.'

What a happy evening we spent, for our Gaucho runner had brought

'Good news from Home!'

[7] 'Ca' Canny' = Drive slowly.

CHAPTER XVI
SUMMER IN THE SILVER WEST

Though it really was not so very long since we had said farewell to our friends in Scotland and the dear ones at home, it seemed an age. So it is no wonder, seeing that all were well, our letters brought us joy. Not for weeks did we cease to read them over and over again and talk about them. One of mine was from Archie Bateman, and, much to my delight and that of my brothers, he told us that he had never ceased worrying his father and mother to let him come out to the Silver West and join us, and that they were yielding fast. He meant, he said, to put the screw on a little harder soon, by running away and taking a cruise as far as Newcastle-on-Tyne in a coalboat. He had no doubt that this would have the desired effect of showing his dearly-beloved *pater et mater* that he was in downright earnest in his desire to go abroad. So we were to expect him next summer—'that is,' he added, 'summer in England, and winter with you.'

Another letter of mine was from Irene M'Rae. I dare say there must have been a deal of romance about me even then, for Irene's delightful little matter-of-fact and prosaic letter gave me much pleasure, and I—I believe I carried it about with me till it was all frayed at every fold, and I finally stowed it away in my desk.

Flora wrote to us all, with a postscript in addition to Dugald. And we were to make haste and get rich enough to send for pa and ma and her.

I did not see Townley's letter to aunt, but I know that much of it related to the 'Coila crime,' as we all call it now. The scoundrel M'Rae had disappeared, and Mr. Townley had failed to trace him. But he could wait. He would not get tired. It was as certain as Fate that as soon as the poacher spent his money—and fellows like him could not keep money long—he would appear again at Coila, to extort more by begging or threatening. Townley had a watch set for him, and as soon as he should appear there would be an interview.

'It would,' the letter went on, 'aid my case very much indeed could I but find the men who assisted him to restore the vault in the old ruin. But they, too, are spirited away, apparently, and all I can do fails to find them. But I live in hope. The good time is bound to come, and may Heaven in justice send it soon!'

Moncrieff had no letters, but I am bound to say that he was as much delighted to see us happy as if we were indeed his own brothers, and our aunt his aunt, if such a thing could have been possible.

But meanwhile the building of our Coila Villa moved on apace, and only those situated as we were could understand the eager interest we took in its gradual rise. At the laying of the foundation-stone we gave all the servants and workmen, and settlers, new and old, an entertainment. We had not an ostrich to roast whole this time, but the supper placed before our guests under Moncrieff's biggest tent was one his cook might well have been proud of. After supper music commenced, only on this special and auspicious occasion the guitars did not have it all their own way, having to give place every now and then to the inspiring strains of the Highland bagpipes. That was a night which was long remembered in our little colony.

While the villa was being built our furniture was being made. This, like that in Moncrieff's mansion, was all, or mostly, Indian work, and manufactured by our half-caste Gauchos. The wood chiefly used was algaroba, which, when polished, looked as bright as mahogany, and quite as beautiful. This Occidental furniture, as we called it, was really very light and elegant, the seats of the couches, fauteuils and sofas, and chairs being worked with thongs, or pieces of hardened skin, in quite a marvellous manner.

We had fences to make all round our fields, and hedges to plant, and even trees. Then there was the whole irrigation system to see to, and the land to sow with grain and lucerne, after the soil had been duly ploughed and attended to. All this kept us young fellows very busy indeed, for we worked with the men almost constantly, not only as simple superintendents, but as labourers.

Yes, the duties about an *estancia*, even after it is fairly established, are very varied; but, nevertheless, I know of no part of the world where the soil responds more quickly or more kindly to the work of the tiller than it does in the Silver West. And this is all the more wonderful when we consider that a great part of the land hereabouts is by nature barren in the extreme.

I do not think I am wrong in saying that sheep, if not first introduced into the *estancias* of the Silver West by the Scotch, have at all events been elevated to the rank of a special feature of produce in the country by them. Moncrieff had done much for the improvement of the breed, not only as regards actual size of body, but in regard to the texture of the wool; and it was his proudest boast to be able to say that the land of his adoption could already compare favourably with Australia itself, and that in the immediate future it was bound to beat that island.

It is no wonder, therefore, that we all looked forward to our first great shearing as a very busy time indeed. Our great wool harvest was, indeed, one of the principal events of the year. Moncrieff said he always felt young again at the sheep-shearing times.

Now there are various styles of wool harvesting. Moncrieff's was simple enough. Preparations were made for it, both out-doors and in, at least a fortnight beforehand. Indoors, hams, &c., were got ready for cooking, and the big tent was erected once more near and behind the mansion, for extra hands to the number of twenty at least were to be imported; several neighbour settlers—they lived ten miles off, and still were neighbours—were coming over to lend a hand, and all had to eat, and most had to sleep, under canvas.

If sheep-shearing prospects made Moncrieff young again, so they did his mother. She was here, there, and everywhere; now in parlour or dining-room, in kitchen and scullery, in out-houses and tent, giving orders, leading, directing, ay, and sometimes even driving, the servants, for few of the Gauchos, whether male or female, could work with speed enough to please old Jenny.

Well, the sheds had to be cleared out, and a system of corralling adopted which was only called for during times like these. Then there were the weighing machines to be seen to; the tally tables and all the packing and pressing machinery—which on this large *estancia* was carried almost to perfection—had all to be got into the very best working order imaginable. For, in the matter of sheep-shearing, Moncrieff was fastidious to a degree.

The sheep were washed the day before. This was hard work, for no animal I know of is more obstinate than a sheep when it makes up its mind to be so.

So the work commenced, and day after day it went merrily on. Moncrieff did not consider this a very large shearing, and yet in six days' time no less than 11,000 sheep were turned away fleeceless.

And what a scene it was, to be sure!

I remember well, when quite a little lad, thinking old Parson McGruer's shearing a wonderful sight. The old man, who was very fat and podgy, and seldom got down to breakfast before eleven in the morning, considered himself a sheep farmer on rather a large scale. Did he not own a flock of nearly six hundred—one shepherd's work—that fed quietly on the heath-clad braes of Coila? One shepherd and two collies; and the collies did nearly all the duty in summer and a great part of it in winter. The shepherd had his bit of shieling in a clump of birch-trees at the glen-foot, and at times, crook in hand, his Highland plaid dangling from his shoulder, he might be seen slowly winding along the braes, or standing, statue-like, on the hill-top, his romantic figure well defined against the horizon, and very much in keeping with the scene. I never yet saw the minister's shepherd running. His life was almost an idyllic one in summer, when the birks waved green and eke, or in autumn, when the hills were all ablaze with the crimson glory of the heather. To be sure, his pay was not a great deal, and his fare for the most part consisted of oatmeal and milk, with now and then a slice of the best part of a 'braxied' sheep. Here, in our home in the Silver West, how different! Every *puestero* had a house or hut as good as the minister's shepherd; and as for living, why, the worthy Mr. McGruer himself never had half so well-found a table. Our dogs in the Silver West lived far more luxuriously than any farm servant or shepherd, or even gamekeeper, 'in a' braid Scotland.'

But our shepherds had to run and to ride both. Wandering over miles upon miles of pasturage, sheep learn to be dainty, and do not stay very long in any one place; so it is considered almost impossible to herd them on foot. It is not necessary to do so; at all events, where one can buy a horse for forty shillings, and where his food costs *nil*, or next to *nil*, one usually prefers riding to walking.

But it was a busy time in May even at the Scotch minister's place when sheep-shearing came round. The minister got up early then, if he did not do so all the year round again. The hurdles were all taken to the river-side, or banks of the stream that, leaving Loch Coila, went meandering through the glen. Here the sheep were washed and penned, and anon turned into the enclosures where the shearers were. Lads and lasses all took part in the work in one capacity or another. The sun would be brightly shining, the 'jouking burnie' sparkling clear in its rays; the glens and hills all green and bonnie; the laughing and joking and lilting and singing, and the constant bleating of sheep and lambs, made altogether a curious medley; but every now and then Donald the piper would tune his pipes and make them 'skirl,' drowning all other sounds in martial melody.

But here on Moncrieff's *estancia* everything was on a grander scale. There was the same bleating of sheep, the same laughing, joking, lilting, singing, and piping; the same hurry-scurry of dogs and men; the same prevailing busy-ness and activity; but everything was multiplied by twenty.

McGruer at home in Coila had his fleeces thrust into a huge sack, which was held up by two stalwart Highlanders. Into this not only were the fleeces put, but also a boy, to jump on them and pack them down. At the *estancia* we had the very newest forms of machinery to do everything.

Day by day, as our shearing went on, Moncrieff grew gayer and gayer, and on the final morning he was as full of life and fun as a Harrow schoolboy out on the range. The wool harvest had turned out well.

It had not been so every year with Moncrieff and his partner. They had had many struggles to come through—sickness had at one time more than decimated the flocks. The Indians, though they do not as a rule drive away sheep, had played sad havoc among them, and scattered them far and wide over the adjoining pampas, and the pampero[8] had several times destroyed its thousands, before the trees had grown up to afford protection and shelter.

I have said before that Moncrieff was fond of doing things in his own fashion. He was willing enough to adopt all the customs of his adopted country so long as he thought they were right, but many of the habits of his native land he considered would engraft well with those of Mendoza. Moncrieff delighted in dancing—that is, in giving a good hearty rout, and he simply did so whenever there was the slightest excuse. The cereal harvest ended thus, the grape harvest also, and making of the wine and preserves, and so of course did the shearing.

The dinner at the mansion itself was a great success; the supper in the marquee, with the romp to follow, was even a greater. Moncrieff himself opened the fun with Aunt Cecilia as a partner, Donald and a charming Spanish girl completing the quartette necessary for a real Highland reel. The piper played, of course (guitars were not good enough for this sort of thing), and I think we must have kept that first 'hoolichin' up for nearly twenty minutes. Then Moncrieff and aunt were fain to retire 'for-fochten.'[9]

Well Moncrieff might have been 'for-fochten,' but neither Donald nor his Spanish lassie were half tired. Nor was the piper.

'Come on, Dugald,' cried Donald, 'get a partner, lad. Hooch!'

'Hooch!' shouted Dugald in response, and lo and behold! he gaily led forth—whom? Why, whom but old Jenny herself? What roars of laughter there was as, keeping time to a heart-stirring strathspey, the little lady cracked her thumbs and danced, reeling, setting, and deeking! roars of laughter, and genuine hearty applause as well.

Moncrieff was delighted with his mother's performance. It was glorious, he said, and so true to time; surely everybody would believe him now that mither was a downright mar-r-r-vel. And everybody did.

During the shearing Donald and I had done duty as clerks; and very busy we had been kept. As for Dugald, it would have been a pity to have parted him and his dear gun, so the work assigned to him was that of lion's provider—we, the shearing folk, being the lion.

For a youth of hardly sixteen Dugald was a splendid shot, and during the shearing he really kept up his credit well. Moncrieff objected to have birds killed when breeding; but in this country, as indeed in any other where game is numerous, there are hosts of birds that do not, for various reasons, breed or mate every season. These generally are to be found either singly and solitary, as if they had some great grief on their minds that they desired to nurse in solitude, or in small flocks of gay young bachelors. Dugald knew such birds well, and it was from the ranks of these he always filled the larder.

To the supply thus brought daily by Dugald were added fowls, ducks, and turkeys from the *estancia's* poultry-yard, to say nothing of joints of beef, mutton, and pork. Nor was it birds alone that Dugald's seemingly inexhaustible creels and bags were laden with, but eggs of the swan[10] and the wild-duck and goose, with—to serve as tit-bits for those who cared for such desert delicacies—cavies, biscachas, and now and then an armadillo. If these were not properly appreciated by the new settlers, the eyes of the old, and especially the Gauchos, sparkled with anticipation of gustatory delight on beholding them.

For some days after the shearing was over comparative peace reigned around and over the great *estancia*. But nevertheless preparations were being made to send off a string of waggons to Villa Mercedes. The market at Mendoza was hardly large enough to suit Moncrieff, nor were the prices so good as could be obtained in the east. Indeed, Moncrieff had purchasing agents from Villa Mercedes to meet his waggons on receipt of a telegram.

So the waggons were loaded up—wool, wine, and preserves, as well as raisins.

To describe the vineyards at our *estancia* would take up far too much space. I must leave them to the reader's imagination; but I hardly think I am wrong in stating that there are no grapes in the world more delicious or more viniferous than those that grow in the province of Mendoza. The usual difficulty is not in the making of wine, but in the supply of barrels and bottles. Moncrieff found a way out of this; and in some hotels in Buenos Ayres, and even Monte Video, the Château Moncrieff had already gained some celebrity.

The manufacture of many different kinds of preserves was quite an industry at the *estancia*, and one that paid fairly well. There were orangeries as well as vineries; and although the making of marmalade had not before been attempted, Moncrieff meant now to go in for it on quite a large scale. This branch was to be superintended by old Jenny herself, and great was her delight to find out that she was of some use on the estate, for 'really 'oman,' she told aunt, 'a body gets tired of the stockin'—shank, shank, shank a' day is hard upon the hands, though a body maun do something.'

Well, the waggons were laden and off at last. With them went Moncrieff's Welsh partner as commander, to see to the sale, and prevent the Gauchos and drivers generally from tapping the casks by the way. The force of men, who were all well armed, was quite sufficient to give an excellent account of any number of prowling Indians who were likely to put in an appearance.

And now summer, in all its glory, was with us. And such glory! Such glory of vegetable life, such profusion of foliage, such wealth of colouring, such splendour of flowers! Such glory of animal life, beast and bird and insect! The flowers themselves were not more gay and gorgeous than some of these latter.

Nor were we very greatly plagued with the hopping and blood-sucking genera. Numerous enough they were at times, it must be confessed, both by day and night; but somehow we got used to them. The summer was wearing to a close, the first wing of our Coila Villa was finished and dry, the furniture was put in, and as soon as the smell of paint left we took possession.

This was made the occasion for another of Moncrieff's festive gatherings. Neighbours came from all directions except the south, for we knew of none in this direction besides the wild Pampean Indians, and they were not included in the invitation. Probably we should make them dance some other day.

About a fortnight after our opening gathering, or 'house-warming,' as Moncrieff called it, we had a spell of terribly hot weather. The heat was of a sultry, close description, difficult to describe: the cattle, sheep, and horses seemed to suffer very much, and even the poor dogs. These last, by the way, we found it a good plan to clip. Long coats did not suit the summer season.

One evening it seemed hotter and sultrier than ever. We were all seated out in the verandah, men-folk smoking, and aunt and Aileen fanning themselves and fighting the insects, when suddenly a low and ominous rumbling was heard which made us all start except Moncrieff.

Is it thunder? No; there is not at present a cloud in the sky, although a strange dark haze is gathering over the peaks on the western horizon.

'Look!' said Moncrieff to me. As he spoke he pointed groundwards. Beetles and ants and crawling insects of every description were heading for the verandah, seeking shelter from the coming storm.

The strange rumbling grew louder!

It was not coming from the sky, but from the earth!

[8] Pampero, a storm wind that blows from the south.

[9] For-fochten = worn out. The term usually applies to barn-yard roosters, who have been settling a quarrel, and pause to pant, with their heads towards the ground.

[10] Swans usually commence laying some time before either ducks or geese; but much depends upon the season.

CHAPTER XVII
THE EARTHQUAKE

With a rapidity that was truly alarming the black haze in the west crept upwards over the sky, the sun was engulfed in a few minutes, and before half an hour, accompanied by a roaring wind and a whirl of dust and decayed leaves, the storm was with us and on us, the whole *estancia* being enveloped in clouds and darkness.

The awful earth sounds still continued—increased, in fact—much to the terror of every one of us. We had retreated to the back sitting-room. Moncrieff had left us for a time, to see to the safety of the cattle and the farm generally, for the Gauchos were almost paralyzed with fear, and it was found afterwards that the very shepherds had left their flocks and fled for safety—if safety it could be called—to their *puestos*.

Yet Gauchos are not as a rule afraid of storms, but—and it is somewhat remarkable—an old Indian seer had for months before been predicting that on this very day and night the city of Mendoza would be destroyed by an earthquake, and that not only the town but every village in the province would be laid low at the same time.

It is difficult to give the reader any idea of the events of this dreadful night. I can only briefly relate my own feelings and experiences. As we all sat there, suddenly a great river of blood appeared to split the dark heavens in two, from zenith to horizon. It hung in the sky for long seconds, and was followed by a peal of thunder of terrific violence, accompanied by sounds as if the whole building and every building on the estate were being rent and riven in pieces. At the self-same moment a strange, dizzy, sleepy feeling rushed through my brain. I could only see those around me as if enshrouded in a blue-white mist. I tried to rise from my chair, but fell back, not as I thought into a chair but into a boat. Floor and roof and walls appeared to meet and clasp. My head swam. I was not only dizzy but deaf apparently, not too deaf, however, to hear the wild, unearthly, frightened screams of twenty at least of our Gaucho servants, who were huddled together in the centre of the garden. It was all over in a few seconds: even the thunder was hushed and the wind no longer bent the poplars or roared through the cloud-like elm-trees. A silence that could be felt succeeded, broken only by the low moan of terror that the Gauchos kept up; a silence that soon checked even that sound itself; a silence that crept round the heart, and held us all spellbound; a silence that was ended at last by terrible thunderings and lightnings and earth-tremblings, with all the same dizzy, sleepy, sickening sensations that had accompanied the first shock. I felt as if chaos had come again, and for a time felt also as if death itself would have been a relief.

But this shock passed next, and once more there was a solemn silence, a drear stillness. And now fear took possession of every one of us, and a desire to flee away somewhere—anywhere. This had almost amounted to panic, when Moncrieff himself appeared in the verandah.

'I've got our fellows to put up the marquee,' he said, almost in a whisper. 'Come—we'll be safer there. Mither, I'll carry you. You're not afraid, are you?'

'Is the worruld comin' tae an end?' asked old Jenny, looking dazed as her son picked her up. 'Is the worruld comin' tae an end, *and the marmalade no made yet*?'

In about an hour after this the storm was at its worst. Flash followed flash, peal followed peal: the world seemed in flames, the hills appeared to be falling on us. The rain and hailstones came down in vast sheets, and with a noise so great that even the thunder itself was heard but as a subdued roar.

We had no light here—we needed none. The lightning, or the reflection of it, ran in under the canvas on the surface of the water, which must have been inches deep. The hail melted as soon as it fell, and finally gave place to rain alone; then the water that flowed through the tent felt warm, if not hot, to the touch. This was no doubt occasioned by the force with which it fell to the ground. The falling rain now looked like cords of gold and silver, so brightly was it illuminated by the lightning.

While the storm was still at its height suddenly there was a shout from one of the Gauchos.

'Run, run! the tent is falling!' was the cry.

It was only too true. A glance upwards told us this. We got into the open air just in time, before, weighted down by tons of water, the great marquee came groundwards with a crash.

But though the rain still came down in torrents and the thunder roared and rattled over and around us, no further shock of earthquake was felt. Fear fled then, and we made a rush for the house once more. Moncrieff reached the casement window first, with a Gaucho carrying a huge lantern. This man entered, but staggered out again immediately.

'The ants! the ants!' he shouted in terror.

Moncrieff had one glance into the room, as if to satisfy himself. I took the lantern from the trembling hands of the Gaucho and held it up, and the sight that met my astonished gaze was one I shall never forget. The whole room was in possession of myriads of black ants of enormous size; they covered everything—walls, furniture, and floor—with one dense and awful pall.

The room looked strange and mysterious in its living, moving covering. Here was indeed the blackness of darkness. Yes, and it was a darkness too that could be felt. Of this I had a speedy proof of a most disagreeable nature. I was glad to hand the lantern back and seek for safety in the rain again.

Luckily the sitting-room door was shut, and this was the only room not taken possession of.

After lights had been lit in the drawing-room the storm did not appear quite so terrible; but no one thought of retiring that night. The vague fear that something more dreadful still might occur kept hanging in our minds, and was only dispelled when daylight began to stream in at the windows.

By breakfast-time there was no sign in the blue sky that so fearful a storm had recently raged there. Nor had any very great violence been done about the farmyards by the earthquake.

Many of the cattle that had sought shelter beneath the trees had been killed, however; and in one spot we found the mangled remains of over one hundred sheep. Here also a huge chestnut-tree had been struck and completely destroyed, pieces of the trunk weighing hundreds of pounds being scattered in every direction over the field.

Earthquakes are of common occurrence in the province of Mendoza, but seldom are they accompanied by such thunder, lightning, and rain as we had on this occasion. It was this demonstration, coupled with the warning words of the Indian seer, which had caused the panic among our worthy Gaucho servants. But the seer had been a false prophet for once, and as the Gauchos seized him on this same day and half drowned him in the lake, there was but little likelihood that he would prophesy the destruction of Mendoza again.

Mendoza had been almost totally destroyed already by an awful earthquake that occurred in 1861. Out of a population of nearly sixteen thousand souls no less than thirteen thousand, we are told, were killed—

swallowed up by the yawning earth. Fire broke out afterwards, and, as if to increase the wretchedness and sad condition of the survivors, robbers from all directions—even from beyond the Andes—flocked to the place to loot and pillage it. But Mendoza is now built almost on the ashes of the destroyed city, and its population must be equal to, even if it does not exceed, its former aggregate.

With the exception of a few losses, trifling enough to one in Moncrieff's position, the whole year was a singularly successful one. Nor had my brothers nor I and the other settlers any occasion to complain, and our prospects began to be very bright indeed.

Nor did the future belie the present, for ere another year had rolled over our heads we found ourselves in a fair way to fortune. We felt by this time that we were indeed old residents. We were thoroughly acclimatized: healthy, hardy, and brown. In age we were, some would say, mere lads; in experience we were already men.

Our letters from home continued to be of the most cheering description, with the exception of Townley's to aunt. He had made little if any progress in his quest. Not that he despaired. Duncan M'Rae was still absent, but sooner or later—so Townley believed—poverty would bring him to bay, and *then*—

Nothing of this did my aunt tell me at the time. I remained in blissful ignorance of anything and everything that our old tutor had done or was doing.

True, the events of that unfortunate evening at the old ruin sometimes arose in my mind to haunt me. My greatest sorrow was my being bound down by oath to keep what seemed to me the secret of a villain—a secret that had deprived our family of the estates of Coila, had deprived my parents—yes, that was the hard and painful part. For, strange as it may appear, I cared nothing for myself. So enamoured had I become of our new home in the Silver West, that I felt but little longing to return to the comparative bleakness and desolation of even Scottish Highland scenery. I must not be considered unpatriotic on this account, or if there was a decay of patriotism in my heart, the fascinating climate of Mendoza was to blame for it. I could not help feeling at times that I had eaten the lotus-leaf. Had we not everything that the heart of young men could desire? On my own account, therefore, I felt no desire to turn the good soldier M'Rae away from Coila, and as for Irene—as for bringing a tear to the eyes of that beautiful and engaging girl, I would rather, I thought, that the dark waters of the laguna should close over my head for ever.

Besides, dear father was happy. His letters told me that. He had even come to like his city life, and he never wrote a word about Coila.

Still, the oath—the oath that bound me! It was a dark spot in my existence.

Did it bind me? I remember thinking that question over one day. Could an oath forced upon any one be binding in the sight of Heaven? I ran off to consult my brother Moncrieff. I found him riding his great bay mare, an especial favourite, along the banks of the highest *estancia* canal—the canal that fed the whole system of irrigation. Here I joined him, myself on my pet brown mule.

'Planning more improvements, Moncrieff?' I asked.

He did not speak for a minute or two.

'I'm not planning improvements,' he said at last, 'but I was just thinking it would be well, in our orra[11] moments, if we were to strengthen this embankment. There is a terrible power o' water here. Now supposing that during some awful storm, with maybe a bit shock of earthquake, it were to burst here or hereabouts, don't you see that the flood would pour right down upon the mansion-house, and clean it almost from its foundations?'

'I trust,' I said, 'so great a catastrophe will not occur in our day.'

'It would be a fearful accident, and a judgment maybe on my want of forethought.'

'I want to ask you a question,' I said, 'on another subject, Moncrieff.'

'You're lookin' scared, laddie. What's the matter?'

I told him as much as I could.

'It's a queer question, laddie—a queer question. Heaven give me help to answer you! I think, as the oath was to keep a secret, you had best keep the oath, and trust to Heaven to set things right in the end, if it be for the best.'

'Thanks, Moncrieff,' I said; 'thanks. I will take your advice.'

That very day Moncrieff set a party of men to strengthen the embankment; and it was probably well he did so, for soon after the work was finished another of those fearful storms, accompanied as usual by shocks of earthquake, swept over our valley, and the canal was filled to overflowing, but gave no signs of bursting. Moncrieff had assuredly taken time by the forelock.

One day a letter arrived, addressed to me, which bore the London post-mark.

It was from Archie, and a most spirited epistle it was. He wanted us to rejoice with him, and, better still, to expect him out by the very first packet. His parents had yielded to his request. It had been the voyage to Newcastle that had turned the scale. There was nothing like pluck, he said; 'But,' he added, 'between you and me, Murdoch, I would not take another voyage in a Newcastle collier, not to win all the honour and glory of Livingstone, Stanley, Gordon-Cumming, and Colonel Frederick Burnaby put in a bushel basket.'

I went tearing away over the *estancia* on my mule, to find my brothers and tell them the joyful tidings. And we rejoiced together. Then I went off to look for Moncrieff, and he rejoiced, to keep me company.

'And mind you,' he said, 'the very day after he arrives we'll have a dinner and a kick-up.'

'Of course we will,' I said. 'We'll have the dinner and fun at Coila Villa, which, remember, can now boast of two wings besides the tower.'

'Very well,' he assented, 'and after that we can give another dinner and rout at my diggings. Just a sort of return match, you see?'

'But I don't see,' I said; 'I don't see the use of two parties.'

'Oh, but I do, Murdoch. We must make more of a man than we do of a nowt[12] beast. Now you mind that bull I had sent out from England — Towsy Jock that lives in the Easter field? — well, I gave a dinner when he came. £250 I paid for him too.'

'Yes, and I remember also you gave a dinner and fun when the prize ram came out. Oh, catch you not finding an excuse for a dinner! However, so be it: one dinner and fun for a bull, two for Archie.'

'That's agreed then,' said Moncrieff.

Now, my brothers and I and a party of Gauchos, with the warlike Bombazo and a Scot or two, had arranged a grand hunt into the guanaco country; but as dear old Archie was coming out so soon we agreed to postpone it, in order that he might join in the fun. Meanwhile we commenced to make all preparations.

They say that the principal joy in life lies in the anticipation of pleasure to come. I think there is a considerable amount of truth in this, and I am sure that not even bluff old King Hal setting out to hunt in the New Forest could have promised himself a greater treat than we did as we got ready for our tour in the land of the guanaco, and country of the condor.

We determined to be quite prepared to start by the time Archie was due. Not that we meant to hurry our dear cockney cousin right away to the wilds as soon as he arrived. No; we would give him a whole week to 'shake down,' as Moncrieff called it, and study life on the *estancia*.

And, indeed, life on the *estancia*, now that we had become thoroughly used to it, was exceedingly pleasant altogether.

I cannot say that either my brothers or I were ever much given to lazing in bed of a morning in Scotland itself. To have done so we should have looked upon as bad form; but to encourage ourselves in matutinal sloth in a climate like this would have seemed a positive crime.

Even by seven in the morning we used to hear the great gong roaring hoarsely on Moncrieff's lawn, and this used to be the signal for us to start and draw aside our mosquito curtains. Our bedrooms adjoined, and all the time we were splashing in our tubs and dressing we kept up an incessant fire of banter and fun. The fact is, we used to feel in such glorious form after a night's rest. Our bedroom windows were very large casements, and were kept wide open all the year round, so that virtually we slept in the open air. We nearly always went to bed in the dark, or if we did have lights we had to shut the windows till we had put them out, else moths as big as one's hand, and all kinds and conditions of insect life, would have entered and speedily extinguished our candles. Even had the windows been protected by glass, this insect life would have been troublesome. In the drawing and dining rooms we had specially prepared blinds of wire to exclude these creatures, while admitting air enough.

The mosquito curtains round our beds effectually kept everything disagreeable at bay, and insured us wholesome rest.

But often we were out of bed and galloping over the country long before the gong sounded. This ride used to give us such appetites for breakfast, that sometimes we had to apologize to aunt and Aileen for our apparent greediness. We were out of doors nearly all day, and just as often as not had a snack of luncheon on the hills at some settler's house or at an outlying *puesto*.

Aunt was now our housekeeper, but nevertheless so accustomed had we and Moncrieff and Aileen become to each other's society that hardly a day passed without our dining together either at his house or ours.

The day, what with one thing and another, used to pass quickly enough, and the evening was most enjoyable, despite even the worry of flying and creeping insects. After dinner my brothers and I, with at times Moncrieff and Bombazo, used to lounge round to see what the servants were doing.

They had a concert, and as often as not some fun, every night with the exception of Sabbath, when Moncrieff insisted that they should retire early.

At many *estancias* wine is far too much in use—even to the extent of inebriety. Our places, however, owing to Moncrieff's strictness, were models of temperance, combined with innocent pleasures. The master, as he was called, encouraged all kinds of games, though he objected to gambling, and drinking he would not permit at any price.

One morning our post-runner came to Coila Villa in greater haste than usual, and from his beaming eyes and merry face I conjectured he had a letter for me.

I took it from him in the verandah, and sent him off round to the kitchen to refresh himself. No sooner had I glanced at its opening sentences than I rushed shouting into the breakfast-room.

'Hurrah!' I cried, waving the letter aloft. 'Archie's coming, and he'll be here to-day. Hurrah! for the hunt, lads, and hurrah! for the hills!'

[11] Orra = leisure, idle. An orra-man is one who does all kinds of odd jobs about a farm.

[12] Nowt = cattle.

CHAPTER XVIII
OUR HUNTING EXPEDITION

If not quite so exuberant as the welcome that awaited us on our arrival in the valley, Archie's was a right hearty one, and assuredly left our cousin nothing to complain of.

He had come by diligence from Villa Mercedes, accomplishing the journey, therefore, in a few days, which had occupied us in our caravan about as many weeks.

We were delighted to see him looking so well. Why, he had even already commenced to get brown, and was altogether hardy and hearty and manlike.

We were old *estancieros*, however, and it gave us unalloyed delight to show him round our place and put him up to all the outs and ins of a settler's life.

Dugald even took him away to the hills with him, and the two of them did not get home until dinner was on the table.

Archie, however, although not without plenty of pluck and willingness to develop into an *estanciero* pure and simple, had not the stamina my brothers and I possessed, but this only made us all the more kind to him. In time, we told him, he would be quite as strong and wiry as any of us.

'There is one thing I don't think I shall ever be able to get over,' said Archie one day. It may be observed that he did not now talk with the London drawl; he had left both his cockney tongue and his tall hat at home.

'What is it you do not think you will ever get over, Arch?' I asked.

'Why, the abominable creepies,' he answered, looking almost miserable.

'Why,' he continued, 'it isn't so much that I mind being bitten by mosquitoes—of which it seems you have brutes that fly by day, and gangs that go on regular duty at night—but it is the other abominations that make my blood run positively cold. Now your cockroaches are all very well down in the coal-cellar, and centipedes are interesting creatures in glass cases with pins stuck through them; but to find cockroaches in your boots and centipedes in your bed is rather too much of a good thing.'

'Well,' said Dugald, laughing, 'you'll get used to even that. I don't really mind now what bites me or what crawls over me. Besides, you know all those creepie-creepies, as you call them, afford one so excellent an opportunity of studying natural history from the life.'

'Oh, bother such life, Dugald! My dear cousin, I would rather remain in blissful ignorance of natural history all my life than have even an earwig reposing under my pillow. Besides, I notice that even your Yahoo servants—'

'I beg your pardon, cousin; Gaucho, not Yahoo.'

'Well, well, Gaucho servants shudder, and even run from our common bedroom creepies.'

'Oh! they are nothing at all to go by, Archie. They think because a thing is not very pretty it is bound to be venomous.'

'But does not the bite of a centipede mean death?'

'Oh dear no. It isn't half as bad as London vermin.'

'Then there are scorpions. Do they kill you? Is not their bite highly dangerous?'

'Not so bad as a bee's sting.'

'Then there are so many flying beetles.'

'Beauties, Archie, beauties. Why, Solomon in all his glory was not arrayed like some of these.'

'Perhaps not. But then, Solomon or not Solomon, how am I to know which sting and which don't?'

'*Experientia docet*, Archie.'

Archie shuddered.

'Again, there are spiders. Oh, they do frighten me. They're as big as lobsters. Ugh!'

'Well, they won't hurt. They help to catch the other things!'

'Yes, and that's just the worst of it. First a lot of creepies come in to suck your blood and inject poison into your veins, to say nothing of half scaring a fellow to death; and then a whole lot of flying creepies, much worse than the former, come in to hunt them up; and bats come next, to say nothing of lizards; and what with the buzzing and singing and hopping and flapping and beating and thumping, poor *me* has to lie awake half the night, falling asleep towards morning to dream I'm in purgatory.'

'Poor *you* indeed!' said Dugald.

'You have told me, too, I must sleep in the dark, but I want to know what is the good of that when about one half of those flying creepies carry a lamp each, and some of them two. Only the night before last I awoke in a fright. I had been dreaming about the great sea-serpent, and the first thing I saw was a huge creature about as long as a yard stick wriggling along my mosquito curtains.'

'Ah! How could you see it in the dark?'

'Why, the beggar carried two lamps ahead of him, and he had a smaller chap with a light. Ugh!'

'These were some good specimens of the *Lampyridæ*, no doubt.'

'Well, perhaps; but having such a nice long name doesn't make them a bit less hideous to me. Then in the morning when I looked into the glass I didn't know myself from Adam. I had a black eye that some bug or other had given me—I dare say he also had a nice long name. I had a lump on my brow as large as a Spanish onion, and my nose was swollen and as big as a bladder of lard. From top to toe I was covered with hard knots, as if I'd been to Donnybrook Fair, and what with aching and itching it would have been a comfort to me to have jumped out of my skin.'

'Was that all?' I said, laughing.

'Not quite. I went to take up a book to fling at a monster spider in the corner, and put my hand on a scorpion. I cracked him and crushed the spider, and went to have my bath, only to find I had to fish out about twenty long-named indescribables that had committed suicide during the night. Other creepies had been drowned in the ewer. I found earwigs in my towels, grasshoppers in my clothes, and wicked-looking little beetles even in my hairbrushes. This may be a land flowing with milk and honey and all the rest of it, Murdoch, but it is also a land crawling with creepie-creepies.'

'Well, anyhow,' said Dugald, 'here comes your mule. Mount and have a ride, and we'll forget everything but the pleasures of the chase. Come, I think I know where there is a jaguar—an immense great brute. I saw him killing geese not three days ago.'

'Oh, that will be grand!' cried Archie, now all excitement.

And five minutes afterwards Dugald and he were off to the hills.

But in two days more we would be off to the hills in earnest.

For this tour we would not of our own free-will have made half the preparations Moncrieff insisted on, and perhaps would hardly have provided ourselves with tents. However, we gave in to his arrangements in every way, and certainly we had no cause to repent it.

The guide—he was to be called our *cacique* for the time being—that Moncrieff appointed had been a Gaucho malo, a pampas Cain. No one ever knew half the crimes the fellow had committed, and I suppose he himself had forgotten. But he was a reformed man and really a Christian, and it is difficult to find such an anomaly among Gauchos. He knew the pampas well, and the Andes too, and was far more at home in the wilds than at the *estancia*. A man like this, Moncrieff told us, was worth ten times his weight in gold.

And so it turned out.

The summer had well-nigh gone when our caravan at length left Moncrieff's beautiful valley. The words 'caravan at length' in the last sentence may be understood in two ways, either as regards space or time. Ours was no caravan on wheels. Not a single wheeled waggon accompanied us, for we should cross deserts, and pass through glens where there would be no road, perhaps hardly even a bridle-path. So the word caravan is to be understood in the Arab sense of the word. And it certainly was a lengthy one. For we had a pack mule for every two men, including our five Gauchos.

Putting it in another way, there were five of us Europeans—Donald, Dugald, Archie Bateman, Sandie Donaldson, and myself; each European had a horse and a Gaucho servant, and each Gaucho had a mule.

Bombazo meant to have come; he said so to the very last, at all events, but an unfortunate attack of toothache confined him to bed. Archie, who had no very exalted idea of the little Spanish captain's courage, was rude enough to tell us in his hearing that he was 'foxing.' I do not pretend to understand what Archie meant, but I feel certain it was nothing very complimentary to Bombazo's bravery.

'Dear laddies,' old Jenny had said, 'if you think you want onybody to darn your hose on the road, I'll gang wi' ye mysel'. As for that feckless loon Bombazo, the peer[13] body is best in bed.'

Our arms consisted of rifles, shot-guns, the bolas, and lasso. Each man carried a revolver as well, and we had also abundance of fishing tackle. Our tents were only three in all, but they were strong and waterproof, a great consideration when traversing a country like this.

We were certainly prepared to rough it, but had the good sense to take with us every contrivance which might add to our comfort, so long as it was fairly portable.

Archie had one particular valise of his own that he declared contained only a few nicknacks which no one ought to travel without. He would not gratify us by even a peep inside, however, so for a time we had to be content with guessing what the nicknacks were. Archie got pretty well chaffed about his Gladstone bag, as he called it.

'You surely haven't got the tall hat in it,' said Dugald.

'Of course you haven't forgotten your nightcap,' said Donald.

'Nor your slippers, Archie?' I added.

'And a dressing-gown would be indispensable in the desert,' said Sandie Donaldson.

Archie only smiled to himself, but kept his secret.

What a lovely morning it was when we set out! So blue was the sky, so green the fields of waving lucerne, so dense the foliage and flowers and hedgerows and trees, it really seemed that summer would last for many and many a month to come.

We were all fresh and happy, and full of buoyant anticipation of pleasures to come. Our very dogs went scampering on ahead, barking for very joy. Of these we had quite a pack—three pure Scotch collies, two huge bloodhound-mastiffs, and at least half a dozen animals belonging to our Gauchos, which really were nondescripts but probably stood by greyhounds. These dogs were on exceedingly good terms with themselves and with each other—the collies jumping up to kiss the horses every minute by way of encouragement, the mastiffs trotting steadily on ahead cheek-by-jowl, and the hounds everywhere—everywhere at once, so it appeared.

Being all so fresh, we determined to make a thorough long day's journey of it. So, as soon as we had left the glen entirely and disappeared among the sand dunes, we let our horses have their heads, the *capataz* Gaucho riding on ahead on a splendid mule as strong as a stallion and as lithe as a Scottish deerhound.

Not long before our start for the hunting grounds men had arrived from the Chilian markets to purchase cattle. The greatest dainty to my mind they had brought with them was a quantity of *Yerba maté*, as it is called. It is the dried leaves of a species of Patagonian ilex, which is used in this country as tea, and very delightful and soothing it is. This was to be our drink during all our tour. More refreshing than tea, less exciting than wine, it not only seems to calm the mind but to invigorate the body. Drunk warm, with or without sugar, all feeling of tiredness passes away, and one is disposed to look at the bright side of life, and that alone.

We camped the first night on high ground nearly forty miles from our own *estancia*. It was a long day's journey in so rough a country, but we had a difficulty earlier in the afternoon in finding water. Here, however, was a stream as clear as crystal, that doubtless made its way from springs in the *sierras* that lay to the west of us at no very great distance. Behind these jagged hills the sun was slowly setting when we erected our tents. The ground chosen was at some little distance from the stream, and on the bare gravel. The cacti that grew on two sides of us were of gigantic height, and ribboned or edged with the most beautiful flowers. Our horses and mules were hobbled and led to the stream, then turned on to the grass which grew green and plentiful all along its banks.

A fire was quickly built and our great stewpan put on. We had already killed our dinner in the shape of a small deer or fawn which had crossed our path on the plains lower down. With biscuits, of which we had a store, some curry, roots, which the Gauchos had found, and a handful or two of rice, we soon had a dinner ready, the very flavour of which would have been enough to make a dying man eat.

The dogs sat around us and around the Gauchos as we dined, and, it must be allowed, behaved in a most mannerly way; only the collies and mastiffs kept together. They must have felt their superiority to those mongrel greyhounds, and desired to show it in as calm and dignified a manner as possible.

After dinner sentries were set, one being mounted to watch the horses and mules. We were in no great fear of their stampeding, but we had promised Moncrieff to run as little risk of any kind as possible on this journey, and therefore commenced even on this our first night to be as good as our word.

The best Gauchos had been chosen for us, and every one of them could talk English after a fashion, especially our bold but not handsome *capataz*, or *cacique* Yambo. About an hour after dinner the latter began serving out the *maté*. This put us all in excellent humour and the best of spirits. As we felt therefore as happy as one could wish to be, we were not surprised when the *capataz* proposed a little music.

'It is the pampas fashion, señor,' he said to me.

'Will you play and sing?' I said.

'Play and sing?' he replied, at once producing his guitar, which lay in a bag not far off. '*Si*, señor, I will play and sing for you. If you bid me, I will dance; every day and night I shall cook for you; when de opportunity come I will fight for you. I am your servant, your slave, and delighted to be so.'

'Thank you, my *capataz*; I have no doubt you are a very excellent fellow.'

'Oh, señor, do not flatter yourself too mooch, too very mooch. It is not for the sake of you young señors I care, but for the sake of the dear master.'

'Sing, *capataz*,' I said, 'and talk after.'

To our surprise, not one but three guitars were handed out, and the songs and melodies were very delightful to listen to.

Then our Sandie Donaldson, after handing his cup to be replenished, sang, *Ye banks and braes* with much feeling and in fine manly tenor. We all joined in each second verse, while the guitars gave excellent accompaniment. One song suggested another, and from singing to conversational story-telling the transition was easy. To be sure, neither my brothers nor I nor Archie had much to tell, but some of the experiences of the Gauchos, and especially those of our *capataz*, were thrilling in the extreme, and we never doubted their truth.

But now it was time for bed, and we returned to the tents and lit our lamps.

Our beds were the hard ground, with a rug and guanaco robe, our saddles turned upside down making as good a pillow as any one could wish.

We had now the satisfaction of knowing something concerning the contents of that mysterious grip-sack of Archie's. So judge of our surprise when this wonderful London cousin of ours first produced a large jar of what he called mosquito cream, and proceeded to smear his face and hands with the odorous compound.

'This cream,' he said, 'I bought at Buenos Ayres, and it is warranted to keep all pampas creepies away, or anything with two wings or four, six legs or sixty. Have a rub, Dugald?'

'Not I,' cried Dugald. 'Why, man, the smell is enough to kill bees.'

Archie proceeded with his preparations. Before enshrouding himself in his guanaco mantle he drew on a huge waterproof canvas sack and fastened it tightly round his chest. He next produced a hooped head-dress. I know no other name for it.

'It is an invention of my own,' said Archie, proudly, 'and is, as you see, composed of hoops of wire—'

'Like a lady's crinoline,' said Dugald.

'Well, yes, if you choose to call it so, and is covered with mosquito muslin. This is how it goes on, and I'm sure it will form a perfect protection.'

He then inserted his head into the wondrous muslin bladder, and the appearance he now presented was comical in the extreme. His body in a sack, his head in a white muslin bag, nothing human-looking about him except his arms, that, encased in huge leather gloves, dangled from his shoulders like an immense pair of flippers.

We three brothers looked at him just for a moment, then simultaneously exploded into a perfect roar of laughter. Sandie Donaldson, who with the *capataz* occupied the next tent, came rushing in, then all the Gauchos and even the dogs. The latter bolted barking when they saw the apparition, but the rest joined the laughing chorus.

And the more we looked at Archie the more we laughed, till the very sand dunes near us must have been shaken to their foundations by the manifestation of our mirth.

'Laugh away, boys,' said our cousin. 'Laugh and grow fat. I don't care how I look, so long as my dress and my cream keep the creepies away.'

[13] Peer = poor.

CHAPTER XIX
IN THE WILDERNESS

Some days afterwards we found ourselves among the mountains in a regio whose rugged grandeur and semi-desolation, whose rock-filled glens, tall, frowning precipices, with the stillness that reigned everywhere around, imparted to it a character approaching even to sublimity.

The *capataz* was still our guide, our foremost man in everything; but close beside him rode our indefatigable hunter, Dugald.

We had already seen pumas, and even the terrible jaguar of the plains; we had killed more than one rhea—the American ostrich—and deer in abundance. Moreover, Dugald had secured about fifty skins of the most lovely humming-birds, with many beetles, whose elytra, painted and adorned by Nature, looked like radiant jewels. All these little skins and beetles were destined to be sent home to Flora. As yet, however, we had not come in contact with the guanaco, although some had been seen at a distance.

But to-day we were in the very country of the guanaco, and pressing onwards and ever upwards, in the hopes of soon being able to draw trigger on some of these strange inhabitants of the wilderness.

Only this morning Dugald and I had been bantering each other as to who should shoot the first.

'I mean to send my first skin to Flora,' Dugald had said.

'And I my first skin to Irene,' I said.

On rounding the corner of a cliff we suddenly came in sight of a whole herd of the creatures, but they were in full retreat up the glen, while out against the sky stood in bold relief a tall buck. It was the trumpet tones of his voice ringing out plaintively but musically on the still mountain air that had warne the herd of our approach.

Another long ride of nearly two hours. And now we must have been many thousands of feet above the sea level, or even the level of the distant plains.

It is long past midday, so we determine to halt, for here, pure, bubbling from a dark green slippery rock, is a spring of water as clear as crystal and deliciously cool. What a treat for our horses and dogs! What a treat even for ourselves!

I notice that Dugald seems extra tired. He has done more riding to-day than any of us, and made many a long *détour* in search of that guanaco which he has hitherto failed to find.

A kind of brotherly rivalry takes possession of me, and I cannot help wishing that the first guanaco would fall to my rifle. The Gauchos are busy preparing the stew and boiling water for the *maté*, so shouldering my rifle, and carelessly singing to myself, I leave my companions and commence sauntering higher up the glen. The hill gets very steep, and I have almost to climb on my hands and knees, starting sometimes in dread as a hideous snake goes wriggling past me or raises head and body from behind a stone, and hisses defiance and hate almost in my face. But I reach the summit at last, and find myself on the very edge of a precipice.

Oh, joy! On a little peak down beneath, and not a hundred yards away, stands one of the noblest guanacos I have ever seen. He has heard something, or scented something, for he stands there as still as a statue, with head and neck in the air sniffing the breeze.

How my heart beats! How my hand trembles! I cannot understand my anxiety. Were I face to face with a lion or tiger I could hardly be more nervous. A thousand thoughts seem to cross my mind with a rush, but uppermost of all is the fear that, having fired, I shall miss.

He whinnies his warning now: only a low and undecided one. He is evidently puzzled; but the herd down in the bottom of the cañon hear it, and every head is elevated. I have judged the distance; I have drawn my bead. If my heart would only keep still, and there were not such a mist before my eyes! Bang! I have fired, and quickly load again. Have I missed? Yes—no, no; hurrah! hurrah! yonder he lies, stark and still, on the very rock on which he stood—my first guanaco!

The startled herd move up the cañon. They must have seen their leader drop.

I am still gazing after them, full of exultation, when a hand is laid on my shoulder, and, lo! there stands Dugald laughing.

'You sly old dog,' he says, 'to steal a march on your poor little brother thus!'

For a moment I am startled, mystified.

'Dugald,' I say, 'did I really kill that guanaco?'

'No one else did.'

'And you've only just come—only just this second? Well, I'm glad to hear it. It was after all a pure accident my shooting the beast. I *did* hold the rifle his way. I *did* draw the trigger— —'

'Well, and the bullet did the rest, boy. Funny, you always kill by the merest chance! Ah, Murdoch, you're a better shot than I am, for all you won't allow it.'

Wandering still onwards and still upwards next day, through lonely glens and deep ravines, through cañons the sides of which were as perpendicular as walls, their flat green or brown bottoms sometimes scattered with huge boulders, casting shadows so dark in the sunlight that a man or horse disappeared in them as if the earth had opened and swallowed him up, we came at length to a dell, or strath, of such charming luxuriance that it looked to us, amid all the barrenness of this dreary wilderness, like an oasis dropped from the clouds, or some sweet green glade where fairies might dwell.

I looked at my brother. The same thought must have struck each of us, at the same moment—Why not make this glen our *habitat* for a time?

'Oh!' cried Archie, 'this is a paradise!'

'Beautiful! lovely!' said Dugald. 'Suppose now—'

'Oh, I know what you are going to say,' cried Donald.

'And I second the motion,' said Sandie Donaldson.

'Well,' I exclaimed, 'seeing, Sandie, that no motion has yet been made—'

'Here is the motion, then,' exclaimed Dugald, jumping out of his saddle.

It was a motion we all followed at once; and as the day was getting near its close, the Gauchos set about looking for a bit of camping-ground at once. As far as comfort was concerned, this might have been chosen almost anywhere, but we wanted to be near to water. Now here was the mystery:

the glen was not three miles long altogether, and nowhere more than a mile broad; all along the bottom it was tolerably level and extremely well wooded with quite a variety of different trees, among which pines, elms, chestnuts, and stunted oak-trees were most abundant; each side of the glen was bounded by rising hills or braes covered with algorroba bushes and patches of charmingly-coloured cacti, with many sorts of prickly shrubs, the very names of which we could not tell. Curious to say, there was very little undergrowth; and, although the trees were close enough in some places to form a jungle, the grass was green beneath. But at first we could find no water. Leaving the others to rest by the edge of the miniature forest, Dugald and I and Archie set out to explore, and had not gone more than a hundred yards when we came to a little lake. We bent down and tasted the water; it was pure and sweet and cool.

'What a glorious find!' said Dugald. 'Why, this place altogether was surely made for us.'

We hurried back to tell the news, and the horses and mules were led to the lake, which was little more than half an acre in extent. But not satisfied with drinking, most of the dogs plunged in; and horses and mules followed suit.

'Come,' cried Donald, 'that is a sort of motion I will willingly second.' He commenced to undress as he spoke. So did we all, and such splashing and dashing, and laughing and shouting, the birds and beasts in this romantic dale had surely never witnessed before.

Dugald was an excellent swimmer, and as bold and headstrong in the water as on the land. He had left us and set out to cross the lake. Suddenly we saw him throw up his arms and shout for help, and we—Donald and I—at once commenced swimming to his assistance. He appeared, however, in no danger of sinking, and, to our surprise, although heading our way all the time, he was borne away from us one minute and brought near us next.

When close enough a thrill of horror went through me to hear poor Dugald cry in a feeble, pleading voice,

'Come no nearer, boys: I soon must sink. Save yourselves: I'm in a whirlpool.'

It was too true, though almost too awful to be borne. I do not know how Donald felt at that moment, but as for myself I was almost paralyzed with terror.

'Back, back, for your lives!' shouted a voice behind us.

It was our Gaucho *capataz*. He was coming towards us with powerful strokes, holding in one hand a lasso. Instead of swimming on with us when he saw Dugald in danger, he had gone ashore at once and brought the longest thong.

We white men could have done nothing. We knew of nothing to do. We should have floated there and seen our dear brother go down before our eyes, or swam recklessly, madly on, only to sink with him.

Dugald, weak as he had become, sees the Gaucho will make an attempt to save him, and tries to steady himself to catch the end of the lasso that now flies in his direction.

But to our horror it falls short, and Dugald is borne away again, the circles round which he is swept being now narrower.

The Gaucho is nearer. He is perilously near. He will save him or perish.

Again the lasso leaves his hand. Dugald had thrown up his hands and almost leapt from the water. He is sinking. Oh, good Gaucho! Oh, good *capataz*, surely Heaven itself directed that aim, for the noose fell over our brother's arms and tightened round the chest!

In a few minutes more we have laid his lifeless body on the green bank.

Lifeless only for a time, however. Presently he breathes, and we carry him away into the evening sunshine and place him on the soft warm moss. He soon speaks, but is very ill and weak; yet our thanks to God for his preservation are very sincere. Surely there is a Providence around one even in the wilderness!

We might have explored our glen this same evening, perhaps we really ought to have done so, but the excitement caused by Dugald's adventure put everything else out of our heads.

In this high region, the nights were even cold enough to make a position near the camp fire rather a thing to be desired than otherwise. It was especially delightful, I thought, on this particular evening to sit around the fire and quietly talk. I reclined near Dugald, who had not yet quite recovered. I made a bed for him with extra rugs; and, as he coughed a good deal, I begged of him to consider himself an invalid for one night at least; but no sooner had he drunk his mug of *maté* than he sat up and joined in the conversation, assuring us he felt as well as ever he had in his life.

It was a lovely evening. The sky was unclouded, the stars shining out very clear, and looking very near, while a round moon was rising slowly over the hill-peaks towards the east, and the tall dark pine-trees were casting gloomy shadows on the lake, near which, in an open glade, we were encamped. I could not look at the dark waters without a shudder, as I thought of the danger poor Dugald had so narrowly escaped. I am not sure that the boy was not always my mother's favourite, and I know he was Flora's. How could I have written and told them of his fearful end? The very idea made me creep nearer to him and put my arm round his shoulder. I suppose he interpreted my thoughts, for he patted my knee in his brotherly fond old fashion.

Our Gaucho *capataz* was just telling a story, an adventure of his own, in the lonely pampas. He looked a strange and far from comely being, with his long, straggling, elf-like locks of hair, his low, receding forehead, his swarthy complexion, and high cheek bones. The mark of a terrible spear wound across his face and nose did not improve his looks.

'Yes, señors,' he was saying, 'that was a fearful moment for me.' He threw back his poncho as he spoke, revealing three ugly scars on his chest. 'You see these, señors? It was that same tiger made the marks. It was a keepsake, ha! ha! that I will take to de grave with me, if any one should trouble to bury me. It was towards evening, and we were journeying across the pampa. We had come far that day, my Indians and me. We felt tired—sometimes even Indians felt tired on de weary wide pampa. De sun has been hot all day. We have been chased far by de white settlers. Dey not love us. Ha! ha! We have five score of de cattle with us. And we have spilt blood, and left dead and wounded Indians plenty on de pampa. Never mind, I swear revenge. Oh, I am a bad man den. Gaucho malo, mucho malo, Nandrin, my brother *cacique*, hate me. I hate him. I wish him dead. But de Indians love him all de same as me. By and by de sun go down, down, down, and we raise de *toldo* [14] in de cañon near a stream. Here grow many ombu-trees. The young señors have not seen this great tree; it is de king of the lonely pampa. Oh, so tall! Oh, so wide! so spreading and shady! Two, three ombu-trees grow near; but I have seen de great tiger sleep in one. My brother *cacique* have seen him too. When de big moon rise, and all is bright like de day, and no sound make itself heard but de woo-hoo-woo of de pampa owl, I get quietly up and go to de ombu-tree. I think myself much more brave as my brother *cacique*. Ha! ha! he think himself more brave as me. When I come near de ombu-trees I shout. Ugh! de scream dat comes from de ombu-tree make me shake and shiver. Den de terrible tiger spring down; I will not run, I am too brave. I shoot. He not fall. Next moment I am down—on my back I lie. One big foot is on me; his blood pour over my face. He pull me close and more close to him. Soon, ah, soon, I think my brother *cacique* will be chief—I will be no more. De tiger licks my arm—my cheek. How he growl and froth! He is now going to eat me. But no! Ha! ha! my brother *cacique* have also leave de camp to come to de ombu-tree. De tiger see him. P'r'aps he suppose his blood more sweet as mine. He leave poor me. Ha! ha! he catch my brother *cacique* and carry him under de shade of de ombu-tree. By and by I listen, and hear my brother's bones go crash! crash! crash! De tiger is enjoying his supper!'

'But, *capataz*,' I said, with a shudder, 'did you make no attempt to save your brother chief?'

'Not much! You see, he all same as dead. Suppose I den shoot, p'r'aps I kill him for true; 'sides, I bad Gaucho den; not love anybody mooch. Next day I kill dat tiger proper, and his skin make good ponchos. Ha! ha!'

Many a time during the Gaucho's recital he had paused and looked uneasily around him, for ever and anon the woods re-echoed with strange cries. We white men had not lived long enough in beast-haunted wildernesses to distinguish what those sounds were, whether they proceeded from bird or beast.

As the *capataz* stopped speaking, and we all sat silent for a short time, the cries were redoubled. They certainly were not calculated to raise our spirits: some were wild and unearthly in the extreme, some were growls of evident anger, some mere groanings, as if they proceeded from creatures dying in pain and torment, while others again began in a low and most mournful moan, rising quickly into a hideous, frightened, broken, or gurgling yell, then dying away again in dreary cadence.

I could not help shuddering a little as I looked behind me into the darkness of the forest. The whole place had an uncanny, haunted sort of look, and I even began to wonder whether we might not possibly be the victims of enchantment. Would we awaken in the morning and find no trees, no wood, no water, only a green cañon, with cliffs and hills on every side?

'Look, look!' I cried, starting half up at last. 'Did none of you see that?'

'What is it? Speak, Murdoch!' cried Archie; 'your face is enough to frighten a fellow.'

I pressed my hand to my forehead.

'Surely,' I said, 'I am going to be ill, but I thought I could distinctly see a tall grey figure standing among the trees.'

We resumed talking, but in a lower, quieter key. The events of the evening, our strange surroundings, the whispering trees, the occasional strange cries, and the mournful beauty of the night, seemed to have cast a glamour over every heart that was here; and though it was now long past our usual hour for bed, no one appeared wishful to retire.

All at once Archie grasped me by the shoulder and glanced fearfully into the forest behind me. I dared scarcely turn my head till the click of Yambo's revolver reassured me.

Yes, there was the figure in grey moving silently towards us.

'Speak, quick, else I fire!' shouted our *capataz*.

'*Ave Maria!*'

Yambo lowered the revolver, and we all started to our feet to confront the figure in grey.

[14] Toldo = a tent.

CHAPTER XX
THE MOUNTAIN CRUSOE

The figure in grey—the grey was a garment of skin, cap, coat, breeches, and even boots, apparently all of the same material—approached with extended hand. We could see now it was no ghost who stood before us, but a man of flesh and blood. Very solid flesh, too, judging from the cheeks that surmounted the silvery beard. The moon shone full on his face, and a very pleasant one it was, with a bright, merry twinkle in the eye.

'Who are you?' said I.

'Nay, pardon me,' was the bold reply, 'but the question would come with greater propriety from my lips. I need not ask it, however. You are right welcome to my little kingdom. You are, I can see, a party of roving hunters. Few of your sort have ever come here before, I can tell you.'

'And you?' I said, smiling.

'*I* am—but there, what need to give myself a name? I have not heard my name for years. Call me Smith, Jones, Robinson; call me a hunter, a trapper, a madman, a fool—anything.'

'A hermit, anyhow,' said Dugald.

'Yes, boy, a hermit.'

'And an Englishman?'

'No; I am a Portuguese by birth, but I have lived in every country under the sun, and here I am at last. Have I introduced myself sufficiently?'

'No,' I said; 'but sit down. You have,' I continued, 'only introduced yourself sufficiently to excite our curiosity. Yours must be a strange story.'

'Oh, anybody and everybody who lives for over fifty years in the world as I have done has a strange story, if he cared to tell it. Mine is too long, and some of it too sad. I have been a soldier, a sailor, a traveller; I have been wealthy, I have been poor; I have been in love—my love left *me*. I forgot *her*. I have done everything except commit crime. I have not run away from anywhere, gentlemen. There is no blood on my hands. I can still pray. I still love. She whom I love is here.'

'Oh!' cried Dugald, 'won't you bring the lady?'

The hermit laughed.

'She *is* here, there, all around us. My mistress is Nature. Ah! boys,' he said, turning to us with such a kind look, 'Nature breaks no hearts; and the more you love her, the more she loves you, and leads you upwards—always upwards, never down.'

It was strange, but from the very moment he began to talk both my brothers and I began to like this hermit. His ways and his manners were quite irresistible, and before we separated we felt as if we had known him all our lives.

He was the last man my brothers and I saw that night, and he was the first we met in the morning. He had donned a light cloth poncho and a broad sombrero hat, and really looked both handsome and picturesque.

We went away together, and bathed, and I told him of Dugald's adventure. He looked interested, patted my brother's shoulder, and said:

'Poor boy, what a narrow escape you have had!

'The stream,' he continued, 'that flows through this strange glen rises in the hills about five miles up. It rises from huge springs—you shall see them—flows through the woods, and is sucked into the earth in the middle of that lake. I have lived here for fifteen years. Walk with me up the glen. Leave your rifles in your tents; there is nothing to hurt.'

We obeyed, and soon joined him, and together we strolled up the path that led close by the banks of a beautiful stream. We were enchanted with the beauty displayed everywhere about us, and our guide seemed pleased.

'Almost all the trees and shrubs you see,' he said, 'I have planted, and many of the beautiful flowers—the orchids, the climbers, and creepers, all are my pets. Those I have not planted I have encouraged, and I believe they all know me.'

At this moment a huge puma came bounding along the path, but stopped when he saw us.

'Don't be afraid, boys,' said the hermit. 'This, too, is a pet. Do not be shy, Jacko. These are friends.'

The puma smelt us, then rubbed his great head against his master's leg, and trotted along by his side.

'I have several. You will not shoot while you live here? Thanks. I have a large family. The woods are filled with my family. I have brought them from far and near, birds and beasts of every kind. They see us now, but are shy.'

'I say, sir,' said Dugald, 'you are Adam, and this is Paradise.'

The hermit smiled in recognition of the compliment, and we now approached his house.

'I must confess,' I said, 'that a more Crusoe-looking establishment it has never been my luck to behold.'

'You are young yet,' replied the hermit, laughing, 'although you speak so like a book.

'Here we are, then, in my compound. The fence, you see, is a very open one, for I desire neither to exclude the sunshine nor the fresh air from my vegetables. Observe,' he continued, 'that my hut, which consists of one large room, stands in the centre of a gravel square.'

'It is strange-looking gravel!' said Dugald.

'It is nearly altogether composed of salt. My house is built of stone, but it is plastered with a kind of cement I can dig here in the hills. There is not a crevice nor hollow in all the wall, and it is four feet thick. The floor is also cemented, and so is the roof.'

'And this,' I remarked, 'is no doubt for coolness in summer.'

'Yes, and warmth in winter, if it comes to that, and also for cleanliness. Yonder is a ladder that leads to the roof. Up there I lounge and think, drink my *maté* and read. Oh yes, I have plenty of books, which I keep in a safe with bitter-herb powder—to save them, you know, from literary ants and other insects who possess an ambition to solve the infinite. Observe again, that I have neither porch nor verandah to my house, and that the windows are small. I object to a porch and to climbing things on the same principle that I do to creeping, crawling creatures. The world is wide enough for us all. But they must keep to their side of the house at night, and I to mine. And mine is the inside. This is also the reason why most of the gravel is composed of salt. As a rule, creepies don't like it.'

'Oh, I'm glad you told us that,' said Archie; 'I shall make my mule carry a bushel of it. I'm glad you don't like creepies, sir.'

'But, boy, I *do*. Only I object to them indoors. Walk in. Observe again, as a showman would say, how very few my articles of furniture are. Notice, however, that they are all scrupulously clean. Nevertheless, I have every convenience. That thong-bottomed sofa is my bed. My skins and rugs are kept in a bag all day, and hermetically sealed against the prying probosces of insectivora. Here is my stove, yonder my kitchen and scullery, and there hangs my armoury. Now I am going to call my servant. He is a Highlander like yourselves, boys; at any rate, he appears to be, for he never wears anything else except the kilt, and he talks a language which, though I have had him for ten years, I do not yet understand. Archie, Archie, where are you?'

'Another Archie!' said Dugald, 'and a countryman, too?'

'He is shy of strangers. Archie, boy! He is swinging in some tree-top, no doubt.'

'What a queer fellow he must be! Wears nothing but the kilt, speaks Gaelic, swings in tree-tops, and is shy! A *rara avis* indeed.'

'Ah! here he comes. Archie, spread the awning out of doors, lay the table, bring a jug of cold *maté* and the cigars.'

Truly Archie was a curious Highlander. He was quite as tall as our Archie, and though the hermit assured us he was only a baby when he bought him in Central Africa for about sevenpence halfpenny in Indian coin, he had now the wrinkled face of an old man of ninety—wrinkled, wizened, and weird. But his eye was singularly bright and young-looking. In his hand he carried a long pole from which he had bitten all the bark, and his only dress was a little petticoat of skunk skin, which the hermit called his kilt. He was, in fact, an African orang-outang.

'Come and shake hands with the good gentlemen, Archie.'

Archie knitted his brows, and looked at us without moving. The hermit laughingly handed him a pair of big horn-rimmed spectacles. These he put on with all the gravity of some ancient professor of Sanscrit, then looked us all over once again.

We could stand this no longer, and so burst into a chorus of laughing.

'Don't laugh longer than you can help, boys. See, Archie is angry.'

Archie was. He showed a mouth full of fearful-looking fangs, and fingered his club in a way that was not pleasant.

'Archie, you may have some peaches presently.'

Archie grew pleasant again in a moment, and advanced and shook hands with us all round, looking all the time, however, as if he had some silent sorrow somewhere. I confess he wrung our hands pretty hard. Neither my brother nor I made any remark, but when it came to Archie's turn—

'Honolulu!' he shouted, shaking his fingers, and blowing on them. 'I believe he has made the blood come!'

'I suppose,' said Dugald, laughing, 'he knows you are a namesake.'

Off went the great baboon, and to our intense astonishment spread the awning, placed table and camp-stools under it, and fetched the cold *maté* with all the gravity and decorum of the chief steward on a first-class liner.

I looked at my brothers, and they looked at me.

'You seem all surprised,' the hermit said, 'but remember that in olden times it was no rare thing to see baboons of this same species waiting at the tables of your English nobility. Well, I am not only a noble, but a king; why should not I also have an anthropoid as a butler and valet?'

'I confess,' I said, 'I for one am very much surprised at all I have seen and all that has happened since last night, and I really cannot help thinking that presently I shall awake and find, as the story-books say, it is all a dream.'

'You will find it all a very substantial dream, I do assure you, sir. But help yourself to the *maté*. You will find it better than any imported stuff.'

'Archie! Archie! Where are you?'

'Ah! ah! Yah, yah, yah!' cried Archie, hopping round behind his master.

'The sugar, Archie.'

'Ah, ah, ah! Yah, yah!'

'Is that Gaelic, Dugald?' said our Archie.

'Not quite, my cockney cousin.'

'I thought not.'

'Why?' said Dugald.

'It is much more intelligible.'

The hermit laughed.

'I think, Dugald,' he said, 'your cousin has the best of you.'

He then made us tell him all our strange though brief history, as the reader already knows it. If he asked us questions, however, it was evidently not for the sake of inquisitiveness, but to exchange experiences, and support the conversation. He was quite as ready to impart as to solicit information; but somehow we felt towards him as if he were an elder brother or uncle; and this only proves the hermit was a perfect gentleman.

'Shall you live much longer in this beautiful wilderness?' asked Donald.

'Well, I will tell you all about that,' replied the hermit. 'And the all is very brief. When I came here first I had no intention of making a long stay. I was a trapper and hunter then pure and simple, and sold my skins and other odds and ends which these hills yield — and what these are I must not even tell to you — journeying over the Andes with mules twice every year for that purpose. But gradually, as my trees and bushes and all the beauty of this wild garden-glen grew up around me, and so many of God's wild children came to keep me company, I got to love my strange life. So from playing at being a hermit, I dare say I have come to be one in reality. And now, though I have money — much more than one would imagine — in the Chilian banks, I do not seem to care to enter civilized life again. For some years back I have been promising myself a city holiday, but I keep putting it off and off. I should not wonder if it never comes, or, to speak more correctly, I should wonder if it ever came. Oh, I dare say I shall die in my own private wilderness here, with no one to close my eyes but old Archie.'

'Do you still go on journeys to Chili?'

'I still go twice a year. I have strong fleet mules. I go once in summer and once in winter.'

'Going in winter across the Andes! That must be a terribly dreary journey.'

'It is. Yet it has its advantages. I never have to flee from hostile Indians then. They do not like the hills in winter.'

'Are you not afraid of the pampas Indians?'

'No, not at all. They visit me occasionally here, but do not stay long. I trust them, I am kind to them, and I have nothing they could find to steal, even if they cared to be dishonest. But they are *not*. They are good-hearted fellows in their own way.'

'Yes,' I said, 'very much in their own way.'

'My dear boy,' said the hermit, 'you do not know all. A different policy would have made those Indians the sworn friends, the faithful allies and servants of the white man. They would have kept then to their own hunting-grounds, they would have brought to you wealth of skins, and wealth of gold and silver, too, for believe me, they (the Indians) have secrets that the white trader little wots of. No, it is the dishonest, blood-stained policy of the Republic that has made the Indian what he is—his hand against every man, every man's hand against him.'

'But they even attack you at times, I think you gave us to understand?'

'Nay, not the pampas or pampean Indians: only prowling gipsy tribes from the far north. Even they will not when they know me better. My fame is spreading as a seer.'

'As a seer?'

'Yes, a kind of prophet. Do not imagine that I foster any such folly, only they will believe that, living here all alone in the wilds, I must have communication with—ha! ha! a worse world than this.'

As we rose to go the hermit held out his hand.

'Come and see me to-night,' he said; 'and let me advise you to make this glen your headquarters for a time. The hills and glens and bush for leagues around abound in game. Then your way back lies across a pampa north and east of here; not the road you have come.'

'By the by,' said Archie, 'before we go, I want to ask you the question which tramps always put in England: "Are the dogs all safe?"'

'Ah,' said the hermit, smiling, 'I know what you mean. Yes, the dogs are safe. My pet pumas will not come near you. I do not think that even my jaguars would object to your presence; but for safety's sake Archie shall go along with you, and he shall also come for you in the evening. Give him these peaches when you reach camp. They are our own growing, and Archie dotes upon them.'

So away back by the banks of the stream we went, our strange guide, club in hand, going hopping on before. It did really seem all like a scene of enchantment.

We gave Archie the peaches, and he looked delighted.

'Good-bye, old man,' said Dugald, as he presented him with his.

'Speak a word or two of Gaelic to him,' said our Archie.

Sandie Donaldson was indeed astonished at all we told him.

'I suppose it's all right,' he said, 'but dear me, that was an uncanny-looking creature you had hirpling on in front of you!'

In the evening, just as we had returned from a most successful guanaco hunt, we found Donaldson's uncanny creature coming along the path.

'I suppose he means us to dine with him,' I remarked.

'Ah, ah, ah! Yah, ah, yah!' cried the baboon.

'Well, will you come, Sandie?'

Sandie shook his head.

'Not to-night,' said Sandie. 'Take care of yourselves, boys. Mind what the old proverb says: "They need a lang spoon wha sup wi' the deil."'

We found the hermit at his gate, and glad he seemed to see us.

'I've been at home all the afternoon,' he said, 'cooking your dinner. Most enjoyable work, I can assure you. All the vegetables are fresh, and even the curry has been grown on the premises. I hope you are fond of armadillo; that is a favourite dish of mine. But here we have roast ducks, partridges, and something that perhaps you have never tasted before, roast or boiled.

For bread we have biscuit; for wine we have *maté* and milk. My goats come every night to be milked. Archie does the milking as well as any man could. Ah, here come my dogs.'

Two deerhounds trotted up and made friends with us.

'I bought them from a roving Scot two years ago while on a visit to Chili.'

'How about the pumas? Don't they—'

'No, they come from the trees to sleep with Rob and Rory. Even the jaguars do not attempt to touch them. Sit down; you see I dine early. We will have time before dusk to visit some of my pets. I hope they did not keep you awake.'

'No, but the noise would have done so, had we not known what they were.'

Conversation never once flagged all the time we sat at table. The hermit himself had put most of the dishes down, but Archie duly waited behind his master's chair, and brought both the *maté* and the milk, as well as the fruit. This dessert was of the most tempting description; and not even at our own *estancia* had I tasted more delicious grapes. But there were many kinds of fruit here we had never even seen before. As soon as we were done the waiter had *his* repast, and the amount of fruit he got through surprised us beyond measure. He squatted on the ground to eat. Well, when he commenced his dinner he looked a little old gentleman of somewhat spare habit; when he rose up—by the aid of his pole—he was decidedly plump, not to say podgy. Even his cheeks were puffed out; and no wonder, they were stuffed with nuts to eat at his leisure. ¯

'I dare say Archie eats at all odd hours,' I said.

'No, he does not,' replied the hermit. 'I never encouraged him to do so, and now he is quite of my way of thinking, and never eats between meals. But come, will you light a cigarette and stroll round with me?'

'We will stroll round without the cigarette,' I said.

'Then fill your pockets with nuts and raisins; you must do something.'

'Feed the birds, Archie.'

'Ah, ah, ah! Yah, ah! Yah, yah!'

'The birds need not come to be fed; there is enough and to spare for them in the woods, but they think whatever we eat must be extra nice. We have all kinds of birds except the British sparrow. I really hope you have not brought him. They say he follows Englishmen to the uttermost parts of the world.'

We waited for a moment, and wondered at the flocks of lovely bright-winged doves and pigeons and other birds that had alighted round the table to receive their daily dole, then followed our hermit guide, to feast our eyes on other wonders not a whit less wonderful than all we had seen.

CHAPTER XXI
WILD ADVENTURES ON PRAIRIE AND PAMPAS

If I were to describe even one half of the strange creatures we saw in the hermit's glen, the reader would be tired before I had finished, and even then I should not have succeeded in conveying anything like a correct impression of this floral wilderness and natural menagerie.

It puzzled me to know, and it puzzles me still, how so many wild creatures could have been got together in one place.

'I brought many of them here,' the hermit told us, 'but the others came, lured, no doubt, by the water, the trees, and the flowers.'

'But was the water here when you arrived?'

'Oh yes, else I would not have settled down here. The glen was a sort of oasis even then, and there were more bushes and trees than ever I had seen before in one place. The ducks and geese and swans, in fact, all the web-footed fraternity, had been here before me, and many birds and beasts besides—the biscachas, the armadilloes, the beetle-eating pichithiego, for instance—the great ant-eater, and the skunk—I have banished that, however—wolves, foxes, kites, owls, and condors. I also found peccaries, and some deer. These latter, and the guanaco, give me a wide berth now. They do not care for dogs, pumas, and jaguars. Insects are rather too numerous, and I have several species of snakes.'

Archie's—*our* Archie's—face fell.

'Are they?' he began, 'are they very—'

'Very beautiful? Yes; indeed, some are charming in colour. One, for example, is of the brightest crimson streaked with black.'

'I was not referring to their beauty; I meant were they dangerous?'

'Well, I never give them a chance to bite me, and I do not think they want to; but all snakes are to be avoided and left severely alone.'

'Or killed, sir?'

'Yes, perhaps, if killed outright; for the pampan Indians have an idea that if a rattlesnake be only wounded, he will come back for revenge. But let us change the subject. You see those splendid butterflies? Well, by and by the moths will be out; they are equally lovely, but when I first came here there were very few of either. They followed the flowers, and the humming-birds came next, and many other lovely gay-coloured little songsters. I introduced most of the parrots and toucans. There are two up there even now. They would come down if you were not here.'

'They are very funny-looking, but very pretty,' said Dugald. 'I could stop and look at them for hours.'

'But we must proceed. Here are the trees where the parrots mostly live. Early as it is, you see they are retiring.'

What a sight! What resplendency of colour and beauty! Such bright metallic green, lustrous orange, crimson and bronze!

'Why do they frequent this particular part of the wood?' said Dugald.

'Ah, boy,' replied the hermit, 'I see you want to know everything. Don't be ashamed of that; you are a true naturalist at heart. Well, the parrots like to be by themselves, and few of my birds care to live among them. You will notice, too, that yonder are some eucalyptus trees, and farther up some wide-spreading, open-branched trees, with flowers creeping and clinging around the stems. Parrots love those trees, because while there they have sunshine, and because birds of prey cannot easily tell which is parrot and which is flower or flame-coloured lichen.'

'That is an advantage.'

'Well, yes; but it is an advantage that also has a disadvantage, for our serpents are so lovely that even they are not easily seen by the parrots when they wriggle up among the orchids.'

'Can the parrots defend themselves against snakes?'

'Yes, they can, and sometimes even kill them. I have noticed this, but as a rule they prefer to scare them off by screaming. And they can scream, too. "As deaf as an adder," is a proverb; well, I believe it was the parrot that first deafened the adder, if deaf it be.'

'Have you many birds of prey?'

'Yes, too many. But, see here.'

'I see nothing.'

'No, but you soon shall. Here in the sunniest bank, and in this sunniest part of the wood, dwell a family of that remarkable creature the blind armadillo, or pichithiego. I wonder if any one is at home.'

As he spoke, the hermit knelt down and buried his hands in the sand, soon bringing to the surface a very curious little animal indeed, one of the tenderest of all armadilloes.

It shivered as it cuddled into the hermit's arms.

Dugald laughed aloud.

'Why,' he cried, 'it seems to end suddenly half-way down; and that droll tail looks stuck on for fun.'

'Yes, it is altogether a freak of Nature, and the wonder to me is how, being so tender, it lives here at all. You see how small and delicate a thing it is. They say it is blind, but you observe it is not; although the creatures live mostly underground. They also say that the *chlamyphorus truncatus*—which is the grand name for my wee friend,—carries its young under this pink or rosy shell jacket, but this I very much doubt. Now go to bed, little one.

'I have prettier pets than even these, two species of agoutis, for instance, very handsome little fellows indeed, and like rats in many of their ways and in many of their droll antics. They are not fond of strangers, but often come out to meet me in my walks about the woods. They live in burrows, but run about plentifully enough in the open air, although their enemies are very numerous. Even the Indians capture and eat them, as often raw as not.

'You have heard of the peccary. Well, I have never encouraged these wild wee pigs, and for some years after I came, there were none in the woods. One morning I found them, however, all over the place in herds. I never knew where they came from, nor how they found us out. But I do know that for more than two years I had to wage constant war with them.'

'They were good to eat?'

'They were tolerably good, especially the young, but I did not want for food; and, besides, they annoyed my wee burrowing pets, and, in fact, they deranged everything, and got themselves thoroughly hated wherever they went.'

'And how did you get rid of them?'

'They disappeared entirely one night as if by magic, and I have never seen nor heard one since. But here we are at my stable.'

'I see no stable,' I said.

'Well, it is an enclosure of half an acre, and my mules and goats are corralled here at night.'

'Do not the pumas or jaguars attempt to molest the mules or goats?'

'Strange to say, they do not, incredible as it may seem. But come in, and you will see a happy family.'

'What are these?' cried Dugald. 'Dogs?'

'No, boy, one is a wolf, the other two are foxes. All three were suckled by one of my dogs, and here they are. You see, they play with the goats, and are exceedingly fond of the mules. They positively prefer the company of the mules to mine, although when I come here with their foster-dam, the deerhound, they all condescend to leave this compound and to follow me through the woods.

'Here come my mules. Are they not beauties?'

We readily admitted they were, never having seen anything in size and shape to equal them.

'Now, you asked me about the jaguars. Mine are but few; they are also very civil; but I do believe that one of these mules would be a match even for a jaguar. If the jaguar had one kick he would never need another. The goats—here they come—herd close to the mules, and the foxes and wolf are sentinels, and give an alarm if even a strange monkey comes near the compound. Ah, here come my pet toucans!'

These strange-beaked birds came floating down from a tree to the number of nearly a dozen, nor did they look at all ungainly, albeit their beaks are so wondrously large.

'What do they eat?'

'Everything; but fruit is the favourite dish with them. But look up. Do you see that speck against the cloud yonder, no bigger in appearance than the lark that sings above the cornfields in England? See how it circles and sweeps round and round. Do you know that bird is a mile above us?'

'That is wonderful!'

'And what think you it is doing? Why, it is eyeing you and me. It is my pet condor. The only bird I do not feed; but the creature loves me well for all that. He is suspicious of your presence. Now watch, and I will bring him down like an arrow.'

The hermit waved a handkerchief in a strange way, and with one fell downward swoop, in a few seconds the monster eagle had alighted near us.

Well may the condor be called 'king of the air,' I thought, for never before had I seen so majestic a bird. He was near us now, and scrutinizing us with that bold fierce eye of his, as some chieftain in the brave days of old might have gazed upon spies that he was about to order away to execution. I believed then—and I am still of the same opinion—that there was something akin to pity and scorn in his steadfast looks, as if we had been brought here for his especial delectation and study.

'Poor wretched bipeds!' he seemed to say; 'not even possessed of feathers, no clothes of their own, obliged to wrap themselves in the hair and skins of dead quadrupeds. No beaks, no talons; not even the wings of a miserable bat. Never knew what it was to mount and soar into the blue sky to meet the morning sun; never floated free as the winds far away in the realms of space; never saw the world spread out beneath them like a living panorama, its woods and forests mere patches of green or purple, its lakes like sheets of shimmering ice, its streams like threads of spiders' webs before the day has drunk the dew, its very deserts dwarfed by distance till the guanacos and the ostriches[15] look like mites, and herds of wild horses appear but crawling ants. Never knew what it was to circle round the loftiest summits of the snow-clad voiceless Andes, while down in the valleys beneath dark clouds rolled fiercely on, and lightnings played across the darkness; nor to perch cool and safe on peak or pinnacle, while below on earth's dull level the hurricane Pampero was levelling house and hut and tree; or the burning breath of the Zonda was sweeping over the land, scorching every flower and leaf, drinking every drop of dew, draining even the blood of moving beings till eyes ache and brains reel, till man himself looks haggard, wild, and worn, and the beasts of the forest, hidden in darkling caves, go mad and rend their young.'

The hermit returned with us to our camping-ground just as great bats began to circle and wheel around, as butterflies were folding their wings and going to sleep beneath the leaves, and the whole woodland glen began to awake to the screaming of night-birds, to the mournful howling of strange monkeys, and hoarse growl of beasts of prey.

We sat together till far into the night listening to story after story of the wild adventures of our new but nameless hero, and till the moon—so high above us now that the pine-trees no longer cast their shadows across the glade—warned us it was time to retire.

'Good night, boys all,' said the hermit; 'I will come again to-morrow.'

He turned and walked away, his *potro* boots making no sound on the sward. We watched him till the gloom of the forest seemed to swallow him up.

'What a strange being!' said Archie, with a sigh.

'And what a lonely life to lead!' said Donald.

'Ah!' said Dugald, 'you may sigh as you like, Archie, and say what you please, I think there is no life so jolly, and I've half a mind to turn hermit myself.'

We lived in the glen for many weeks. No better or more idyllic headquarters could possibly have been found or even imagined, while all around us was a hunter's paradise. We came at last to look upon the hermit's dell as our home, but we did not bivouac there every night. There were times when we wandered too far away in pursuit of the guanaco, the puma, jaguar, or even the ostrich, which we found feeding on plains at no great distance from our camp.

It was a glorious treat for all of us to find ourselves on these miniature pampas, across which we could gallop unfettered and free.

Under the tuition of Yambo, our *capataz*, and the other Gauchos, we became adepts in the use of both bolas and lasso. Away up among the beetling crags and in the deep, gloomy caverns we had to stalk the guanacos as the Swiss mountaineer stalks the chamois. Oh, our adventures among the rocks were sometimes thrilling enough! But here on the plains another kind of tactics was pursued. I doubt if we could have ridden near enough to the ostriches to bola them, so our plan was to make *détours* on the pampas until we had outflanked, encircled, and altogether puzzled our quarry. Then riding in a zigzag fashion, gradually we narrowed the ring till near enough to fire. When nearer still the battue and stampede commenced, and the scene was then wild and confusing in the extreme. The frightened whinny or neigh of the guanacos, the hoarse whirr of the flying ostriches, the shouts of the Gauchos, the bark and yell of dogs, the whistling noise of lasso or bolas, the sharp ringing of rifle and revolver—all combined to form a medley, a huntsman's chorus which no one who has once heard it and taken part in it is likely to forget.

When too far from the camp, then we hobbled our horses at the nearest spot where grass and water could be found, and after supping on broiled guanaco steak and ostrich's gizzard—in reality right dainty morsels—we would roll ourselves in our guanaco robes, and with saddles for pillows go quietly to sleep. Ah, I never sleep so soundly now as I used to then beneath the stars, fanned by the night breeze; and although the dews lay heavy on our robes in the morning, we awoke as fresh as the daisies and as happy as puma cubs that only wake to play.

We began to get wealthy ere long with a weight of skins of birds and beasts. Some of the most valuable of these were procured from a species of otter that lived in the blackest, deepest pools of a stream we had fallen in with in our wanderings. The Gauchos had a kind of superstitious dread of the huge beast, whom they not inappropriately termed the river tiger.

We had found our dogs of the greatest use in the hills, especially our monster bloodhound-mastiffs. These animals possessed nearly all the tracking qualities of the bloodhound, with more fierceness and speed than the mastiff, and nearly the same amount of strength. Their courage, too, and general hardiness were very great.

Among our spoils we could count the skins of no less than fifteen splendid pumas. Several of these had shown fight. Once, I remember, Archie had leapt from his horse and was making his way through a patch of bush on the plains, in pursuit of a young guanaco which he had wounded. He was all alone: not even a dog with him; but Yambo's quick ear had detected the growl of a lion in that bit of scrub, and he at once started off three of his best dogs to the scene of Archie's adventure. Not two hundred yards away myself, but on high ground, I could see everything, though powerless to aid. I could see Archie hurrying back through the bush. I could see the puma spring, and my poor cousin fall beneath the blow—then the death struggle began. It was fearful while it lasted, which was only the briefest possible time, for, even as I looked, the dogs were on the puma. The worrying, yelling, and gurgling sounds were terrible. I saw the puma on its hind legs, I saw one dog thrown high in the air, two others on the wild beast's neck, and next moment Yambo himself was there, with every other horseman save myself tearing along full tilt for the battle-field.

Yambo's long spear had done the work, and all the noise soon ceased. Though stunned and frightened, Archie was but little the worse. One dog was killed. It seemed to have been Yambo's favourite. I could not help expressing my astonishment at the exhibition of Yambo's grief. Here was a man, once one of the cruellest and most remorseless of desert wanderers, whose spear and knife had many a time and oft drunk human blood, shedding tears over the body of his poor dog! Nor would he leave the place until he had dug a grave, and, placing the bleeding remains therein, sadly and slowly covered them up.

But Yambo would meet his faithful hound again in the happy hunting-grounds somewhere beyond the sky. That, at least, was Yambo's creed, and who should dare deny him the comfort and joy the thought brings him!

It was now the sweetest season of all the year in the hills—the Indian summer. The fierce heat had fled to the north, fled beyond the salt plains of San Juan, beyond the wild desert lands of Rioja and arid sands of Catamarca, lingering still, perhaps, among the dreamland gardens of Tucuman, and reaching its eternal home among the sun-kissed forests of leafy Brazil and

Bolivia. The autumn days were getting shorter, the sky was now more soft, the air more cool and balmy, while evening after evening the sun went down amidst a fiery magnificence of colouring that held us spellbound and silent to behold.

A month and more in the hermit's glen! We could hardly believe it. How quickly the time had flown! How quickly time always does fly when one is happy!

And now our tents are struck, our mules are laden. We have but to say good-bye to the solitary being who has made the garden in the wilderness his home, and go on our way.

'Good-bye!'

'Good-bye!'

Little words, but sometimes *so* hard to say.

We had actually begun to like—ay, even to love the hermit, and we had not found it out till now. But I noticed tears in Dugald's eye, and I am not quite sure my own were not moist as we said farewell.

We glanced back as we rode away to wave our hands once more. The hermit was leaning against a tree. Just then the sun came struggling out from under a cloud, the shadow beneath the tree darkened and darkened, till it swallowed him up.

And we never saw the hermit more.

[15] The *Rhea Americana*.

CHAPTER XXII
ADVENTURE WITH A TIGER

Two years more have passed away, four years in all, since we first set foot in the Silver West. What happy, blithesome years they had been, too! Every day had brought its duties, every duty its pleasures as well. During all this time we could not look back with regret to one unpleasant hour. Sometimes we had endured some crosses as well, but we brothers bore them, I believe, without a murmur, and Moncrieff without one complaining word.

'Boys,' he would say, quietly, 'nobody gets it all his own way in this world. We must just learn to take the thick wi' the thin.'

Moncrieff was somewhat of a proverbial philosopher; but had he been entrusted with the task of selecting proverbs that should smooth one's path in life, I feel sure they would have been good ones.

Strath Coila New, as we called the now green valley in which our little colony had been founded, had improved to a wonderful extent in so brief a time. The settlers had completed their houses long ago; they, like ourselves, had laid out their fields and farms and planted their vineyards; the hedges were green and flowering; the poplar-trees and willows had sprung skywards as if influenced by magic—the magic of a virgin soil; the fields were green with waving grain and succulent lucerne; the vines needed the help of man to aid them in supporting their wondrous wealth of grapes; fruit grew everywhere; birds sang everywhere, and to their music were added sounds even sweeter still to our ears—the lowing of herds of sleek fat cattle, the bleating armies of sheep, the home-like noise of poultry and satisfied grunting of lazy pigs. The latter sometimes fed on peaches that would have brought tears of joy to the eyes of many an English market gardener.

Our villa was complete now; wings and tower, and terraced lawns leading down to the lake, close beside which Dugald had erected a boat-house that was in itself like a little fairy palace. Dugald had always a turn for the romantic, and nothing would suit him by way of a boat except a gondola. What an amount of time and taste he had bestowed on it too! and how the Gaucho carpenters had worked and slaved to please him and make it complete! But there it was at last, a thing of beauty, in all conscience— prows and bows, cushioned seats, and oars, and awnings, all complete.

It was his greatest pleasure to take auntie, Aileen, and old Jenny out to skim the lake in this gondola, and sit for long happy hours reading or fishing.

Even Bombazo used to form an item in these pleasant little excursions. He certainly was no use with an oar, but it was the 'bravo' captain's delight to dress as a troubadour and sit twanging the light guitar under the awnings, while Aileen and auntie plied the oars.

Dugald was still our mighty hunter, the fearless Nimrod of hill and strath and glen. But he was amply supported in all his adventures by Archie, who had wonderfully changed for the better. He was brown and hard now, an excellent horseman, and crack shot with either the revolver or rifle.

Between the two of them, though ably assisted by a Gaucho or two, they had fitted up the ancient ruined monastery far away among the hills as a kind of shooting-box, and here they spent many a day, and many a night as well. Archie had long since become acclimatized to all kinds of creepies— they no longer possessed any terrors for him.

The ruin, as I have before hinted, must have, at some bygone period, belonged to the Jesuits; but so blown up with sand was it when Dugald took possession that the work of restoration to something like its pristine form had been a task of no little difficulty. The building stood on a slight eminence, and at one side grew a huge ombu-tree. It was under this that the only inhabitable room lay. This room had two windows, one on each side, facing each other, one looking east, the other west. Neither glass nor frames were in these windows, and probably had not existed even in the Jesuits' time. The room was cooler without any such civilized arrangements.

It was a lonesome, eerie place at the very best, and that weird looking ombu-tree, spreading its dark arms above the grey old walls, did not detract from the air of gloom that surrounded it. Sometimes Archie said laughingly that the tree was like a funeral pall. Well, the half-caste Indians of the *estancias* used to give this ruin a wide berth; they had nasty stories to tell about it, stories that had been handed down through generations. There were few indeed of even the Gauchos who would have cared to remain here after night-fall, much less sleep within its walls. But when Dugald's big lamp stood lighted on the table, when a fire of wood burned on the low hearth, and a plentiful repast, with bowls of steaming fragrant *maté*, stood before the young men, then the room looked far from uncomfortable.

There was at each side a hammock hung, which our two hunters slept in on nights when they had remained too long on the hill, or wanted to be early at the chase in the morning.

'Whose turn is it to light the fire to-night?' said Dugald, one winter evening, as the two jogged along together on their mules towards the ruin.

'I think it is mine, cousin. Anyhow, if you feel lazy I'll make it so.'

'No, I'm not lazy, but I want to take home a bird or two to-morrow that auntie's very soul loveth, so if you go on and get supper ready I shall go round the red dune and try to find them.'

'You won't be long?'

'I sha'n't be over an hour.'

Archie rode on, humming a tune to himself. Arrived at the ruin, he cast the mule loose, knowing he would not wander far away, and would find juicy nourishment among the more tender of the cacti sprouts.

Having lit a roaring fire, and seen it burn up, Archie spread asunder some of the ashes, and placed thereon a huge pie-dish—not an empty one—to warm. Meanwhile he hung a kettle of water on the hook above the fire, and, taking up a book, sat down by the window to read by the light of the setting sun until the water should boil.

⌐A whole half-hour passed away. The kettle had rattled its lid, and Archie had hooked it up a few links, so that the water should not be wasted. It was very still and quiet up here to-night, and very lonesome too. The sun had just gone down, and all the western sky was aglow with clouds, whose ever-changing beauty it was a pleasure to watch. Archie was beginning to wish that Dugald would come, when he was startled at hearing a strange and piercing cry far down below him in the cactus jungle. It was a cry that made his flesh quiver and his very spine feel cold. It came from no human lips, and yet it was not even the scream of a terror-struck mule. Next minute the mystery was unravelled, and Dugald's favourite mule came galloping towards the ruin, pursued by an enormous tiger, as the jaguar is called here.

Just as he had reached the ruin the awful beast had made his spring. His talons drew blood, but the next moment he was rolling on the ground with one eye apparently knocked out, and the foam around his fang-filled mouth mixed with blood; and the mule was over the hills and safe, while the jaguar was venting his fume and fury on Archie's rugs, which, with his gun, he had left out there.

There is no occasion to deny that the young man was almost petrified with fear, but this did not last long: he must seek for safety somehow, somewhere. To leave the ruin seems certain death, to remain is impossible. Look, the tiger even already has scented him; he utters another fearful yell, and makes direct for the window. The tree! the tree! Something seems to utter those words in his ear as he springs from the open window. The jaguar has entered the room as Archie, with a strength he never knew he possessed, catches a lower limb and hoists himself up into the tree. He hears yell after yell; now first in the ruin, next at the tree foot, and then in the tree itself. Archie creeps higher and higher up, till the branches can no longer bear him, and after him creeps death in the most awful form imaginable. Already the brute is so close that he sees his glaring eye and hears his awful scenting and snuffling. Archie is fascinated by that tiger's face so near him—on the same limb of the tree, he himself far out towards the point. This must be fascination. He feels like one in a strange dream, for as the time goes by and the tiger springs not, he takes to speculating almost calmly on his fate, and wondering where the beast will seize him first, and if it will be very painful; if he will hear his own bones crash, and so faint and forget everything. What fangs the tiger has! How broad the head, and terribly fierce the grin! But how the blood trickles from the wound in the skull! He can hear it pattering on the dead leaves far beneath.

Why doesn't the tiger spring and have it over? Why does—but look, look, the brute has let go the branch and fallen down, down with a crash, and Archie hears the dull thud of the body on the ground.

Dead—to all intents and purposes. The good mule's hoof had cloven the skull.

'Archie! Archie! where on earth are you? Oh, Archie!'

It is Dugald's voice. The last words are almost a shriek.

Then away goes fear from Archie's heart, and joy unspeakable takes its place.

'Up here, Dugald,' he shouts, 'safe and sound.'

I leave the reader to guess whether Dugald was glad or not to see his cousin drop intact from the ombu-tree, or whether or not they enjoyed their pie and *maté* that evening after this terrible adventure.

'I wonder,' said Archie, later on, and just as they were preparing for hammock, 'I wonder, Dugald, if that tiger has a wife. I hope she won't come prowling round after her dead lord in the middle of the night.'

'Well, anyhow, Archie, we'll have our rifles ready, and Dash will give us ample warning, you know. So good-night.'

'Good-night. Don't be astonished if you hear me scream in my sleep. I feel sure I'll dream I'm up in that dark ombu-tree, and perhaps in the clutches of that fearsome tiger.'

About a month after the above related adventure the young men had another at that very ruin, which, if not quite so stirring, was at all events far more mysterious.

It happened soon after a wild storm, a kind of semi-pampero, had swept over the glen with much thunder and lightning and heavy rains. It had cleared the atmosphere, however, which previously had been hazy and close. It had cooled it as well, so that one afternoon, Dugald, addressing Archie, said,

'What do you say to an early morning among the birds to-morrow, cousin?'

'Oh, I'm ready, Dugald, if you are,' was the reply.

'Well, then, off you trot to the kitchen, and get food ready, and I'll see to the shooting tackle and the mules.'

When Dugald ran over to say good-night to Moncrieff and Aileen before they started, he met old Jenny in the door.

'Dear laddie,' she said, when she heard he was bound for the hills, 'I hope nae ill will come over ye; but I wot I had an unco' ugly dream last night. Put your trust in Providence, laddie. And ye winna forget to say your prayers, will ye?'

'That we won't, mother. Ta, ta!'

Moncrieff saw Dugald to his own gate. With them went Wolf, the largest bloodhound-mastiff.

'Dreams,' said Moncrieff, 'may be neither here nor there; but you'll be none the worse for taking Wolf.'

'Thank you,' said Dugald; 'he shall come, and welcome.'

The sun had quite set before they reached the ruin, but there was a beautiful after-glow in the west—a golden haze beneath, with a kind of crimson blush over it higher up. When they were on a level with the ruin, the two windows of which, as already stated, were opposite to each other, Archie said, musingly,

'Look, Dugald, what a strange and beautiful light is streaming through the windows!'

'Yes,' replied Dugald, 'but there is something solemn, even ghostly, about it. Don't you think so?'

'True; there always is something ghostly about an empty ruin, I think. Are you superstitious?'

'No; but—see. What was that? Why, there is some one there! Look to your rifle, Archie. It was an Indian, I am certain.'

What had they seen? Why, only the head and shoulders of a passing figure in the orange light of the two windows. It had appeared but one moment—next it was gone. Rifles in left hand, revolvers in right, they cautiously approached the ruin and entered. Never a soul was here. They went out again, and looked around; they even searched the ombu-tree, but all in vain.

'Our eyes must have deceived us,' said Dugald.

'I think,' said Archie, 'I have a theory that might explain the mystery.'

'What is it, then?'

'Well, that was no living figure we saw.'

'What! You don't mean to say, Archie, it was a ghost?'

'No, but a branch of that ghostly ombu-tree moved by a passing wind between us and the light.'

As he spoke they rounded the farthest off gable of the ruin, and there both stopped as suddenly as if shot. Close beside the wall, with some rude digging tools lying near, was a newly-opened grave!

'This is indeed strange,' said Dugald, remembering old Jenny's warning and dream; 'I cannot make it out.'

'Nor can I. However, we must make the best of it.'

By the time supper was finished they had almost forgotten all about it. Only before lying down that night—

'I say, Archie,' said Dugald, 'why didn't we think of it?'

'Think of what?'

'Why, of putting Wolf the mastiff on the track. If there have been Indians here he would have found them out.'

'It will not be too late to-morrow, perhaps.'

Dugald lay awake till it must have been long past midnight. He tried to sleep, but failed, though he could tell from his regular breathing that nothing was disturbing Archie's repose. It was a beautiful night outside, and the light from a full moon streamed in at one window and fell on the form of good Wolf, who was curled up on the floor; the other window was shaded by the branches of the ombu-tree. No matter how calm it might be in the valley below, away up here there was always a light breeze blowing, and to-night the whispering in the tree at times resembled the sound of human voices. So thought Dugald. Several times he started and listened, and once he felt almost sure he heard footsteps as of people moving outside. Then again all sounds—if sounds there had been—ceased, and nothing was audible save the sighing wind in the ombu-tree. Oh, that strange waving ombu-tree! He wondered if it really had some dark secret to whisper to him, and had chosen this silent hour of night to reveal it.

Hark, that was a sound this time! The mournful but piercing cry of a night-bird. 'Chee-hee-ee! chee-hee-ee!' It was repeated farther up the hill.

But could the dog be deceived? Scarcely; and growling low as if in anger, Wolf had arisen and stood pointing towards the ombu-shaded window.

With one accord both Dugald and Archie, seizing their revolvers and jumping from their hammocks, ran out just in time to see a tall figure cross a patch of moonlit sward and disappear in the cactus jungle.

Both fired in the direction, but of course aimlessly, and it was with the greatest difficulty they succeeded in keeping the great dog from following into the bush.

They were disturbed no more that night; and daylight quite banished their fears, though it could not dispel the mystery of the newly-dug grave.

Indeed, they could even afford to joke a little over the matter now.

'There is something in it, depend upon that,' said Dugald, as the two stood together looking into the hole.

'There doesn't seem to be,' said Archie, quizzingly.

'And I mean to probe it to the bottom.'

'Suppose you commence now, Dugald. Believe me, there is no time like the present. Here are the tools. They look quite antediluvian. Do you think now that it really was a flesh-and-blood Indian we saw here; or was it the ghost of some murdered priest? And has he been digging down here to excavate his own old bones, or have a peep to see that they are safe?'

'Archie,' said Dugald, at last, as if he had not listened to a word of his companion's previous remarks, 'Archie, we won't go shooting to-day.'

'No?'

'No, we will go home instead, and bring Moncrieff and my brothers here. I begin to think this is no grave after all.'

'Indeed, Dugald, and why?'

'Why, simply for this reason: Yambo has told me a wonderful blood-curdling story of two hermit priests who lived here, and who had found treasure among the hills, and were eventually murdered and buried in this very ruin. According to the tradition the slaughtering Indians were themselves afterwards killed, and since then strange appearances have taken place from time to time, and until we made a shooting-box of the ruin no Gauchos could be found bold enough to go inside it, nor would any Indian come within half a mile of the place. That they have got more courageous now we had ample evidence last night.'

'And you think that—'

'I think that Indians are not far away, and that—but come, let us saddle our mules and be off.'

It was high time, for at that very moment over a dozen pairs of fierce eyes were watching them from the cactus jungle. Spears were even poised ready for an attack, and only perhaps the sight of that ferocious-looking dog restrained them.

No one could come more speedily to a conclusion than Moncrieff. He hardly waited to hear Dugald's story before he had summoned Yambo, and bade him get ready with five trusty Gauchos to accompany them to the hills.

'Guns, señor?'

'Ay, guns, Yambo, and the other dog. We may have to draw a trigger or two. Sharp is the word, Yambo!'

In two hours more, and just as the winter's sun was at its highest, we all reached the cactus near the old monastic ruin. Here a spear flew close past Moncrieff's head. A quick, fierce glance of anger shot from the eyes of this buirdly Scot. He called a dog, and in a moment more disappeared in the jungle. A minute after there was the sharp ring of a revolver, a shriek, a second shot, and all was still. Presently Moncrieff rode back, looking grim, but calm and self-possessed.

There was no one near the ruin when we advanced, but the Indians had been here. The grave was a grave no longer in shape, but a huge hole.

'Set to work, Yambo, with your men. They have saved us trouble. Dugald and Archie and Donald, take three men and the dogs and scour the bush round here. Then place sentinels about, and post yourselves on top of the red dune.'

Yambo and his men set to work in earnest, and laboured untiringly for hours and hours, but without finding anything. A halt was called at last for rest and refreshment; then the work was commenced with greater heart than ever.

I had ridden away to the red dune to carry food to my brothers and the dogs and the sentinels.

The day was beginning already to draw to a close. The sky all above was blue and clear, but along the horizon lay a bank of grey rolling clouds, that soon would be changed to crimson and gold by the rays of the setting sun. Hawks were poised high in the air, and flocks of kites were slowly winging their way to the eastward.

From our position on the summit of the red dune we had a most extended view on all sides. We could even see the tall waving poplars of our own *estancias*, and away westward a vast rolling prairie of pampa land, bounded by the distant *sierras*. My eyes were directed to one level and snow-white patch in the plain, which might have been about three square miles in extent, when suddenly out from behind some dunes that lay beyond rode a party of horsemen. We could tell at a glance they were Indians, and that they were coming as fast as fleet horses could carry them, straight for the hill on which we stood. There was not a moment to lose, so, leaping to the back of my mule, I hurried away to warn our party.

CHAPTER XXIII
A RIDE FOR LIFE

'Moncrieff!' I cried, as soon as I got within hail, 'the Indians will be on us in less than half an hour!'

'Then, boy,' replied Moncrieff, 'call in your brothers and the men; they cannot hold the dune. We must fight them here, if it be fighting they mean. Hurry back, I have something to show you.'

We had all returned in less than ten minutes. Greatly to our astonishment, we found no one in the pit now, but we heard voices beneath, and I hurried in and down.

They had found a cave; whether natural or not we could not at present say. At one side lay a heap of mouldering bones, in the opposite corner a huge wooden chest. Moncrieff had improvised a torch, and surely Aladdin in his cave could not have been more astonished at what he saw than we were now! The smoky light fell on the golden gleam of nuggets! Yes, there they were, of all shapes and sizes. Moncrieff plunged his hand to the bottom of the box and stirred them up as he might have done roots or beans.

This, then, was the secret the ruin had held so long—the mystery of the giant ombu-tree.

That the Indians in some way or other had got scent of this treasure was evident, and as these wandering savages care little if anything for gold on their own account, it was equally evident that some white man—himself not caring to take the lead or even appear—was hounding them on to find it, with the promise doubtless of a handsome reward.

Not a moment was there to be lost now. The treasure must be removed. An attempt was first made to lift the chest bodily. This was found to be impossible owing to the decayed condition of the wood. The grain-sacks, therefore, which formed a portion of the Gaucho's mule-trappings, were requisitioned, and in a very short time every gold nugget was carried out and placed in safety in a corner of our principal room in the hunting-box.

The beasts were placed for safety in another room of the ruin, a trench being dug before the door, which could be commanded from one of our windows.

'How many horsemen did you count?' said Moncrieff to me.

'As near as I could judge,' I replied, 'there must be fifty.'

'Yes, there may be a swarm more. One of you boys must ride to-night to the *estancia* and get assistance. Who volunteers?'

'I do,' said Dugald at once.

'Then it will be well to start without delay before we are surrounded. See, it is already dusk, and we may expect our Indian friends at any moment. Mount, lad, and Heaven preserve you!'

Dugald hardly waited to say another word. He saw to the revolvers in his saddle-bows, slung his rifle over his shoulder, sprang to the saddle, and had disappeared like a flash.

And now we had but to wait the turn of events — turn how they might.

Dugald told us afterwards that during that memorable ride to the *estancia* he felt as if the beast beneath him was a winged horse instead of his own old-fashioned and affectionate mule. Perhaps it was fear that lent him such speed, and possibly it was fear transmitted even from his rider. Times without number since we had come out to our new home in the Silver West my brother had shown what sort of stuff he was made of, but a ride like this is trying to a heart like oak or nerves like steel, and a young man must be destitute of soul itself not to feel fear on such an occasion. Besides, the very fact of flying from unseen foes adds to the terror.

Down through the cactus jungle he went, galloping in and out and out and in, himself hardly knowing the road, trusting everything to the sagacity of the wondrous mule. Oftentimes when returning from a day on the hills, tired and weary, he had thought the way through this strange green bushland interminably long; but now, fleetly though he was speeding on, he thought it would never, never end, that he would never, never come out into the open braeland, and see, miles away beneath him, the twinkling lights of the *estancia*. Many an anxious glance, too, did he cast around him or into the gloomiest shades of the jungle, more than once imagining he saw dusky figures therein with long spears ready to launch at him.

He is out at last, however; but the path is now loose and rough and stony. After riding for some hundred yards he has to cut across at right angles to the jungle he has left. To his horror, a dozen armed Indians at that very moment leave the cactus, and with levelled spears and wild shouts dash onward to intercept him. This is indeed a ride for life, for to his immediate left is a precipice full twenty feet in height. He must gain the end of this before he can put even a yard of actual distance betwixt himself and the savages who are thirsting for his life. More than once he has half made up his mind to dare the leap, but the venture is far too great.

Nearer and nearer sweep the Indians. Dugald is close at the turning-point now, but he sees the foremost savage getting the deadly lasso ready. He must shoot, though he has to slacken speed slightly to take better aim.

He fires. Down roll horse and man, and Dugald is saved.

They have heard that rifle-shot far away on the *estancia*. Quick eyes are turned towards the braelands, and, dusk though it is, they notice that something more than usual is up. Five minutes afterwards half a dozen armed horsemen thunder out to meet Dugald. They hear his story, and all return to alarm the colony and put the whole place in a state of defence. Then under the guidance of Dugald they turn back once more—a party of twenty strong now—towards the hills, just as the moon, which is almost full, is rising and shining through between the solemn steeple-like poplars.

To avoid the jungle, and a probable ambuscade, they have to make a long *détour*, but they reach the ruin at last, to find all safe and sound. The Indians know that for a time their game is played, and they have lost; and they disappeared as quickly and mysteriously as they came leaving not a trace behind.

The gold is now loaded on the backs of the mules, and the journey home commenced.

As they ride down through the giant cacti two huge vultures rise with flapping wings and heavy bodies at no great distance. It was into that very thicket that Moncrieff rode this morning. It was there he fired his revolver. The vultures had been disturbed at a feast—nothing more.

Great was the rejoicing at the safe return of Moncrieff and his party from the hills. Our poor aunt had been troubled, indeed, but Aileen was frantic, and threw herself into her husband's arms when she saw him in quite a passion of hysterical joy.

Now although there was but little if any danger of an attack to-night on the *estancias*, no one thought of retiring to bed. There was much to be done by way of preparation, for we were determined not to lose a horse, nor even a sheep, if we could help it. So we arranged a code of signals by means of rifle-shots, and spent the whole of the hours that intervened betwixt the time of our return and sunrise in riding round the farms and visiting even distant *puestos*.

My brothers and I and Moncrieff lay down when day broke to snatch a few hours of much-needed rest.

It was well on in the forenoon when I went over to Moncrieff's mansion. I had already been told that strangers had arrived from distant *estancias* bringing evil tidings. The poor men whom I found in the drawing-room with Moncrieff had indeed brought dreadful news. They had escaped from their burned *estancias* after seeing their people massacred by savages before their eyes. They had seen others on the road who had suffered even worse, and did not know what to do or where to fly. Many had been hunted into the bush and killed there. Forts had been attacked further south, and even the soldiers of the republic in some instances had been defeated and scattered over the country.

The year, indeed, was one that will be long remembered by the citizens of the Argentine Republic. Happily things have now changed for the better, and the Indians have been driven back south of the Rio Negro, which will for ever form a boundary which they must not cross on pain of death.

More fugitives dropped in that day, and all had pitiful, heartrending stories to tell.

Moncrieff made every one welcome, and so did we all, trying our very best to soothe the grief and anguish they felt for those dear ones they would never see more on earth.

And now hardly a day passed that did not bring news of some kind of the doings of the Indians. Success had rendered them bold, while it appeared to have cowed for a time the Government of this noble republic, or, at all events, had confused and paralyzed all its action. Forts were overcome almost without resistance. Indeed, some of them were destitute of the means of resisting, the men having no proper supply of ammunition. *Estancia* after *estancia* on the frontier had been raided and burned, with the usual shocking barbarities that make one shudder even to think of.

It was but little likely that our small but wealthy colony would escape, for the fact that we were now possessed of the long-buried treasure—many thousands of pounds in value—must have spread like wild-fire.

One morning Moncrieff and I started early, and rode to a distant *estancia*, which we were told had been attacked and utterly destroyed, not a creature being left alive about the place with the exception of the cattle and horses, which the Indians had captured. We had known this family. They had often attended Moncrieff's happy little evening parties, and the children had played in our garden and rowed with us in the gondola.

Heaven forbid I should attempt to draw a graphic picture of all we saw! Let it be sufficient to say that the rumours which had reached us were all too true, and that Moncrieff and I saw sights which will haunt us both until our dying day.

The silence all round the *estancia* when we rode up was eloquent, terribly eloquent. The buildings were blackened ruins, and it was painful to notice the half-scorched trailing flowers, many still in bloom, clinging around the wrecked and charred verandah. But everywhere about, in the out-buildings, on the lawn, in the garden itself, were the remains of the poor creatures who had suffered.

'Alas! for love of this were all,
And none beyond, O earth!'

Moncrieff spoke but little all the way back. While standing near the verandah I had seen him move his hand to his eyes and impatiently brush away a tear, but after that his face became firm and set, and for many a day after this I never saw him smile.

At this period of our strange family story I lay down my pen and lean wearily back in my chair. It is not that I am tired of writing. Oh, no! Evening after evening for many and many a long week I have repaired up here to my turret chamber—my beautiful study in our Castle of Coila—and with my faithful hound by my feet I have bent over my sheets and transcribed as faithfully as I could events as I remember them. But it is the very multiplicity of these events as I near the end of my story that causes me to pause and think.

Ah! here comes aunt, gliding into my room, pausing for a moment, curtain in hand, half apologetically, as she did on that evening described in our first chapter.

'No, auntie, you do not disturb me. Far from it. I was longing for your company.'

She is by my side now, and looking down at my manuscript.

'Yes,' she says many times—nodding assent to every sentence, and ever turning back the pages for reference—'yes, and now you come near the last events of this story of the M'Crimmans of Coila. Come out to the castle roof, and breathe the evening air, and I will talk.'

We sit there nearly an hour. Aunt's memory is better even than mine, and I listen to her without ever once opening my lips. Then I lead her back to the tower, and point smilingly to the harp.

She has gone at last, and I resume my story.

We, Moncrieff and I, saw no signs of Indians during our long ride that day. We had gone on this journey with our lives in our hands. The very daringness and dash of it was probably our salvation. The enemy were about—they might be here, there, anywhere. Every bush might conceal a foe, but they certainly made no appearance.

All was the same apparently about our *estancias*; *but* I wondered a little that my brothers had not come out to meet me as usual, and that faithful, though plain-faced Yambo looked at me strangely, and I thought pityingly, as he took my mule to lead away to the compound.

I went straight away through our gardens, and entered the drawing-room by the verandah window.

I paused a moment, holding the casement in my hand. Coming straight out of the glare of the evening sunset, the room appeared somewhat dark, but I noticed Dugald sitting at the table with his face bent down over his hand, and Donald lying on the couch.

'Dugald!'

He started up and ran towards me, seizing and wringing my hand.

'Oh, Murdoch,' he cried, 'our poor father!'

'You have had a letter—he is ill?'

'He is ill.'

'Dugald,' I cried, 'tell me all! Dugald—is—father—dead?'

No reply.

I staggered towards the table, and dropped limp and stricken and helpless into a chair.

I think I must have been ill for many, many days after this sad news. I have little recollection of the events of the next week—I was engrossed, engulfed in the one great sorrow. The unexpected death of so well-beloved a father in the meridian of life was a terrible blow to us all, but more so to me, with all I had on my mind.

'And so, and so,' I thought, as I began to recover, 'there is an end to my bright dreams of future happiness—*the* dream of all my dreams, to have father out here among us in our new home in the Silver West, and all the dark portions of the past forgotten. Heaven give me strength to bear it!'

I had spoken the last words aloud, for a voice at my elbow said—

'Amen! Poor boy! Amen!'

I turned, and—*there stood Townley.*

'You wonder to see me here,' he said, as he took my hand. 'Nay, but nobody should ever wonder at anything I do. I am erratic. I did not come over before, because I did not wish to influence your mind. You have been ill, but—I'm glad to see you weeping.'

I did really sob and cry then as if my very heart would burst and break.

I was well enough in a day or two to hear the rest of the news. Townley, who was very wise, had hesitated to tell me everything at once.

But if anything could be called joyful news now surely this was— mother and Flora were at Villa Mercedes, and would be here in a day or two. Townley had come on before, even at considerable personal risk, to break the news to us, and prepare us all. Mother and sister were waiting an escort, not got up specially for them certainly, but that would see to their safety. It consisted of a large party of officers and men who were passing on to the frontiers to repel, or try to repel, the Indian invasion.

We all went to meet mother and sister at the far-off cross roads. There was quite a large and very well-armed party of us, and we encamped for three days near an *estancia* to await their coming.

It was on the morning of the fourth day that one of the Gauchos reported an immense cloud of dust far away eastwards on the Mendoza road.

'They might be Indians,' he added.

'Perhaps,' said Moncrieff, 'but we will risk it.'

So camp was struck and off we rode, my brothers and I forming the vanguard, Moncrieff and Archie bringing up the rear. How my heart beat with emotion when the first horsemen of the advancing party became visible through the cloud of dust, and I saw they were soldiers!

On we rode now at the gallop.

Yes, mother was there, and sister, and they were well. Our meeting may be better imagined than described.

Both mother and Flora were established at the *estancia*, and so days and weeks flew by, and I was pleased to see them smile, though mother looked sad, so sad, yet so beautiful, just as she had ever looked to me.

Dugald was the first to recover anything approaching to a chastened happiness. He had his darling sister with him. He was never tired taking her out and showing her all the outs-and-ins and workings of our new home.

It appeared to give him the chiefest delight, however, to see her in the gondola.

I remember him saying one evening:

'Dear Flora! What a time it seems to look back since we parted in old Edina. But through all these long years I have worked for you and thought about you, and strange, I have always pictured you just as you are now, sitting under the gondola awnings, looking piquant and pretty, and on just such a lovely evening as this. But I didn't think you would be so big, Flora.'

'Dear stupid Dugald!' replied Flora, blushing slightly because Archie's eyes were bent on her in admiration, respectful but unconcealable. 'Did you think I would always remain a child?'

'You'll always be a child to me, Flo,' said Dugald.

But where had the Indians gone?

Had our bold troops beaten them back? or was the cloud still floating over the *estancia*, and floating only to burst?

CHAPTER XXIV
THE ATTACK ON THE ESTANCIA

Shortly after we had all settled down at the *estancia*, and things began to resume their wonted appearance, albeit we lived in a state of constant preparation to repel attack, an interview took place one day in Moncrieff's drawing-room, at which, though I was not present, I now know all that happened.

To one remark of Townley's my mother replied as follows:

'No, Mr. Townley, I think with you. I feel even more firmly, I believe, than you do on the subject, for you speak with, pardon me, some little doubt or hesitancy. Our boy's conscience must not be tampered with, not for all the estates in the world. Much though I love Coila, from which villainy may have banished us, let it remain for ever in the possession of the M'Rae sooner than even hint to Murdoch that an oath, however imposed, is not binding.'

'Yes,' said Townley, 'you are right, Mrs. M'Crimman; but the present possessor of Coila, the younger Le Roi, or M'Rae, as he was called before his father's death, has what he is pleased to call broader views on the subject than we have.'

'Mr. Townley, the M'Rae is welcome to retain his broad views, and we will stick to the simple faith of our forefathers. The M'Rae is of French education.'

'Yes, and at our meeting, though he behaved like a perfect gentleman— indeed, he is a gentleman—'

'True, in spite of the feud I cannot forget that the M'Raes are distant relatives of the M'Crimmans. He must, therefore, be a gentleman.'

'"My dear sir," he said to me, "I cannot conceive of such folly"— superstitious folly, he called it—"as that which your young friend Murdoch M'Crimman is guilty of. Let him come to me and say boldly that the ring found in the box and in the vault was on the finger of Duncan—villain he is, at all events—on the night he threatened to shoot him, and I will give up all claim to the estates of Coila; but till he does so, or until you bring me other proof, I must be excused for remaining where I am."'

'Then let him,' said my mother quietly.

'Nay, but,' said Townley, 'I do not *mean* to let him. It has become the one dream of my existence to see justice and right done to my dear old pupil Murdoch, and I think I begin to see land.'

'Yes?'

'I believe I do. I waited and watched untiringly. Good Gilmore, who still lives in Coila, watched for me too. I knew one thing was certain—namely, that the ex-poacher Duncan M'Rae would turn up again at the castle. He did. He went to beg money from the M'Rae. The M'Rae is a man of the world; he saw that this visit of Duncan's was but the beginning of a never-ending persecution. He refused Duncan's request point-blank. Then the man changed flank and breathed dark threatenings. The M'Rae, he hinted, had better not make him (Duncan) his enemy. He (M'Rae) was obliged to him for the house and position he occupied, but the same hand that *did* could *undo*. At this juncture the M'Rae had simply rung the bell, and the ex-poacher had to retire foiled, but threatening still. It was on that same day I confronted him and told him all I knew. Then I showed him the spurious ring, which, as I placed it on my finger, even he could not tell from the original. Even this did not overawe him, but when I ventured a guess that this very ring had belonged to a dead man, and pretended I knew more than I did, he turned pale. He was silent for a time—thinking, I suppose. Then he put a question which staggered me with its very coolness, and, clergyman though I am, I felt inclined at that moment to throttle the man where he stood. Would we pay him handsomely for turning king's evidence on himself and confessing the whole was a conspiracy, and would we save him from the legal penalty of the confessed crime?

'I assure you, Mrs. M'Crimman, that till then I had leaned towards the belief that, scoundrel though this Duncan be, some little spark of humanity remained in his nature, and that he might be inclined to do justice for justice's sake. I dare say he read my answer in my eyes, and he judged too that for the time being I was powerless to act. Could he have killed me then, I know he would have done so. Once more he was silent for a time. He did not dare to repeat his first question, but he put another, "Have you any charge to make against me about *anything*?" He placed a terribly-meaning emphasis on that word "anything." I looked at him. I was wondering whether he really had had anything to do with the death of old Mawsie, and if the ring of which I had the facsimile on my finger had in reality belonged to a murdered man. Seeing me hesitate, he played a bold card; it was, I suppose, suggested to him by the appearance at that moment of the village policeman walking calmly past the window of the little inn where we sat. He knocked, and beckoned to him, while I sat wondering and thinking that verily the man before me was cleverer by far than I. On the entrance of the policeman—"This gentleman, policeman," he said, quietly and slowly, "makes or insinuates charges against me in private which now in your presence I dare him to repeat." Then turning to me—"The ball is with you," he said. And what could I reply? Nothing. I do believe that at that very moment even the worthy village policeman noticed and pitied my position, for he turned to Duncan, and, nodding, made this remark in Gaelic: "I know Mr. Townley as a gentleman, and I know you, Duncan M'Rae, to be something very different. If Mr. Townley makes no charge against you it is no doubt because he is not prepared with proofs. But, Duncan, boy, if you like to remain in the glen for a few days, I'm not sure there isn't a charge or two I could rub up against you myself."

'I left the room with the policeman. Now I knew that, although foiled, Duncan did not consider himself beaten. I had him watched therefore, and followed by a detective. I wanted to find out his next move. It was precisely what I thought it would be. He had heard of our poor chief M'Crimman's death, remember. Well, a day or two after our conversation in the little inn at Coila, Duncan presented himself at the M'Rae's advocate's office and so pleaded his case—so begged and partially hinted at disclosures and confessions—that this solicitor, not possessed of the extraordinary pride and independence of the M'Rae—'

'A pride and independence, Mr. Townley,' said my aunt, 'which the M'Raes take from their relatedness to our family.'

'That is true,' said my mother.

'Well, I was going to say,' continued Townley, 'that Duncan so far overcame the advocate that this gentleman thought it would be for his client's interest to accede in part to his demands, or rather to one of them— viz., to pay him a sum of money to leave the country for ever. But this money was not to be paid until he had taken his passage and was about to sail for some—any—country, not nearer than the United States of America, Mr. Moir's—the advocate's—clerk was to see him on board ship, and see him sail.'

'And did he sail?' said my aunt, as Townley paused and looked at her.

'Yes, in a passenger ship, for Buenos Ayres.'

'I see it all now,' said my aunt. 'He thinks that no charge can be made against him there for conspiracy or crime committed at home.'

'Yes, and he thinks still further: he thinks that he will be more successful with dear Murdoch than he was with either the M'Rae or myself.'

There was a few minutes' pause, my aunt being the first to break the silence.

'What a depth of well-schemed villainy!' was the remark she made.

Moncrieff had listened to all the conversation without once putting in a word. Now all he said was—

'Dinna forget, Miss M'Crimman, the words o' the immortal Bobbie Burns:

> "The best laid schemes o' mice and men
> Gang aft agley,
> And leave us naught but grief and pain
> For promised joy."'

To the fear and fever consequent upon the depredations committed by the Indians there succeeded a calmness and lull which the canny Moncrieff thought almost unnatural, considering all that had gone before. He took pains to find out whether, as had been currently reported, our Argentine troops had been victorious all along the frontier line. He found that the report, like many others, had been grossly exaggerated. If a foe retires, a foe is beaten by the army which *sees* that foe retire. This seems too often to be the logic of the war-path. In the present instance, however, the Indians belonged to races that lived a nomad life. They were constantly advancing and retreating. When they chose to advance in this particular year there was not a sufficient number of cavalry to oppose them, nor were the soldiers well mounted. The savages knew precisely on what part of the stage to enter, and they did not think it incumbent on them to previously warn our Argentine troops. Indeed, they, like sensible savages, rather avoided a conflict than courted one. It was not conflict but cattle they were after principally; then if at any time strategy directed retreat, why, they simply turned their horses' heads to the desert, the pampas, or mountain wilds, and the troops for a time had seen the last of them.

I think Moncrieff would have made a capital general, for fancied security never sent him to sleep. What had happened once might happen again, he thought, and his *estancias* were big prizes for Indians to try for, especially as there was plenty to gain by success, and little to lose by defeat.

I have said that our Coila Villa was some distance from the fortified Moncrieff houses. It was now connected with the general rampart and ditches. It was part and parcel of the whole system of fortification; so my brothers and I might rest assured it would be defended, if ever there was any occasion.

'It seems hard,' said Townley to Moncrieff one day, 'that you should be put to so much trouble and expense. Why does not the Government protect its settlers?'

'The Government will in course of time,' replied Moncrieff. 'At present, as we lie pretty low down in the western map, we are looked upon as rich pioneers, and left to protect ourselves.'

They were riding then round the *estancias*, visiting outlying *puestos*.

'You have your rockets and red-lights for night signals, and your flags for day use?' Moncrieff was saying to each *puestero* or shepherd.

'We have,' was the invariable reply.

'Well, if the Indians are sighted, signal at once, pointing the fan in their direction, then proceed to drive the flocks towards the *estancias*. There,' continued Moncrieff, 'there is plenty of corraling room, and we can concentrate a fire that will, I believe, effectually hold back these raiding thieves.'

One day there came a report that a fort had been carried by a cloud of Indians.

This was in the forenoon. Towards evening some Gauchos came in from a distant *estancia*. They brought the old ugly story of conflagration and murder, to which Moncrieff and his Welsh partner had long since become used.

But now the cloud was about to burst over our *estancia*. We all ate our meals together at the present awful crisis, just, I think, to be company to each other, and to talk and keep up each other's heart.

But to-day Moncrieff had ordered an early dinner, and this was ominous. Hardly any one spoke much during the meal. A heaviness was on every heart, and if any one of us made an effort to smile and look cheerful, others saw that this was only assumed, and scarcely responded.

Perhaps old Jenny spoke more than all of us put together. And her remarks at times made us laugh, gloomy though the situation was.

'They reeving Philistines are coming again, are they? Well, laddie, if the worst should happen I'll just treat them to a drap parridge.'

'What, mither?'

'A drap parridge, laddie. It was boiled maize I poured ower the shoulders o' them in the caravan. But oatmeal is better, weel scalded. Na, na, naething beats a drap parridge. Bombazo,' she said presently,'you've been unco quiet and douce for days back, I hope you'll no show the white feather this time and bury yoursel' in the moold like a rabbit.'

Poor Bombazo winced, and really, judging from his appearance, he had been ill at ease for weeks back. There was no singing now, and the guitar lay unheeded in its case.

'Do not fear for me, lady. I am burning already to see the foe.'

'Weel, Bombazo man, ye dinna look vera warlike. You're unco white about the gills already, but wae worth the rigging o' you if ye dinna fecht. My arm is strong to wield the auld ginghamrella yet.'

'Hush, mither, hush!' said Moncrieff.

Immediately after dinner Moncrieff beckoned to Townley, and the two left the room and the house together.

'You think the Indians will come to-night?' said Townley, after a time.

'I know they will, and in force too.'

'Well, I feel like an idler. You, General Moncrieff, have not appointed me any station.'

Moncrieff smiled.

'I am now going to do so,' he said, 'and it is probably the most important position and trust on the *estancia*.'

They walked up as far as the great canal while they conversed.

Arrived there, Moncrieff pointed to what looked like a bundle of brushwood.

'You see those branches?'

'Yes.'

'And you see that wooden lock or huge doorway?'

'I do.'

'Well, my friend, the brushwood conceals a sentry-box. It overlooks the whole *estancia*. It conceals something else, a small barrel of gunpowder, which you are to hang to the hook yonder on the wooden lock, and explode the moment you have the signal.'

'And the signal will be?'

'A huge rocket sent up from either my *estancia* house or Coila Villa. There may be several, but you must act when you see the first. There is fuse enough to the bomb to give you time to escape, and the bomb is big enough to burst the lock and flood the whole ditch system in and around the *estancia*. You are to run as soon as you fire. Further on you will find another brushwood place of concealment. Hide there. Heaven forbid I should endanger a hair of your head! Now you know your station!'

'I do,' said Townley, 'and thankful I am to think I can be of service in this great emergency.'

Before dark all the most valuable portion of our stock was safely corraled, and silence, broken only by the occasional lowing of the cattle or the usual night sounds of farm life, reigned around and over the *estancia*.

Later on Townley stole quietly out, and betook himself to his station.

Still later on Yambo rode in and right up to the verandah of our chief sitting-room. The horse he bestrode was drenched in sweat. He had seen Indians in force; they were even now advancing. He had ridden for his life.

The order 'Every man to his quarters!' was now given.

The night which was to be so terrible and so memorable in the annals of Moncrieff's *estancia* had begun. It was very still, and at present very dark. But by and by the moon would rise.

'A rocket, sir!' we heard Archie shout from his post as sentinel; 'a rocket from the south-western *puesto*.'

We waited, listening, starting almost at every sound. At length in the distance we could plainly hear the sound of horses' hoofs on the road, and before many minutes the first *puestero* rode to the gate and was admitted. The men from the other *puestos* were not far behind; and, all being safe inside, the gates were fastened and fortified by triple bars of wood.

All along the ditches, and out for many yards, was spread such a thorny spikework of pointed wood as to defy the approach of the cleverest Indian for hours at least.

While we waited I found time to run round to the drawing-room. There was no sign of fear on any face there, with the exception perhaps of that of poor Irish Aileen. And I could well believe her when she told me it was not for herself she cared, but for her 'winsome man.'

I was talking to them as cheerfully as I could, when I heard the sound of a rifle, and, waving them good-bye, I rushed off to my station.

Slowly the moon rose, and before many minutes the whole *estancia* was flooded with its light. And how we thanked Heaven for that light only those who have been situated as we were now can fully understand.

Up it sailed between the dark whispering poplars. Never had these trees seemed to me more stately, more noble. Towering up into the starry sky, they seemed like sentinels set to guard and defend us, while their taper fingers, piercing heavenwards, carried our thoughts to One who never deserts those who call on Him in faith in their hour of need.

The moon rose higher and higher, and its light—for it was a full moon—got still more silvery as it mounted towards its zenith. But as yet there was no sign that a foe as remorseless and implacable as the tiger of the jungle was abroad on the plains.

A huge fire had been erected behind the mansion, and about ten o'clock the female servants came round our lines with food, and huge bowls of steaming *maté*.

Almost immediately after we were at our quarters again.

I was stationed near our own villa. Leaning over a parapet, I could not help, as I gazed around me, being struck with the exceeding beauty of the night. Not far off the lake shone in the moon's rays like a silver mirror, but over the distant hills and among the trees and hedges was spread a thin blue gauzy mist that toned and softened the whole landscape.

As I gazed, and was falling into a reverie, a puff of white smoke and a flash not fifty yards away, and the ping of a bullet close to my ear, warned me that the attack had commenced.

There had been no living thing visible just before then, but the field on one side of our villa was now one moving mass of armed Indians, rushing on towards the ditch and breastwork.

At the same moment all along our lines ran the rattle of rifle-firing. That savage crowd, kept at bay by the spikework, made a target for our men that could hardly be missed. The war-cry, which they had expected to change in less than a minute to the savage shout of victory, was mingled now with groans and yells of anger and pain.

But this, after all, was not the main attack. From a red signal-light far along the lines I soon discovered that Moncrieff was concentrating his strength there, and I hastened in that direction with five of my best men. The Indians were under the charge of a *cacique* on horseback, whose shrill voice sounded high over the din of battle and shrieks of the wounded. He literally hurled his men like seas against the gates and ramparts here.

But all in vain. Our fellows stood; and the *cacique* at length withdrew his men, firing a volley or two as they disappeared behind the hedges.

There was comparative silence for a space now. It was soon broken, however, by the thunder of Indian cavalry. The savages were going to change their tactics.

CHAPTER XXV
THE LAST ASSAULT

Never before, perhaps, in all the annals of Indian warfare had a more determined attack been made upon a settler's *estancia*. The *cacique* or *caciques* who led the enemy seemed determined to purchase victory at any cost or hazard. Nor did the principal *cacique* hesitate to expose himself to danger. During the whole of the first onset he moved about on horseback close in the rear of his men, and appeared to bear a charmed life. The bullets must have been whizzing past him as thick as flies. Moncrieff himself tried more than once to bring him down, but all in vain.

During the final assault he was equally conspicuous; he was here, there, and everywhere, and his voice and appearance, even for a moment, among them never failed to cause his men to redouble their efforts.

It was not, however, until far on into the night that this last and awful charge was made.

The savage foe advanced with a wild shout all along the line of rampart that connected the Moncrieff main *estancia* with our villa. This was really our weakest part.

The assault was made on horseback. We heard them coming thundering on some time before we saw them and could fire. They seemed mad, furious; their tall feather-bedecked spears were waved high in air; they sat like huge baboons on their high saddles, and their very horses had been imbued with the recklessness of their riders, and came on bounding and flying over our frail field of spikes. It was to be all spear work till they came to close quarters; then they would use their deadly knives.

Hardly had the first sound of the horses' hoofs reached our ears ere one, two, three rockets left Coila Villa; and scarcely had they exploded in the air and cast their golden showers of sparks abroad, before the roar of an explosion was heard high up on the braeland that shook the houses to their very foundations—and then—there is the awful rush of foaming, seething water.

Nothing could withstand that unexpected flood; men and horses were floated and washed away, struggling and helpless, before it.

Just at the time when the last assault was nearly at its grim close I felt my arm pulled, and looking quickly round found Yambo at my side. He still clutched me by the arm, but he was waving his blood-stained sword in the direction of Moncrieff's house, and I could see by the motions of his mouth and face he wished me to come with him.

Something had occurred, something dreadful surely, and despite the excitement of battle a momentary cold wave of fear seemed to rush over my frame.

Sandie Donaldson was near me. This bold big fellow had been everywhere conspicuous to-night for his bravery. He had fought all through with extraordinary intrepidity.

Wherever I had glanced that night I had seen Sandie, the moon shining down on the white shirt and trousers he wore, and which made him altogether so conspicuous a figure, as he took aim with rifle or revolver, or dashed into a crowd of spear-armed Indians, his claymore hardly visible, so swiftly was it moved to and fro. I grasped his shoulder, pointed in the direction indicated by Yambo, and on we flew.

As soon as we had rounded the wing of an outbuilding and reached Moncrieff's terraced lawn, the din of the fight we had just left became more indistinct, but we now heard sounds that, while they thrilled us with terror and anger, made us rush on across the grass with the speed of the panther.

They were the voices of shrieking women, the crashing of glass and furniture, and the savage and exultant yell of the Indians.

Looking back now to this episode of the night, I can hardly realize that so many terrible events could have occurred in so brief a time, for, from the moment we charged up across the lawn not six minutes could have elapsed ere all was over. It is like a dream, but a dream every turn of which has been burned into my memory, to remain while life shall last. Yonder is a tall *cacique* hurrying out into the bright moonlight from under the verandah. He bears in his arms the inanimate form of my dear sister Flora. Is it really *I* myself who rush up to meet him? Have *I* fired that shot that causes the savage to reel and fall? Is it I who lift poor Flora and lay her in the shade of a mimosa-tree? It must be I, yet every action seems governed by instinct; I am for the time being a strange psychological study. It is as if my soul had left the body, but still commanded it, standing aside, ruling every motion, directing every blow from first to last, and being implicitly obeyed by the other *ego*, the *ego*-incorporate. There is a crowd, nay, a cloud even it seems, around me; but see, I have cut my way through them at last: they have fallen before me, fallen at my side—fallen or fled. I step over bodies, I enter the room, I stumble over other bodies. Now a light is struck and a lamp is lit, and standing beside the table, calm, but very pale, I see my aunt dimly through the smoke. My mother is near her—my own brave mother. Both have revolvers in their hands; and I know now why bodies are stretched on the floor. One glance shows me Aileen, lying like a dead thing in a chair, and beside her, smoothing her brow, chafing her hands, Moncrieff's marvellous mother.

But in this life the humorous is ever mixed up with the tragic or sad, for lo! as I hurry away to join the fight that is still going on near the verandah I almost stumble across something else. Not a body this time—not quite— only Bombazo's ankles sticking out from under the sofa. I could swear to those striped silk socks anywhere, and the boots are the boots of Bombazo. I administer a kick to those shins, and they speedily disappear. I am out on the moonlit lawn now, and what do I see? First, good brave Yambo, down on one knee, being borne backwards, fierce hands at his throat, a short knife at his chest. The would-be assassin falls; Yambo rises intact, and together we rush on further down to where, on a terrace, Donaldson has just been overpowered. But see, a new combatant has come upon the scene; several revolver shots are fired in quick succession. A tall dark figure in semi-clerical garb is cutting right and left with a good broadsword. And now—why, now it is all over, and Townley stands beside us panting.

Well might he pant—he had done brave work. But he had come all too late to save Sandie. He lies there quietly enough on the grass. His shirt is stained with blood, and it is his own blood this time.

Townley bends over and quietly feels his arm. No pulse there. Then he breathes a half audible prayer and reverently closes the eyes.

I am hurrying back now to the room with Flora.

'All is safe, mother, now. Flora is safe. See, she is smiling: she knows us all. Oh, Heaven be praised, she is safe!'

We leave Townley there, and hurry back to the ramparts.

The stillness alone would have told us that the fight was finished and the victory won.

A few minutes after this, standing high up on the rampart there, Moncrieff is mustering his people. One name after another is called. Alas! there are many who do not answer, many who will never answer more, for our victory has been dearly bought.

Four of our Scottish settlers were found dead in the trench; over a dozen Gauchos had been killed. Moncrieff and his partner were both wounded, though neither severely. Archie and Dugald were also badly cut, and answered but faintly and feebly to the roll-call. Sandie we know is dead, and Bombazo is—under the sofa. So I thought; but listen.

'Captain Rodrigo de Bombazo!'

'Here, general, here,' says a bold voice close behind me, and Bombazo himself presses further to the front.

I can hardly believe my eyes and ears. Could those have been Bombazo's boots? Had I really kicked the shins of Bombazo? Surely the events of the night had turned my brain. Bombazo's boots indeed! Bombazo skulk and hide beneath a sofa! Impossible. Look at him now. His hair is dishevelled; there is blood on his brow. He is dressed only in shirt and trousers, and these are marked with blood; so is his right arm, which is bared over the elbow, and the sword he carries in his hand. Bold Bombazo! How I have wronged him! But the silk striped socks? No; I cannot get over that.

Barely a month before the events just narrated took place at the *estancias* of Moncrieff there landed from a sailing ship at the port of Buenos Ayres a man whose age might have been represented by any number of years 'twixt thirty and forty. There were grey hairs on his temples, but these count for nothing in a man whose life has been a struggle with Fortune and Fate. The individual in question, whom his shipmates called Dalston, was tall and tough and wiry. He had shown what he was and what he could do in less than a week from the time of his joining. At first he had been a passenger, and had lived away aft somewhere, no one could tell exactly where, for he did not dine in the saloon with the other passengers, and he looked above messing with the stewards. As the mate and he were much together it was supposed that Dalston made use of the first officer's cabin. The ship had encountered dirty weather from the very outset; head winds and choppy seas all the way down Channel, so that she was still 'kicking about off the coast'—this is how the seamen phrased it—when she ought to have been crossing the Bay or stretching away out into the broad Atlantic. She fared worse by far when she reached the Bay, having met with a gale of wind that blew most of her cloth to ribbons, carried away her bowsprit, and made hurdles of her bulwarks both forward and amidships. Worse than all, two men were blown from aloft while trying to reef a sail during a squall of more than hurricane violence. I say blown from aloft, and I say so advisedly, for the squall came on after they had gone up, a squall that even the men on deck could not stand against, a squall that levelled the very waves, and made the sea away to leeward—no one could see to windward—look like boiling milk.

The storm began to go down immediately after the squall, and next day the weather was fine enough to make sail, and mend sail. But the ship was short-handed, for the skipper had made no provision against loss by accident. He was glad then when the mate informed him that the 'gentleman' Dalston was as good as any two men on board.

'Send him to me,' said the skipper.

'Good morning. Ahem, I hear, sir, you would be willing to assist in the working of the ship. May I ask on what terms?'

'Certainly,' said Dalston. 'I'm going out to the Argentine, to buy a bit of land; well, naturally, money is some object to me. You see?'

'I understand.'

'Well, my terms are the return of my passage money and civility.'

'Agreed; but why do you mention civility?'

'Because I've heard you using rather rough language to your men. Now, if you forgot yourself so far as to call me a bad name I'd — —'

He paused, and there was a look in his eyes the captain hardly relished.

'Well! What would you do?'

'Why, I'd—retire to my cabin.'

'All right then, I think we understand each other.'

So Dalston was installed, and now dined forward. He became a favourite with his messmates. No one could tell a more thrilling and adventuresome yarn than Dalston, no one could sing a better song than himself or join more heartily in the chorus when another sang, and no one could work more cheerily on deck, or fly more quickly to tack a sheet.

Smyth had been the big man in the forecastle before Dalston's day. But Smyth was eclipsed now, and I dare say did not like his rival. One day, near the quarter-deck, Smyth called Dalston an ugly name. Dalston's answer was a blow which sent the fellow reeling to leeward, where he lay stunned.

'Have you killed him, Dalston?' said the captain.

'Not quite, sir; but I could have.'

'Well, Dalston, you are working for two men now; don't let us lose another hand, else you'll have to work for three.'

Dalston laughed.

Smyth gathered himself up and slunk away, but his look was one Dalston would have cause to remember.

This good ship—Sevenoaks she was called, after the captain's wife's birthplace—had a long and a rough passage all along. The owners were Dutchmen, so it did not matter a very great deal. There was plenty of time, and the ship was worked on the cheap. Perhaps the wonder is she kept afloat at all, for at one period of the voyage she leaked so badly that the crew had to pump three hours out of every watch. Then she crossed a bank on the South American coast, and the men said she had sucked in a bit of seaweed, for she did not leak much after this.

The longest voyage has an end, however, and when the Sevenoaks arrived at Buenos Ayres, Dalston bade his messmates adieu, had his passage money duly returned, and went on shore, happy because he had many more golden sovereigns to rattle than he had expected.

Dalston went to a good hotel, found out all about the trains, and next day set out, in company with a waiter who had volunteered to be his escort, to purchase a proper outfit—only light clothes, a rifle, a good revolver, and a knife or two to wear in his belt, for he was going west to a rough country.

In the evening, after the waiter and he had dined well at another hotel:

'You go home now,' said Dalston; 'I'm going round to have a look at the town,'

'Take care of yourself,' the waiter said.

'No fear of me,' was the laughing reply.

But that very night he was borne back to his inn, cut, bruised, and faint.

And robbed of all his gold.

'Who has done this?' said the waiter, aghast at his friend's appearance.

'Smyth!' That was all the reply.

Dalston lay for weeks between life and death. Then he came round almost at once, and soon started away on his journey. The waiter—good-natured fellow—had lent him money to carry him to Mendoza.

But Dalston's adventures were not over yet.

He arrived at Villa Mercedes well and hopeful, and was lucky enough to secure a passage in the diligence about to start under mounted escort to Mendoza. After a jolting ride of days, the like of which he had never been used to in the old country, the ancient-looking coach had completed three-quarters of the journey, and the rest of the road being considered safe the escort was allowed to go on its way to the frontier.

They had not departed two hours, however, before the travellers were attacked, the driver speared, and the horses captured. The only passenger who made the slightest resistance was Dalston. He was speedily overpowered, and would have been killed on the spot had not the *cacique* of the party whom Dalston had wounded interfered and spared his life.

Spared his life! But for what? He did not know. Some of the passengers were permitted to go free, the rest were killed. He alone was mounted on horseback, his legs tied with thongs and his horse led by an Indian.

All that night and all next day his captors journeyed on, taking, as far as Dalston could judge, a south-west course. His sufferings were extreme. His legs were swollen, cut, and bleeding; his naked shoulders—for they had stripped him almost naked—burned and blistered with the sun; and although his tongue was parched and his head drooping wearily on his breast, no one offered him a mouthful of water.

He begged them to kill him. Perhaps the *cacique*, who was almost a white man, understood his meaning, for he grinned in derision and pointed to his own bullet-wounded arm. The *cacique* knew well there were sufferings possible compared to which death itself would be as pleasure.

When the Indians at last went into camp—which they did but for a night—he was released, but guarded; a hunk of raw guanaco meat was thrown to him, which he tried to suck for the juices it contained.

Next day they went on and on again, over a wild pampa land now, with here and there a bush or tussock of grass or thistles, and here and there a giant ombu-tree. His ankles were more painful than ever, his shoulders were raw, the horse he rode was often prodded with a spear, and he too was wounded at the same time. Once or twice the *cacique*, maddened by the pain of his wound, rushed at Dalston with uplifted knife, and the wretched prisoner begged that the blow might fall.

Towards evening they reached a kind of hill and forest land, where the flowering cacti rose high above the tallest spear. Then they came to a ruin. Indians here were in full force, horses dashed to and fro, and it was evident from the bustle and stir that they were on the war-path, and soon either to attack or be attacked.

The prisoner was now roughly unhorsed and cruelly lashed to a tree, and left unheeded by all. For a moment or two he felt grateful for the shade, but his position after a time became painful in the extreme. At night-fall all the Indians left, and soon after the sufferings of the poor wretch grew more dreadful than pen can describe. He was being slowly eaten alive by myriads of insects that crept and crawled or flew; horrid spiders with hairy legs and of enormous size ran over his neck and naked chest, loathsome centipedes wriggled over his shoulders and face and bit him, and ants covered him black from head to feet. Towards dusk a great jaguar went prowling past, looked at him with green fierce eyes, snarled low, and went on. Vultures alighted near him, but they too passed by; they could wait. Then it was night, and many of the insect pests grew luminous. They flitted and danced before his eyes till tortured nature could bear no more, and insensibility ended his sufferings for a time.

The Indians must have thought that, although their attack on our *estancia* had failed, we were too weak or too frightened to pursue them. They did not know Moncrieff. Wounded though he was, he had issued forth from behind the ramparts with thirty well-armed and splendidly-mounted men. They followed the enemy up for seven long hours, and succeeded in teaching them such a lesson that they have never been seen in that district since.

Towards noon we were riding homewards, tired and weary enough now, when Donald suggested our visiting the old Jesuit ruin, and so we turned our horses' heads in that direction.

Donald had ridden on before, and as I drew near I heard him cry, 'Oh, Moncrieff, come quickly! Here is some poor fellow lashed to the ombu-tree!'

CHAPTER XXV
FAREWELL TO THE SILVER WEST

We cut the man's cords of thongs, we spread rugs on the grass and laid him gently down, then bathed his poor body with wine, and poured a little down his throat.

In about half an hour the wretched being we had thought dead slowly raised himself on his elbow and gazed at *me* as well as his swollen eyes would permit him. His lips moved as if to speak, but no intelligible sound escaped them. The recollection dawned on my mind all at once, and in that sadly-distorted face I discovered traces of the man who had wrought us so much sorrow and evil.

I took his hand in mine.

'Am I right?' I said. 'Are you Duncan M'Rae?'

He nodded drowsily, closed his eyes again, and lay back.

We cut branches from the ombu-tree, tied them together with the thongs that had bound the victim's limbs, and so made a litter. On this we placed rugs and laid the man; and between two mules he was borne by the Gauchos slowly homewards to the *estancias*. Poor wretch! he had expected to come here all but a conqueror, and in a position to dictate his own terms—he arrived a dying man.

Our *estancia* for many weeks was now turned almost into a hospital, for even those Indians who had crept wounded into the bush, preferring to die at the sides of hedges to falling into our hands, we had brought in and treated with kindness, and many recovered.

All the dead we could find we buried in the humble little graveyard on the braeside. We buried them without respect of nationality, only a few feet of clay separating the white man's grave from that of his Indian foe.

'It matters little,' said Moncrieff. 'where one rests,

"For still and peaceful is the grave,
Where, life's vain tumults past,
The appointed house, by Heaven's decree,
Receives us all at last."'

Both Dugald and Archie made excellent patients, and Flora and Aileen the best of nurses. But *the* nurse over even these was old Jenny. She was hospital superintendent, and saw to all the arrangements, even making the poultices and spreading the salves and plasters with her own hands.

'My mither's a marrvel at herrbs!' said Moncrieff over and over again, when he saw the old lady busy at work.

There was one patient, and only one, whom old Jenny did not nurse. This was Duncan himself. For him Townley did all his skill could suggest, and was seldom two consecutive hours away from the room where he lay.

In spite of all this it was evident that the ex-poacher was sinking fast.

Then came a day when Moncrieff, Archie, and myself were called into the dying man's apartment, and heard him make the fullest confession of all his villainy, and beg for our forgiveness with the tears roiling down his wan, worn face.

Yes, we forgave him willingly.

May Heaven forgive him too!

At the time of his confession he was strong enough to read over and sign the document that Townley placed before him. He told Townley too the addresses of the men who had assisted him in the old vault at the ruined kirk in Coila.

And Duncan had seemed brighter and calmer for several days after this. But he told us he had no desire to live now.

Then, one morning the change came, and so he sank and died.

It was several months before we could make up our minds to leave 'Our Home in the Silver West.' Indeed, there was considerable preparation to be made for the long homeward voyage that was before us; besides, Townley had no inclination to hurry matters now that he felt sure of victory.

Victory was not even yet a certainty, however. The estate of Coila was well worth fighting for. Was there not the possibility, the bare possibility, that the solicitors or advocates of Le Roi, or the M'Rae, who now held the castle and glen, might find some fatal flaw in the evidence which Townley had spent so much time and care in working out and collecting?

It was not at all probable. In fact, despite the blood-feud, that ancient family folly, I believed that M'Rae would act the part of a gentleman.

'If,' said Townley to me one day, as we walked for almost the last time in the beautiful gardens around Moncrieff's mansion-house, 'we have anything to fear, I believe it is from the legal advisers of the present "occupier'"—Townley would not say 'owner'—'of the estate. These men, you know, Murdoch, can hardly expect to be *our* advocates. They are well aware that if they lose hold of Coila now the title-deeds thereof will never again rest in the fireproof safes of their offices.'

'I am afraid,' I said, 'you have but a poor opinion of Edinburgh advocates.'

'Not so, Murdoch, not so. But,' he added, meaningly 'I have lived longer in life than you, and I have but a poor opinion of human nature.'

'I suppose,' I said, 'that the M'Rae will know nothing of what is coming till our arrival on Scottish shores!'

'On the contrary,' answered Townley; 'although it may really seem like playing into our opponent's hands, I have written a friendly letter to the M'Rae, and have told him to be prepared; that I have irrefragable evidence— mind, I do not particularize—that you, Murdoch M'Crimman, are the true and only proprietor of the estates of Coila. I want him to see and feel that I am treating him as the man of honour I believe him to be, and that the only thing we really desire is justice to all concerned.'

I smiled, and could not help saying, 'Townley, my best of friends, what an excellent advocate you would have made!'

Townley smiled in turn.

'Say, rather,' he replied, 'what an excellent detective I should have made! But, after all, Murdoch, it may turn out that there is a spice of selfishness in all I am doing.'

'I do not believe a word of it, Townley.'

Townley only laughed, and looked mysterious.

'Hold on a little,' he said; 'don't be too quick to express your judgment.'

'I will wait, then,' I answered; 'but really I cannot altogether understand you.'

Perhaps nothing shows true physical courage better than the power to say 'Farewell' apparently unmoved. It is a kind of courage, however, that is very rare indeed, and all sorts of stratagems have been adopted to soften the grief of parting. I am not sure that I myself was not guilty of adopting one of these on the morning we left that pleasant home by the lake.

'I'm not going to say "farewell" at all,' I insisted, as I shook hands with Irish Aileen and poor old Jenny, Moncrieff's 'marvellous mither.' 'I'm coming out again to see you all as soon as ever I can get settled. Do you think I could leave this beautiful country entirely, without spending at least a few more years in it? Not I! And even if I do succeed in getting old Coila back once more—even that, mind, is uncertain—I sha'n't quite give up Coila New. So *au revoir*, Moncrieff; *au revoir!*'

Then, turning to Jenny, '*Au revoir*, Jenny,' I said.

'Guid-bye, laddie, and God be wi' ye. I canna speak French. I've tried a word or twa mair than once, and nearly knocked my jaws out o' the joint; so I'll just say "Guid-bye." Lang, lang ere you can come back to Coila New puir old Jenny's bones will be in the mools.'

I felt a big lump in my throat just then, and was positively grateful when Bombazo strutted up dressed in full uniform.

'*A dios*', he said; 'my friend, *a dios*. And now you have but to say the word, and if you have the least fear of being molested by Indians, my trusty sword is at your service, and I will gladly escort you as far as Villa Mercedes.'

It is needless to say that I declined this truly heroic offer.

Our party—the departing one—consisted of mother, aunt, Townley, Archie, and myself. My sister and my brothers came many miles on the road with us; then we bade them good-bye, and I felt glad when that was over.

But Moncrieff's convoy was a truly Scottish one. He and his good men never thought of turning back till they had seen us safely on board the train, and rapidly being whirled away southwards.

As long as I could see this honest settler he was waving his broad bonnet in the air, and—I felt sure of this—commending us all to a kind Providence.

The vessel in which we took passage was a steamer that bore us straight to the Clyde. Our voyage was a splendid one; in fact, I believe we were all just a little sorry when it was finished.

Landing there in the Broomielaw on a cold forenoon in early spring would have possessed but little of interest for any of us—so full were our minds with the meeting that was before us, the meeting of M'Crimman and M'Rae—only we received a welcome that, being all so unexpected, caused tears of joy to spring to my eyes. For hardly was the gangway thrust on board from the quay ere more than twenty sturdy Highlanders, who somehow had got possession of it, came rushing and shouting on board. I knew every face at once, though some were changed—with illness, years, or sorrow.

Perhaps few such scenes had ever before been witnessed on the Broomielaw, for those men were arrayed in the full Scottish costume and wore the M'Crimman tartan, and their shouts of joy might have been heard a good half-mile off, despite the noises of the great city.

How they had heard of our coming it never occurred to me to inquire. Suffice it to say that here they were, and I leave the reader to guess the kind of welcome they gave us.

No, nothing would satisfy them short of escorting us to our hotel.

Our carriages, therefore, to please these kindly souls from Coila, were obliged to proceed but slowly, for five pipers marched in front, playing the bold old air of 'The March of the Cameron Men,' while the rest, with drawn claymores, brought up the rear.

On the very next day Townley, Archie, and I received a message from M'Rae himself, announcing that he would gladly meet us at the Royal Hotel in Edinburgh. We were to bring no advocate with us, the letter advised; if any dispute arose, then, and not till then, would be the time to call in the aid of the law.

I confess that I entered M'Rae's room with a beating heart. How would he receive us?

We found him quietly smoking a cigar and gazing out of the window.

But he turned with a kindly smile towards us as soon as we entered, and the next minute we were all seated round the table, and business—*the* business—was entered into.

M'Rae listened without a word. He never even moved a muscle while Townley told all his long story, or rather read it from paper after paper, which he took from his bag. The last of these papers was Duncan's own confession, with Archie's signature and mine as witnesses alongside Moncrieff's.

He opened his lips at last.

'This is your signature, and you duly attest all this?'

He put the question first to Archie and then to me.

Receiving a reply in the affirmative, it was but natural that I should look for some show of emotion in M'Rae's face. I looked in vain. I have never seen more consummate coolness before nor since. Indeed, it was a coolness that alarmed me.

And when he rose from the table after a few minutes of apparently engrossing thought, and walked directly towards a casket that stood on the writing-table, I thought that after all our cause was lost.

In that casket, I felt sure, lay some strange document that should utterly undo all Townley's work of years.

M'Rae is now at the table. He opens the casket, and for a moment looks critically at its contents.

I can hear my heart beating. I'm sure I look pale with anxiety.

Now M'Rae puts his hand inside and quietly takes out—a fresh cigar.

Then, humming a tune the while, he brings the casket towards Townley, and bids him help himself.

Townley does as he is told, but at the same time bursts into a hearty laugh.

'Mr. M'Rae,' he says, 'you are the coolest man that ever I met. I do believe that if you were taken out to be shot—'

'Stay,' said M'Rae, 'I *was* once. I was tried for a traitor—tried for a crime in France called "Treason," that I was as guiltless of as an unborn babe—and condemned.'

'And what did you do?'

'Some one on the ground handed me a cigar, and—I lit it.

'Nay, my dear friends, I have lost my case here. Indeed, I never, it would seem, had one.

'M'Crimman,' he continued, shaking me by the hand, 'Coila is yours.'

'Strathtoul,' I answered, 'is our blood feud at an end?'

'It is,' was the answer; and once again hand met hand across the table.

Need I tell of the home-coming of the M'Crimmans of Coila? Of the clansmen who met us in the glen and marched along with us? Of the cheering strains of music that re-echoed from every rock? Of the flags that fluttered over and around our Castle Coila? Of the bonfires that blazed that night on every hill, and cast their lurid light across the darkling lake? Or of the tears my mother shed when, looking round the tartan drawing-room, the cosiest in all the castle, she thought of father, dead and gone? No, for some things are better left to the reader's imagination.

I throw down my pen with a sigh of relief.

I think I have finished my story; my noble deerhound thinks so too. He gets slowly up from the hearthrug, conies towards me, and places his honest head on my arm, but his eyes are fixed on mine.

It is not patting that he wants, nor petting either.

'Come out now, master,' he seems to say, speaking with soft brown eyes and wagging tail; 'come out, master; mount your fleetest horse, and let us have a glorious gallop across the hills. See how the sun shines and glitters on grass, on leaves and lake! While you have been writing there day after day, I, your faithful dog, have been languishing. Come, master, come!'

And we go together.

When I return, refreshed, and run up stairs to the room in the tower, I find dear auntie there. She has been reading my manuscript.

'There is,' she says, 'only one addition to make.'

'Name it, auntie,' I say; 'it is not yet too late.'

But she hesitates.

'It is almost a secret,' she says at last, bending down and smoothing the deerhound.

'A secret, auntie? Ha, ha!' I laugh. 'I have it, auntie! I have it!'

And I kiss her there and then.

'It is Townley's secret and yours. He has proposed, and you are to—'

But auntie has run out of the room.

And now, come to think of it, there is something to add to all this.

Can you guess *my* secret, reader mine?

Irene, my darling Irene and I, Murdoch M'Crimman, are also to be—

But, there, you have guessed my secret, as I guessed auntie's.

And just let me ask this: Could any better plan have been devised of burying the hatchet betwixt two rival Highland clans, and putting an end for ever to a blood feud?